I0622071

IN SAECULA SAECULORUM

Keith Massey

Lingua Sacra Publishing
Roxbury, New Jersey

In Saecula Saeculorum
Copyright © 2012 by Keith Massey

Published in the United States by Lingua Sacra
Publishing.
www.linguasacrapublishing.com
ISBN 978-0-9843432-5-6

Dedication

In memory of Professor Fanny LeMoine, who once taught me Latin. *Requiem aeternam dona ei, Domine, et lux perpetua luceat ei.*

About the Author

Keith Massey, Ph.D., is the author of *Intermediate Arabic for Dummies, Next Stop: Spanish*, and *A Place of Brightness.* He is a former linguist with the National Security Agency and is currently a language instructor.

Legal Disclaimer

The views and opinions expressed in this work are the author's and not that of the National Security Agency or the U.S. Government.

Chapter One

Will's eyes shot toward the open classroom door. His heart leapt to the sound of approaching footsteps. There were only four students in the class. The faint click sounded feminine, so it couldn't be Jonathan. And that guy always came late anyway. Not Carmen either. She'd be walking more quickly. A smile exploded onto his face at the only logical conclusion.

"Layla."

He suddenly realized he had spoken her name out loud.

The delicate steps grew closer. His mind reeled with the possibilities of what she might be wearing.

"*Oh, Jesus, please let it be that red and orange dress she had on last Tuesday!*" This was an actual prayer from his pious heart.

As Layla approached the door, she saw that the lights inside the room were already on.

"*Please let it be Will—and Will alone!*" she thought.

He was the reason she tried to get there early every day. Pausing before the entrance, she looked down to double-check her appearance.

"*He didn't even notice that red and orange dress from last week*," she thought with a sigh.

Today she had selected a white—and tight—dress which, she believed, pleasantly contrasted with her coffee-colored skin. She made a minor adjustment

1

about the bust. With a nod of approval, she stepped into the room.

"*Salve*, Will," she said, greeting him in the Latin they studied together. "*Quid agis hodie?*" Her eyes caressed a vibrant purple shirt she thought nicely complimented his light brown hair.

"*Bene*, Layla," he answered, smiling broadly and sitting back. "*Et tu?*"

Her heart stirred with delight at how his British accent invaded even his Latin pronunciation.

"*Quoque bene,*" she said, taking the desk on his right.

Will, Layla, and Carmen always sat in the front row; Jonathan usually sat in the back of the wide classroom. Several tall windows faced the front door and poured sunlight into the space. A single long chalkboard filled the wall behind the large wooden desk at the front of the room. The other walls were bare. The various posters their Latin teacher Dr. Valquist annually put up with weak tape had again fallen and formed a pile in the corner by the door.

"Are you ready for the test today?" he asked, continuing in Latin. They were required to speak only that language in their Latin and History classes.

"I don't know," she said. "I always feel like I could have studied a bit more."

"You're probably the only one who's going to get an A+. We all speak pretty well at this point, but you're just on another level, Layla. Didn't Dr. Valquist himself say that your abilities surpassed his sometime during Junior Year?"

She felt a blush come over her at his compliment. "I already spoke Spanish and Arabic before I came to this school."

"You're so lucky," he said. "An Arab family growing up in Brownsville, Texas. It's a linguist's dream."

She smiled. "That had a lot to do with it. Anyway, today's going to be so strange. A normal day here and then we leave tonight for Rome!"

"I know it. Like they couldn't give us the day off to get ready?"

"And you've known about this trip for how long, Mr. Stanhope?" Layla said, imitating the voice of their Latin teacher.

He laughed. "I'm actually almost done packing. How about you?"

"I just need to double-check with Carmen on what she's bringing. You know, we want to avoid the disaster we had at the awards assembly."

Will recalled the fact that Layla and Carmen had both shown up to that event wearing the exact same blue dress. In his mind, he saw them standing beside each other that evening. Carmen's long straight platinum-blonde hair and fair skin were a stark contrast to Layla's jet-black curls and dark complexion. The dress was tight to Layla's body, the skirt just above the knees. Slender straps left plenty of her skin visible at her shoulders. The front plunged such that he had exercised extraordinary discipline to maintain eye contact with her throughout the event. That night she had worn her curly black hair down. He imagined running his fingers through...

"*Bona Dies!*" Carmen shouted in his ear, dropping her neon-green backpack on the desk to his left.

"I'm sorry," he mumbled, shaking his head to return to the classroom.

"I've said 'good morning' to you five times, made fun of your ridiculous purple shirt, and all you do is stare into space."

"Let's start over," he said. "*Salve*, Carmen."

"*Salve, Domine*," she giggled.

Will rolled his eyes. He hated it when she called him "Lord." Yes, he was the only British student at the school and his father was actually a duke, hence her use of the title. Even so, he had never asked for any special treatment.

Carmen unzipped her bag and took out a piece of paper. "Let's review one of the passages I just know we'll see on the test," she said, heading for the blackboard. She began copying from the sheet in large letters across the entire length of the wall.

Will curled his eyebrows as she wrote. "We've done three hundred lines of Vergil since the last test. You really think you can guess one of the passages he's going to throw at us?"

Layla watched the lines emerge and began to nod. "Carmen's on to something. Don't you remember?

That's the passage where he made a special point of telling us about the rare use of a dative of direction."

Will rubbed his forehead. "I actually don't remember that—at all. And now I suddenly feel a whole lot less prepared. Even so, I'll bet an ice cream at lunch that you're wrong."

"Agreed," Carmen said.

From down the hall, the students heard loud whistling and rapid footsteps.

"What is it today?" Will asked.

"*Eine kleine Nachmusik*, by Mozart," Layla replied.

Their teacher entered the room, but finished the musical bar he was on before taking a deep breath. "*Salvete, discipuli*," he said with a kind smile.

"*Salve, Magister*," the students said in unison.

He set a burgundy leather bag on the desk at the front of the room. While most of their teachers carried briefcases or even pushed around carts covered with files, Dr. Valquist seemed to live out of that simple satchel. The students assumed it was a quirk he had picked up during his days as a linguist with the National Security Agency, a period of his life he only occasionally discussed. As with all days, the headmaster of the Fairfax Classical Academy in Virginia was dressed in khaki slacks and a white dress shirt. Today's tie was maroon. Premature gray hair made him look a bit older than his actual mid-forties. After extracting a pile of papers from his satchel, he set them face down on his desk.

"When the bell rings, you can take ten extra minutes to study," he said, looking at the lines written on the board. "Your handwriting, Carmen?"

"*Sic, Magister,*" she replied.

"I love this passage," he said.

Carmen smiled and looked at Will.

"It means nothing," he whispered.

"Game on," she returned.

The bell for period one rang and Dr. Valquist sat down at his desk. "*Ubi est* Jonathan?" he asked.

Carmen, Will, and Layla looked back at the empty desk where their classmate should have been sitting by now.

"Ten minutes," Dr. Valquist said.

They began to study. A few minutes after the bell, Jonathan entered the room silently and was heading to his usual seat. His reddish hair was tussled as if he had just gotten out of a bed in the next room.

"Mr. Drake, do you have a late pass from the office?"

Jonathan put his book bag on the desk and left the room without a word. Five minutes later, he returned with a bright yellow slip of paper and handed it to Dr. Valquist.

"How about I give everyone a few more minutes to study?"

As the other students furiously started back into their notes, Jonathan walked to the back of the room, took his seat, and put his forehead on the desk.

Dr. Valquist sighed as he watched the young man. When Jonathan had made no motion to study for a full minute, the teacher stood from his chair.

"Time's up," he said, erasing the board behind him. "Let's get started." He placed several stapled pages face down on each student's desk. "You'll have the rest of the period. You may begin."

As each turned the sheets over, Carmen laughed out loud.

"I think I'll have strawberry, Will."

****

Near the end of the period, Dr. Valquist again stood from his desk. "Just a few minutes left. Make any final marks on the test and be prepared to hand it in as you leave."

With the bell still ringing, Jonathan shot from his seat and slapped his test on Dr. Valquist's desk before bolting out of the room.

"How do you think you did?" Carmen asked Layla as the two handed in their papers.

"Thanks to your intuition, pretty good," she answered.

Will stood back and waited for the young women to leave.

"Mr. Stanhope, you should be getting to gym class, right?"

"Yes, sir, but could I speak with you a moment?"

Dr. Valquist had a prep period before Freshman Latin. He nodded. "What's on your mind?"

"What's going to happen with Jonathan?"

"Well, he's going to graduate no problem, if that's your worry."

"That's not what I'm asking, I guess." Will looked at his teacher seriously. "Sir, what's happening to him? It's like he's totally shutting down."

Dr. Valquist reached into his satchel and took out a pad of late passes. "I'm giving you safe transit into your gym class," he said, filling out the form. "Mr. Cole will probably still punish you somehow."

"I know. But, sir, I— I miss Jonathan."

"Me too," Dr. Valquist said. "After his parents died that summer—the boy we knew Freshman Year—he just never came back."

"But he seemed okay for the next two years," Will said. "Why would he be having so many problems just now?"

"Have you asked him about this?"

Will shook his head. "We don't talk anymore outside of classes."

"That's too bad. I know you two were close friends once."

"Carmen and Layla and I—we've all tried so hard to get him to open up."

Dr. Valquist smiled gently. "Then don't quit now. Graduation is a time for celebrating with your families. All Jonathan's got is his uncle. And every time he sees your parents at school events, it's probably opening old wounds for him."

"I guess."

"So be his friend right now, even if he can't yet be one in return. Go on to your gym class."

"Yes, sir." Will walked briskly from the room.

Dr. Valquist sat back down at his desk and turned the papers over to grade them. He looked at Jonathan's test first. There he saw a fully accurate translation only of the first passage, as well as a description of Vergil's rare use of a dative of direction. The rest of the test was left blank.

****

Will raced through the wide double doors of the gymnasium. The sprawling space held two basketball courts. A large blue mat was in the center of the broad polished wood floor. Large banks of light bulbs hummed loudly from the ceiling. The other three seniors were already seated on the mat, dressed in shorts and t-shirts.

Mr. Cole was standing in front of them, crew-cut black hair, arms crossed, and wearing a gray t-shirt straining to contain his advanced musculature. Will slowed to a stop a few feet from the teacher.

"Here's a pass from Dr. Valquist," he said, lifting the yellow slip of paper up to the well over six-foot tall man.

"That only lets you in this gym," he said in his low and gravelly voice, taking the paper and crumpling it in his fist.

"So I'm good?"

"*Tace!*" Mr. Cole shouted, telling Will to be quiet in Latin. It was one of the few phrases he had asked Dr. Valquist to teach him. "You have exactly one minute to be out here ready to work out."

Will turned and sprinted for the boys' locker room.

"We're going to review some of the defensive moves today," Cole said, turning back to the other students. "That way you'll be ready for your trip."

"You really think we'll need them over there?" Carmen asked.

"Americans on vacation are always a target."

"Have you been to Rome yourself?" Layla asked him.

Mr. Cole made the faintest smile. "Not yet, but I plan on visiting it soon."

"It's too bad you couldn't be a chaperone, along with Dr. Valquist and Miss Maple," Carmen said.

"Well, someone has to stay and help run the Academy for the lower grades," he said. "And our baseball team plays St. Benet's next week. The boosters want to see a win over our biggest rivalry."

Will emerged from the locker room, hopping on one foot as he struggled to put a gym shoe on the other.

"One minute!" he shouted. "I made it!" He walked toward the group and plopped down beside Jonathan.

"Being ready to work out means being seated with your fellow students," Cole said, looking at his watch. "You were two seconds late."

Will huffed. "Alright. What's my punishment?"

"Fifty push-ups, after class," he said. "Let's go back to basics. First lesson I taught you in Freshman Year. What's the most basic defensive maneuver?"

Carmen, Will, and Layla's hands all shot up. Jonathan sat, his eyes focused on a point a hundred miles away.

"Stay with us, Mr. Drake!" Cole barked.

Jonathan turned toward him, startled. "I'm sorry, sir."

"You can join Will for sixty push-ups after class."

"I still only have fifty, though, right?" Will asked.

"It's seventy now. Do I hear eighty?"

"*Tace*," Jonathan whispered to Will.

"Miss Ramzy, remind us all about the most basic defensive maneuver."

"It's to avoid danger in the first place," Layla said. "If you suspect a conflict, you consider yourself as standing on top of a large X. And you need to get off the X."

"Exactly. The most stupid thing you'll ever hear someone say is that only cowards run from a fight. Avoid fighting at all costs. But even despite your best efforts, you can still get into a situation where you do have to fight. Miss Mattila, come forward and prepare to defend yourself."

Carmen jumped up and assumed a position several feet from her teacher.

"Now, why have I chosen Miss Mattila for this demonstration? Speak freely."

"Because she's the best fighter in the group," Will replied.

"You're half right," he said. "This is an exercise on defensive techniques. She's the best fighter among you primarily because she has mastered defense. A final reminder. If possible, always let your opponent throw the first blow. To attack, your opponent will have to go off balance. And that's when your counterattack will be the most effective. Let's begin."

He took a casual step forward and Carmen instantly moved a foot backward.

"Did you all see that?" he asked loudly. "She has chosen the distance she intends to fight me from. And just because I moved forward, she didn't surrender that gap."

Mr. Cole assumed a stance, squatting slightly at the knees and raising his hands in fists before him. In one lightning motion he had bounded forward and shot a foot toward her. Carmen stepped sideways and blocked the attack with her forearm. Spinning around, she again assumed her defensive stance.

"Nice," he said, turning toward the other three students. "Now, who here can tell me when..."

He turned and lunged again at Carmen. She dropped to the floor, shooting both feet upwards and kicking her teacher squarely in the chest. He flew through the air above her and landed in a somersault several feet away.

Mr. Cole laughed and stood up. "Excellent work. Notice, even as I spoke to the rest of you, she never let her guard down. You can take a seat, Miss Mattila. Mr. Drake, it's your turn."

Jonathan reluctantly stood and walked forward.

"Obviously Carmen is in a class of her own when it comes to combat," Cole said. "The thing to keep in mind is that the typical thug you'll face is nowhere near the fighter she is. And that means that all of you should still be ready to do your part."

Jonathan took a deep breath and released it. "So you pick on me as the example of the worst in the class, is that it?"

Mr. Cole looked at him puzzled. "That was not my intent. I only wanted to..."

"You can't all be Carmen, but even Jonathan can do something, right?"

"That's enough now," Mr. Cole said sadly.

"You know, I've had it with this school," he said. "We learn to actually speak Latin, a stupid dead language no one knows anymore."

Carmen, Will, and Layla sat breathlessly watching the scene, afraid to even move.

"Assume a defensive stance and prepare to deflect a simple blow," Mr. Cole said sternly.

"How about 'no'?" Jonathan returned. "And all our other classes are just one worthless history lesson after another. Horseback riding. Ancient geography. Even sword fighting. And the kicker—literally—is that in gym class we get beat up on by some Army wannabe."

Mr. Cole stepped forward and kicked Jonathan's legs out from under him, dropping him squarely onto his back. Jonathan released a loud moan as his lungs were suddenly emptied of all their air.

Cole turned in the direction of the other students. They could see a genuinely pained look on his face.

"Don't ever let your guard down like that in the field," he said loudly. "You three break off and practice defense and offense while I talk to Jonathan."

They walked quickly to the other side of the gym.

"What did he mean by 'in the field'?" Layla asked.

"Our trip to Rome, I guess," Will said.

Mr. Cole squatted beside Jonathan, who was now curled in a fetal position and gasping.

"I...can't...breathe..." he managed, gulping for air.

"You've just had the wind knocked out of you," Cole said gently. "Press your finger against the muscles on your bottom right rib."

Jonathan reached up and did as told.

"Now you'll feel a bit more braced. Slowly draw air back into your lungs."

Jonathan took a deep and painful breath.

"Release it gently."

As he followed his teacher's instructions, he felt well enough to sit up.

"I'm really sorry," Jonathan said. "I was very inappropriate, I know."

"Don't worry about it. I think you said some things you needed to let out."

"But it wasn't fair to insult you."

Cole chuckled. "I was in the Navy, not the Army. But at least you didn't call me Air Force."

Jonathan smiled and felt a spasm return.

"Keep breathing slowly," Mr. Cole said. "Listen, I know you've had a tough hand dealt to you in life. Graduation coming and everything—it must be kinda depressing."

Jonathan nodded. "I just want these last six weeks of school to be over."

"Well, before they're done, you're going to go through some very dark places, Jonathan."

"What do you mean?"

"The world can be cruel and dangerous. Remember your training and lean on your friends as well."

Jonathan looked at him in confusion. "I will, sir."

Mr. Cole stood. "Alright, students!" he bellowed. "Get ready for your next class."

Will ran up, breathing heavily from practicing the fighting moves. "Can I get started on those push-ups?"

Mr. Cole looked down at Jonathan, still seated on the floor. "You're both pardoned—this time."

"Thank you, sir," Jonathan said. "I probably would've thrown up if I even tried them."

"I wouldn't have to clean it up, so don't think I'm getting soft or anything."

Jonathan and Will looked at each other and could barely suppress a laugh. Mr. Cole chuckled himself.

"Enjoy Rome, if I don't see you before you leave."

****

The four seniors walked up a stairwell toward their next class—Roman History with Miss Maple. Sky-blue ceramic tiled walls reflected the sunlight from a high window above them. Underclassmen were coming down the stairs on their way to the gym, slowing their ascent.

"Remember when we had this entire school to ourselves?" Layla asked.

"Yeah," Carmen replied. "I recall that as the most boring year of our lives. A student-teacher ratio of four to five. Literally, four of us and five of them."

They left the stairwell and continued down a long hallway. Reflections of passing students danced on the polished floor.

"Hey, Jonathan," Will said. "Are you excited about going to Rome tonight?"

The other three waited, hoping he would join in their conversation.

"I guess," Jonathan returned simply.

Will opened his mouth, searching for a follow-on question, but found none as they arrived at their classroom.

Miss Maple stood just outside the door. She was dressed in one of the many brown tweed dress suits the students had observed from her wardrobe. With her thick horn-rimmed glasses and tightly-bunned blonde hair, they had long privately joked that if she weren't a history teacher, she'd make the perfect naughty librarian.

"*Salve*, Will," she said.

"*Salve, Magistra*," he answered. "*Quid agis hodie*?"

"*Bene*," she replied. "*Et tu?*"

"*Quoque bene*," he said.

"*Salve*, Layla."

"*Salve, Magistra.*"

After greeting each of the students, she followed them into the room.

Entering Miss Maple's class was like stepping back into Ancient Rome itself. While Dr. Valquist's room was stark, hers was rich in the images of her topic. On her desk sat a model of the three columns from the Temple of Castor and Pollux in the Roman Forum. The walls were covered with Roman period maps of Miss Maple's native England, as well as ancient Gaul, Italy, and maps of the whole Empire. She had spent the last four years teaching them Roman history and culture using an innovative technique she called "Period Immersion." Since she herself spoke Latin as well as

Dr. Valquist, her class, like his, was conducted only in that language. Everything they studied was somehow connected to the *Cursus Publicus*, the system of imperial roads, inns, and stables that allowed dignitaries and other approved users to make cost-free and rapid travel throughout the Roman Empire. The students had made the imaginary journey from Roman Britannia to the city of Rome and back a total of twelve times in great detail. They had completed class projects focused on the major cities, towns, and roads along this route. Their trip always took place in what Miss Maple considered her favorite period of Roman history—the reign of Antoninus Pius, the enlightened civil servant emperor. The students had come to joke that they could probably do the journey for real if they ever had to.

Laptops were already set up on their desks in preparation for the project Miss Maple had in mind for that day.

"*Bene, discipuli*," Miss Maple chimed. "Today we have the chance to be ancient detectives. Imagine you are actually back in time in the year AD 157. Remember that this is the year 910 *Ab Urbe Condita*, from the founding of the City of Rome. Imagine you're in the Roman Forum. But before you get there, you have the chance to use the internet to find any information you can on how to solve the problem on the board."

The four sat down in their assigned seats. Unlike Dr. Valquist, who let Jonathan hide out in the back of the room, Miss Maple made him sit in the front row far left, flanked by Carmen, with Will next, and then Layla on the far right. The four opened their laptops and spied the single sentence written on the chalkboard: "How would you find a book in the Bibliotheca Ulpia, if it were <u>necessary</u> to do so?"

As they began pulling various searches, no one had to look up what the Bibliotheca Ulpia was. As part of their many runnings of the *Cursus*, they had come to know quite well that it was a library in the Forum of Trajan, just west of the Roman Forum itself. They had studied how it consisted of two buildings facing each other across a courtyard. The building on the east housed books in Latin; the western building held Greek works. During the reign of the Emperor Antoninus Pius it was a rival in scope and significance to the more famous ancient library in Alexandria. Today's research, however, focused on a practical matter they had never before studied.

"Miss Maple," Layla started. "May I ask the significance of the word 'necessary' being underlined in your question?"

"I'm asking, hypothetically, if your very life depended on it, how would you find a book there?"

They all puzzled over the stark importance she had put on the task.

The students explored dozens of websites on the topic given to them. A half hour later, Miss Maple again approached the front of the class.

"What have we discovered, students? I'm not going to call on you. Let's just have a free discussion."

Carmen spoke first. "Most scholars believe that the Bibliotheca Ulpia was not really a library in the modern sense. It was more of a book depository."

"The public couldn't check things out," Layla added. "Only approved scholars could enter and ask to look at items."

"How were the books filed?" she asked.

"By the Dewey Decimal system," Will said. "But in Roman numerals." He alone laughed at his joke.

"Very funny, Mr. Stanhope."

"I'm sorry, Miss Maple. They were arranged in the library by topic."

"Right. So what would you actually do if you needed to see a book you believed was in that library? Let's say, for the sake of argument, a specific work on agriculture."

"Can we make it astronomy?" Will asked. "I just adore studying the stars."

"We all know you do," Miss Maple said, smiling. "Back to the question at hand. How do you see a book in that library?"

"You'd need permission to be there," Carmen said. "And you'd need the name of the work and its author so someone there could help you find it."

"And what if you didn't have that information? Let's say you aren't even allowed to enter the library at all?"

"Then you're going to have to break in and find the book yourself," Jonathan said.

The others looked at him curiously.

"You're going to get our library card revoked!" Carmen said.

"I'm serious," Jonathan said. "Miss Maple specifically described this as a life and death assignment. I'm not going to choose death just because someone doesn't let me enter a library. I'd rather die breaking in than just sitting there and taking it."

The room was filled with a momentary awkward silence.

"Was that a cry for help?" Layla asked with a smirk.

Jonathan laughed. "No, don't worry. I'm not contemplating 'Death by Librarian'."

"But I guess Jonathan's right," Will said. "Short of having permission from an official to view anything you want, getting a look at a whole section of that library is not going to happen."

"The purpose of this discussion is to make you think about the classical world as a real and complicated place," Miss Maple said. "Something as simple as using a library probably involved a lot of frustration there."

"Isn't it also possible that there are things about the library that we just don't know today?" Layla asked. "Maybe you could check books out."

"Possibly, Miss Ramzy," she said, "but unlikely." The bell rang. "You did good work today. Obviously there's no homework. And Dr. Valquist asked me to tell you four that you've been given the rest of the day off. Get ready for our trip and I'll see you this evening. Remember, six o'clock sharp at the circle."

"*Gratias Deo*!" Will said. "Thank God!"

The students stood and gathered their things to leave.

"Call me when you get home," Layla said to Carmen. "I want to make sure we aren't packing the same things."

"Good idea," she said. "We don't want to repeat..."

"The awards assembly," they said in unison.

"Hey, Jonathan, call me when you get home," Will said, as they followed the girls out of the room. "We should probably coordinate our wardrobes too."

"*Tace*!" Carmen said.

Chapter Two

The assembly of teachers, students, and their parents stood outside the vine-encrusted school building, surrounded by suitcases sitting randomly about. A pink and purple light washed upon the horizon in the gathering dusk.

"The bus is almost here," Dr. Valquist said, switching off his cell phone and looking over the broad circle of green lawn set inside the road that looped alongside the school.

"Thank you again for organizing this trip," Mr. Ramzy said.

"Dr. Valquist, will I get a trip to Rome in three years?" asked Marwan Ramzy, there to see his sister off.

The teacher smiled. "It's our plan to take every graduating Senior Class on such a trip."

"That's awesome," Mrs. Mattila said. "Carmen's been talking about the Senior Trip to Rome since she first came to the school. God, was that already four years ago?"

"It's amazing how the time has flown, Phyllis," Lord Stanhope said.

Miss Maple looked at her watch. "Now, if only Jonathan could show up on time for once."

"I spoke to his uncle an hour ago," Dr. Valquist said. "They're on their way."

A few yards from the others, the three seniors stood together, looking at their school.

"So many memories," Carmen said. "I'm really going to miss this place next year."

Will put his hand on her shoulder. "And to think, now we cap it all off with the trip of a lifetime."

"Trip of a lifetime?!" Layla protested. "I, for one, hope that a week in Rome won't be that at all. I'm planning to see the entire world some day."

"But Rome's a good start," he said.

Engines roared in the distance. The entire group looked down the long road leading to the school and saw a blue compact, followed immediately by a large yellow bus.

"Jonathan, and then our transportation, I presume," Carmen said.

The vehicles turned around the circle and came to a stop in front of the group.

"I'm so sorry, Dr. Valquist," a thirty-something man said, jumping out of the driver's side of the car. "Traffic was crazy all the way from Adams Morgan."

"No worries, Mr. Drake," Dr. Valquist said, stepping toward him and shaking his hand. "I booked plenty of extra time into the trip."

Jonathan got out of the car and went to the trunk. He slung a computer bag over his shoulder and took out a large black suitcase.

The students gravitated toward their parents and began their goodbyes.

"Have a great time, Willie," Lady Stanhope said, pulling her son into an embrace.

"We love you," Lord Stanhope added, patting his son's back.

Carmen's mom and dad each put a hand on their daughter's shoulder.

"Be careful, baby," her mom said.

"We're not going to war!" Carmen said with a laugh. "Listen, Snowflake was favoring her front left leg this afternoon. No one rides her until I get back."

"Understood," her dad said, smiling.

"And don't overfeed her."

"Your dad and I will do our best," her mother said, pulling her daughter into a hug. "Have fun—but be careful."

Layla's mom hugged her daughter and began to cry. "*BaHabbik, yaa binti*. You've never been away so long!"

"It's just eight days," she said.

"Call us as soon as you land," her father said, joining the embrace.

Jonathan stood looking at his uncle Frank. "I guess I'll see you in a week," he said.

Frank nodded eagerly. "Yeah. Um, have a good time."

"I will," Jonathan said. He smiled awkwardly and picked up his bags. He put his large suitcase in the open compartment at the side of the bus and then boarded the vehicle.

"All aboard, folks!" Dr. Valquist shouted.

As students embraced their parents one last time, Jonathan had sat down in the bus. Through the window, he watched his uncle's car pulling away. "Goodbye, Frank," he whispered.

Dr. Valquist boarded the bus and took the seat directly behind the Academy's regular bus driver, Juan.

"*Cómo estás, Señor?*" Dr. Valquist asked.

"*Muy bien, Doctor,*" the driver responded.

Dr. Valquist reached into his satchel and took out a pile of papers. "I still need to double-check that you have a valid passport," he said, turning around toward Jonathan. "The others all showed me theirs days ago."

Jonathan smiled and produced the blue document from his shirt pocket.

Dr. Valquist looked at the inside page. "Issued just this week, huh?"

Jonathan nodded. "I lucked out. I didn't even know you could pay more for an expedite, but the thing still came in just a few days."

"Your uncle works at the Department of Transportation, as I recall. Does he have a connection with someone at State?"

"Maybe that's it, sir."

"Even so, it was dangerous putting off something so important until the last minute. You would have missed this trip if you didn't get your passport in time."

"I know it, sir."

Miss Maple came aboard and took the seat beside Dr. Valquist. "This will be how many times in Rome for you, Andrew?"

He looked up in thought. "Seven…" he answered slowly, as if unsure of the number.

"Such a newbie," she said. "This will be thirteen for me!"

The other students boarded one by one. Layla sat down and slid over, making room for another passenger.

Carmen was right behind her. Knowing her friend's unconfessed interest in Will, she slid in next to Jonathan.

"Move over," she said. "*Ego sum* Carmen. Who are you again?"

Will's heart fluttered when he saw the open spot next to Layla. "Is this seat taken?" he asked.

"No," she said, smiling nervously.

Dr. Valquist got up and walked slowly down the aisle, handing tickets to the students. "Before we get on our way to the airport, there's something I want you all to be doing throughout this trip. From time to time, take a moment to make a mental snapshot of the scene you are in. Believe it or not, the day may come in your lives when even the memory of sitting in this bus will be something sweet to cherish."

"I knew he was going to say something to make me cry," Carmen whispered, wiping away tears.

"*Estamos listos para salir, Señor,*" Dr. Valquist said to the driver.

As the bus pulled away from the school, the students looked back at the building with a strange sense of finality, as if they would never see it again. They sat mostly in silence as they watched their progress toward Reagan International Airport. Across the Potomac River, the Washington Monument appeared on the horizon.

Carmen leaned past Jonathan toward the window. "It gets me every time," she said.

"I know what you mean. It just makes you want to serve your country somehow."

"You mean like join the army or something?" Will asked.

"I don't know," Jonathan said.

"There are many ways to serve your countries," Dr. Valquist stated, overhearing the conversation. "You're all destined to contribute to society even if all that means is that you prosper in your chosen careers."

"But I want more than that," Jonathan said quickly. "I want my life to matter somehow. Maybe that's because…"

The teachers and students looked at him, hoping he would continue speaking. Jonathan finally turned away and looked out the window.

"*Llegamos pronto, Doctor,*" the bus driver said.

"*Muchas gracias, Señor*," Dr. Valquist said. "Students, check your seats to make sure you have everything."

The bus pulled up to the international departures terminal. Each of the students grabbed their hand bags and headed to the front exit. The driver had opened the side compartment for their larger luggage. As they each began moving toward the rotating glass doors of the terminal, Will noticed that Dr. Valquist was only carrying his leather satchel and a single small carry-on.

"We're going to be gone over a week, sir," he said. "Is that really all you need?"

"Years of international travel have taught me to pack very light," he answered. "Two changes of clothes, which I will wash in the hotel sink as necessary."

"This is something you learned in your spy days?" Carmen asked.

"Indeed," he replied. "One day you may end up doing similar things."

As they got in the long line waiting to check their baggage for coach travel on the airplane, Will saw a desk attendant answer her cell phone. Immediately after closing the call, she walked up to their group.

"Are you all on a school trip?" she asked.

"Yes, ma'am," Miss Maple answered.

"Let me process you through the First Class check-in, since no one's there right now."

"Excellent," Dr. Valquist said. "I guess there are some perks left for simple school teachers."

As they walked toward the counter, Will nudged Layla with his elbow. "Does this special treatment seem strange to you somehow?"

"Why?"

"I don't know."

Each in turn presented their passports and had their baggage weighed and processed. Once relieved of the burden of their larger luggage, they were holding their boarding passes and ready to go through security. The group passed through the metal detectors uneventfully and at last were seated by their gate, waiting for a direct flight to Rome.

"There's no good way to minimize jetlag on a flight across the Atlantic," Dr. Valquist said casually. "It'll take a day for every hour difference before you feel completely recovered."

"So, in other words, we'll feel normal again just in time to head home," Carmen said.

"Correct," Miss Maple replied. "But the good news is that it's always easier on your body to travel westward. We'll leave Rome in the morning and arrive back in Washington on the afternoon of the same day. Stay awake until at least nine that night and you'll normalize very quickly."

"I didn't realize you'd also done so much foreign travel," Layla said.

"Going back to England twice a year to see my Mum is enough to make me experienced," she said, pushing up her glasses.

"We'll begin pre-boarding for Flight 543 with direct service to Rome shortly," an announcement sounded.

"Has anyone else here never been on a plane before?" Jonathan asked.

The group exchanged quick glances to see who might reply.

"I don't think so," Dr. Valquist said. "This is really your first time?"

"Yeah, and I'll admit I'm nervous."

"You do know all the statistics about it being safer than automobile travel?" Will asked.

"I've heard it. But the thought of being thousands of feet in the air over the Atlantic Ocean doesn't seem safe to me."

"Let's stay scientific about it," Dr. Valquist said. "It is, of course, an inherently dangerous thing to fly. That said, a modern airplane has many safety checks and redundant systems such that in practice it's not something to worry about."

"That doesn't make me feel any better," Jonathan said. "And I'm worried I might get sick during the flight."

Dr. Valquist laughed. "I'm seated right next to you. And I've seen it all. It wouldn't affect me in the least."

"That actually does relieve me a bit," Jonathan said.

"We will now begin boarding rows 20 through 35," an announcement called.

"That's us," Layla said. "Let's go fly to Rome!"

****

The group was more than half way through the flight as Jonathan sat awake in the darkened cabin. He looked at a TV screen jutting from the ceiling of the plane, displaying their location, altitude, and even the temperature outside the aircraft. Pulling open the shade of the window beside him, Jonathan saw nothing but blackness over what he knew was the North Atlantic.

"*Thalassa, thalassa,*" he whispered.

"The sea, the sea," Dr. Valquist said softly from beside him.

"I'm sorry, sir," Jonathan whispered back. "Did I wake you?"

"I can never sleep on planes. *Thalassa*, the sea. We taught you all some Greek. Only Layla speaks it with any real ability, I admit. But we never covered Xenophon. Where did you pick up that quote?"

"I did a presentation on it in Miss Maple's class Freshman Year. What a story! After fighting their way through a thousand miles of enemy territory, the Greeks knew they were finally out of trouble only when they spotted the sea. And so they called out '*Thalassa! Thalassa!*' in celebration of finally reaching home."

Dr. Valquist nodded. "Very good. And this reference was somehow meaningful to you? That's why you chose it?"

Jonathan's face fell.

"I'm sorry. This is evidently something sensitive."

"No. Well, yes." Jonathan sighed and shook his head. "I have to stop doing this. I know what I've become, sir."

"And what's that?"

"The only real problem student you have at the Fairfax Classical Academy."

The teacher turned himself toward Jonathan. "Now *that* I am going to reject, Mr. Drake. First off, that thing last year with the computer— You served your suspension. That's over and done with. And if your academic achievement this year was below what I think your true potential is, I am not disappointed in *you*. If anything, I continue to be disappointed in myself that I never found a way to help you more."

"It wasn't your fault," Jonathan whispered. "Sometime this year, I just stopped feeling like I had the energy to keep going through the motions. Layla's the master of languages. Carmen's the fighter and horse expert. Will's just good at everything and a science whiz to boot. Me? I don't excel at anything. So I guess I quit trying to compete with them."

Dr. Valquist nodded. "So tell me what you want to do from here."

"I meant what I said earlier today about wanting to be of service somehow. Don't laugh, but a part of me is seriously thinking about not going to college and instead joining the military."

Dr. Valquist looked at him and smiled. "When have I ever laughed at you?"

"You haven't."

"Then of course I won't now. There's nothing wrong with that plan, if that's really what you want. I spent four years in the Army myself."

"But then another part of me thinks that everything I've learned at the Academy will be wasted if I did that."

"Wasted? Why?"

"Well, how many other enlisted men in the Army can speak Latin?"

"How many officers in the entire U.S. Armed Forces can speak it?"

Jonathan chuckled. "I suppose none."

"Speaking Latin is all fine and good, Jonathan," he said. "But because of Latin you have also acquired functional Spanish, French, and Italian. The Army would probably send you to their language institute and make you into a linguist. That's what I did for the NSA."

"But I don't know if that's what I really want."

"One thing I do know about how the world works is that once you sign on the dotted line to something bigger than yourself, like the Army, you have to do things you don't choose."

"Maybe I'll just go to college then."

"Mr. Drake, do whatever you *want* to do. Go to college. Or join the Army. And good luck not being a linguist, if you do. But take over your life."

"It sounds easier than it is."

"Go with me a little ways, Jonathon. I lost my own parents when I was about your age. But I had a twin brother and we helped each other through a lot of things. When your parents were killed, you probably felt like your world had been destroyed and you had no control over it."

"Yes, but that's not my biggest problem anymore."

"Okay, then what is?"

Jonathan pursed his lips. "I just don't feel like I have anyone in my life to be proud of me."

"What about your uncle?"

"Are you kidding? He's spent the last three years telling me that he can never replace my parents."

"It was proper of him to stress that," Dr. Valquist said. "But I've also seen for the last three years how that man has been as much a parent to you as anyone could be."

Jonathan's lower lip began to tremble. "And that's the problem. He's the greatest man I know. I love him dearly. And I've never told him that. I miss my parents, but they're gone. And now I kinda wish that I could just...call Frank...my dad."

"What a sad situation," Dr. Valquist said. "You two have no one in this world but each other. You're a family. And you can't admit that's what you've become."

"I've wanted to know if he's proud of me. But if I asked him, I'm sure he'd just say something like he knows my parents would be proud."

"And so..."

"So maybe that's why I'm the underachiever of the Academy," Jonathan said.

"Subconsciously doing nothing to be proud of."

"I don't know, I guess that all makes sense."

"Now tell me about *thalassa*," Dr. Valquist said.

Jonathan nodded. "My dad owned a sail boat."

"Nice. I've never ridden on a boat smaller than a cruise ship. It's fun?"

"It's more. The feeling of the cool air. The mist of the water in your face. The smell and taste of the salt. It's just so calming."

"He taught you how to control the boat as well?"

"Oh yes," Jonathan said. "And I'm damn good at it."

"So..."

"I guess because of what I just said, *thalassa* reminds me of a happier and simpler time. The Greeks saw the sea and knew they were almost home. And for me, it's a home I know I can never get back to. And in dreams sometimes I see the wide open water and I feel like somehow the sea holds my destiny."

"Then it sounds like the Coast Guard or Navy would be a better choice for you than the Army. But let's move back to the present. Who do you want to be, Jonathan Drake?"

"I want to stop being the pitiful orphan," he answered, wiping his eyes.

"Good," Dr. Valquist said, wiping his as well. "That never did get anyone very far."

"And I want my friends back. But I don't think I fit into that group of three anymore."

"You don't fit into that group of three," Dr. Valquist said. "But I know for a fact that they wish they were a group of four again. Make it so."

"You're a very wise man, Dr. Valquist."

"Age and more sins and mistakes than you'll ever make have created what I am today, Mr. Drake. Now, let's try to get some rest so we can enjoy tomorrow a bit more."

Jonathan closed his eyes and sleep instantly found him.

****

The plane arrived back in morning light and the group enjoyed a breakfast while gazing down upon European terrain. As they landed in Rome, they saw the Mediterranean Sea just a few kilometers away through the right-hand windows.

"*Thalassa! Thalassa!*" Jonathan shouted with a smile.

The group laughed, as much at Jonathan's sudden exuberance as at their own knowledge of the obscure reference, still remembering his report in Miss Maple's class.

"Somehow we have a new Jonathan this morning," Carmen said smiling. "And I like him."

As they disembarked, they entered into the large terminal of Rome's airport and were suddenly assaulted by brightly illuminated Italian language signs. Their linguistically trained minds whirled to translate each of them and soon the whole group was pouring into Italian conversations.

A shuttle picked them up from the airport and they arrived at their hotel after thirty minutes of congested Roman street traffic. They stepped into the lobby and saw a space almost over-packed with potted trees. A dark brown wooden reception counter was at their left, behind which stood a young and smiling woman in a bright green blazer. Dr. Valquist handled the check-in procedures and distributed key cards to the group. In a row of rooms on the third floor, the girls were together, followed by Miss Maple, then Dr. Valquist, and finally the boys.

"We've got a big day planned for tomorrow," Miss Maple said, as they walked toward the elevator. "For today it will be enough to get settled into our rooms and then make a brief and initial exploration of the Forum."

"So get cleaned up as you wish, and let's meet back here in the lobby after an hour," Dr. Valquist said.

"We'll see the Forum a bit and then get a meal at a wonderful little place I know just south of this area."

Carmen and Layla showered quickly, changed clothes, and arrived back at the lobby, finding Dr. Valquist already there.

"I can't believe I'm about to see them!" Carmen said.

"You mean the pillars of Castor and Pollux?" Dr. Valquist said.

"Yes!" she exclaimed. "How did you know?"

"I remember you talking about them four years ago when I was showing you slides from one of my trips."

"Slides!" Layla laughed. "I remember you used to bring in those cartridges and click through them one by one. I'm glad you've advanced since then to computer presentations."

"We must keep up with the times."

Miss Maple now arrived, carrying an umbrella.

"I don't think there's any rain in the forecast," Carmen said.

"This is to fight off street urchins, if necessary," she said. "The area of the Forum is crawling with beggars, pickpockets, and other swindlers."

"Just stay close to me," Dr. Valquist said. "No one will bother us."

"And why is that?" she asked, pushing up her glasses.

"I have city presence. It's just an air one develops that makes petty thieves know you aren't a target to consider."

"Whatever it is, I'll be happy for any help you can give."

The elevator opened and the boys poured out, each dressed in the same clothes they had flown in.

"I do hope you guys plan on changing before tomorrow," Layla said.

"It just seemed like a waste of clean clothes to wear them only a few hours," Will said.

"What about putting on new clothes for tonight and then wearing those tomorrow as well?" Carmen asked. "That's my plan."

"And won't your clothes be just as old tomorrow night as ours are now?" Jonathan asked.

Carmen smirked. "*Touché*, new Jonathan," she said, putting her arm around his shoulder and pulling him along. "Let me show you the Roman Forum."

As the group crossed the busy Via Celio Vibenna, they looked down upon the Roman Forum, which lay several feet lower than the towering Coliseum ahead of them. Banks of green grass filled the spaces not covered by concrete walkways.

"There's your first look at the economic artery of ancient Rome, *mi amici*," Dr. Valquist said.

The students all smiled and looked at each other, hearing him use the word "friends."

"The entrance to the Forum is on the other side of the Coliseum," he said. "Follow me."

The shadow of the tall Coliseum cast a welcome coolness on the six weary travelers.

"Hello, my old friend," Miss Maple said, craning her neck to look up at the structure.

The four students stood breathless, seeing it for the first time. Above them loomed story after story of ancient gray concrete proudly standing against time and a brilliant blue sky.

"Bloody hell!" Will gasped. "It's even bigger than I imagined!"

Carmen and Layla looked at each other and smirked. Neither had to say it out loud.

"Let's move along, lads and lasses," Miss Maple chimed, holding her umbrella in one hand and pushing her glasses up her nose with the other. "We'll explore the inside of the Coliseum tomorrow when we're more rested."

"Yes," Dr. Valquist said. "So let's head down."

The four students followed their teachers along a busy walkway lined with a metal chain fence on each side. Carmen and Jonathan were directly behind them, each noticing that Dr. Valquist's gray hair somehow complimented Miss Maple's blonde bun.

Carmen poked Jonathan in the ribs. "When are they gonna hook up?" she whispered.

A cushion of heat fell upon the group as they stepped out of the Coliseum's shadow and descended toward an explosion of white marble artifacts. Columns lay randomly beside the path, as if cast to the ground like cigarette butts.

Layla and Will followed next in the procession.

"*Nos sumus in Roma!*" he exclaimed. "We're finally in Rome. I've been dreaming of this trip for four years!"

"I know," she returned. "Just think, we're about to see the original of that thing that sits on Miss Maple's desk."

"The three columns of Castor and Pollux," Will said. "They're at your eleven o'clock."

She acquired the coordinates. "*Sic!*" she squealed. "Yes!"

"Let me get a picture of you with that in the background," he said, taking out his phone.

She stepped forward and turned toward him. Running her hands over her head to fix her hair, she smiled broadly at Will.

"*Tu es pulchra,*" he whispered to himself as he pressed the button. "You're so beautiful."

They walked quickly to catch up with the group.

"That's the old Senate building ahead, right?" Carmen asked.

"*Sic,*" Dr. Valquist replied. "Remember, that isn't where Caesar was assassinated because..."

"They were meeting in the Theater of Pompey," Will said. "Score!"

"*Sic,* Mr. Stanhope," he chuckled. "Let's stop here for a moment, students."

The group slowly spread out and took in the scene from the center of the Roman Forum. Remnants of once grand buildings stretched to the sky in lonely columns, only hinting at the scale of their original glory.

"Anyone who could ever again see this place in its ancient grandeur would truly be blessed," Dr. Valquist stated.

"Fairfax Classical Academy!" Miss Maple shouted. "Time for a picture!"

The students quickly reassembled next to their teachers.

"Go over by the three columns," she said. "I'm going to put this photo on my desk right next to the replica."

They walked across the open space and formed a tight group, arms around each other's shoulders and faces full of smiles.

Miss Maple looked through her camera at the four. She sighed to see the exquisite picture they formed. Love and fear surged in her heart. "God help you all," she whispered.

"Hurry up," Will shouted. "I'm starving."

"Smile!" She snapped the picture.

"Let's go get some dinner," Dr. Valquist declared.

"Sounds like a plan," Carmen said, raising her eyebrow as she saw a tall man dressed in a plastic gladiator suit approaching.

"Take picture with gladiator, pretty lady!" the man said in an Italian accent. He put his arm around

Carmen's shoulder, letting his hand dangle well down her chest.

"You have exactly one second to leave," Carmen said.

The man pressed his face toward hers. "What you say?"

Carmen's elbow shot into his stomach. He doubled over, gasping for breath. She spun around and kicked the man squarely in the chest. He crumbled to the ground, his plastic armor falling off as he landed on the dusty gravel.

In an instant, a uniformed police officer was on the scene, slapping handcuffs on the stunned man writhing about on the ground.

"We are so sorry," a second officer said, stepping toward the group. "We do not tolerate harassment of tourists. But how did you...?"

"Thank you, officer," Dr. Valquist said, walking backward toward the Coliseum. "Come, students. Let's avoid an international incident and move along."

"Sorry, sir," Carmen said, catching up to him.

"You were magnificent," he returned, suppressing a smile.

The group continued past the Coliseum and soon they were standing back at the Via Celio Vibenna, watching oncoming traffic from the left, followed by a thin median strip and another lane of cars from the right.

"Move fast when we get the walk light," Miss Maple shouted. "There's barely enough time to get across."

"Hold my satchel, would you?" Dr. Valquist said, handing the small burgundy leather case to Carmen.

"Certainly, sir," she said, looking at it curiously.

The walk light flashed green.

"Let's go, students!" Miss Maple said, starting across the road.

The young people moved quickly, reaching the median and continuing past the second set of lanes.

Miss Maple's umbrella slipped from her fingers, sliding backwards on the street.

"I've got it," Dr. Valquist said, turning and scooping up the item.

He stepped with her onto the median strip just as the light changed. The students had reached the other side of the thoroughfare.

"Don't worry," Dr. Valquist shouted. "We'll be with you at the next walk light."

"Look," Layla said. "The sun's setting behind the Forum."

All of the students except Carmen gazed at the swirls of yellow and orange on the horizon.

"Alert," Carmen said. "We are a split team. Focus on the other members."

"This isn't Mr. Cole's gym class, Carm," Jonathan said. "What do you think's gonna happen here?"

A van screeched to a stop in front of Dr. Valquist and Miss Maple. Two men wearing black ski masks burst from the back of the vehicle. One of them lunged at the headmaster and punched him in the midsection. Dr. Valquist crumbled to the ground.

"What the hell!" Carmen shouted. She stepped into the street toward her teachers.

"Look out!" Jonathan shouted, pulling her back just as a car flew by.

The second man lifted Miss Maple into the air and threw her into the back of the van. A third man scrambled out and grabbed Dr. Valquist's feet as the first assailant dragged him by the hands toward the vehicle.

"We have to help them!" Carmen said, diving again out into traffic.

A horn blared as a car barely missed hitting her. She reached the back of the vehicle just as the doors slammed shut. Tires screamed and the van accelerated down the street.

****

The four students huddled together on a bed in the boys' hotel room. A sudden rap at the door startled them all.

"I've got it," Jonathan said, standing up from the bed to peer through the peep-hole. "Who's there?" he shouted through the door.

"Bruce Harper, from the United States Embassy," came a muffled voice.

Jonathan turned to the group. "He looks official."

Will gave a nod.

Carmen got up and took a defensive stance in the middle of the room.

Jonathan unlatched the chain lock and opened the door.

A tall blue-suited man stepped in. "Thank you," he said. "First off, how are you all doing?"

"We're pretty shook up," Layla answered. "I still can't believe this is happening."

Mr. Harper looked between the two boys. "Which one of you is Will?"

"Here," he said, raising his hand.

"I've been in touch with the British Embassy on behalf of you and Miss Maple. They would like us to continue as the lead in this thing."

"Thank you," Will said.

"Now, we've got you all booked on the first flight out in the morning. Have you spoken to your parents?"

"They have," Jonathan said. "And I've spoken to my uncle."

The man nodded knowingly, having learned of Jonathan's situation. "Can I get a bit more background on this trip you're on?"

Will spoke for the group. "We're the Senior Class at the Fairfax Classical Academy in Virginia. This is our Spring Break trip."

"You're the entire Senior Class?"

The students chuckled in concert.

"We were the only students when they first opened," Layla explained. "But now there's a hundred more in the lower grades."

"What does it mean that it's a classical academy?"

"It's a normal high school," Jonathan started, "but we focus on Latin and ancient Roman culture."

"Like mythology?"

"Everything," Carmen said. "We even practice horseback riding and sword fighting."

"What a strange place."

"Mr. Harper, what happened here today?" Jonathan asked.

"It seems to be a random kidnapping. It's not common here in Rome, but it's also not unprecedented."

"Excuse me," Carmen said. "I assume you are aware that Dr. Valquist is a former NSA agent."

"Yes, that fact certainly popped up when I entered his name in my database."

"Could that be connected to this?"

He shook his head. "We have no reason right now to believe it is."

"Any chance these people will come after us too?" Layla asked.

"There are Roman police outside in the hall here and in the lobby downstairs. You'll be fine."

"That makes me feel a little better," Jonathan said.

The man opened the door and stepped into the hall. "An embassy van will pick you up tomorrow morning at six to take you to the airport."

"Thank you, sir," Will said.

As the door gently closed, the students exchanged silent glances for a moment.

Layla closed her eyes. "I'm...so...scared," she managed through broken breaths.

Will took a half and hesitant step toward her and then stopped. Jonathan saw his caution and rolled his eyes. Carmen sat down beside her friend and put her arm around her shoulder.

"It's alright, Layla," she said, pulling her into a hug.

"I can't imagine never seeing them again," she said.

"I know," Jonathan said, sitting down on the other side of Layla and adding another layer to the embrace.

Will stood by, wanting to be there but not knowing how at that point.

Suddenly the hotel phone rang as if screaming for attention.

"Who could that be?" Jonathan mumbled, breaking the hug and rolling across the bed toward the dresser. He lifted the receiver. "Yes?"

The others looked on as horror seized Jonathan's face. He listened carefully for a moment then set the receiver back down.

"What is it?!" Carmen asked insistently.

He shook his head, mouth agape. "Here's what I just heard. Be ready to deliver the bag to us or your teachers die."

"Bloody Hell!" Will shouted. "What does that even mean?"

"What bag?" Layla asked.

"Wait a minute," Carmen said. "Dr. Valquist handed me his satchel when we were by the Coliseum."

"Where is it now?" Jonathan asked.

"In our room. Just a sec." She opened the door and disappeared into the hall. A moment later, she stepped back in, holding the satchel to her chest. She set it on the bed between her fellow students.

"Should we really open this?" Will asked. "I mean, this is his private stuff."

"We don't have a choice," Carmen said, undoing the buckle on the leather bag. "We have to figure out why they want this thing." She emptied the contents onto the bed. An assortment of various nations' currencies, a stick of gum, a weathered passport, and a single folded piece of paper tumbled and bounced on the bed.

"What's this?" Jonathan asked, unfolding the paper.

The students gasped in unison as they spotted the header:

TOP SECRET/COMINT/GAMMA/X-1

"Top Secret?" Layla whispered. "This is a classified document!"

"He's not supposed to have something like this in his bag, right?" Will asked.

"I would assume not," Carmen said. "What's 'COMINT'?"

"Communications Intelligence," Jonathan replied. "That's what the NSA does, wiretaps and stuff like that. I would guess that GAMMA and X-1 have something to do with Area 51 maybe."

"Yeah, right," Will chuckled.

They all looked into the body of the message, a jumble of upper case letters.

"That's a lot of question marks and very few vowels," Carmen said. "Any idea what it says?"

"Some kind of secret code," Will said.

"This is what alien language looks like," Jonathan added. "They're so smart they don't need vowels."

Layla laughed. "It's Arabic, written in an English transcription system."

"What's it say?" Carmen asked.

"Greetings, my brother. God willing, soon you will hear news," she said, running her finger along the page.

"Sounds ominous," Jonathan said.

"It's really not," she returned. "This is the kind of thing my dad would write to my uncle. I don't see why this would even be classified."

"We gotta call Mr. Harper back," Will said. "He has to know about all this."

"But they're gonna kill them," Carmen whispered.

"And we assume that Dr. Valquist and Miss Maple really go free if we give this sheet to the kidnappers?" Jonathan asked.

"Think, people," Will said, standing up from the bed. "What are our options?"

"Give them the satchel and hope for the best," Layla said. "That's one option."

They looked at each other and shook their heads.

"Doing nothing isn't really an option either," Jonathan said.

"Then there's only one other course of action," Carmen said. "And we know it."

"Fight back?" Will said. "We're a high school group on Spring Break. What can we do about kidnappers?"

"Not just kidnappers," Jonathan noted. "Probably these are intelligence officers of a hostile nation."

"Oh, great," Layla said.

"But we're not just high school students," Carmen countered. "We're pretty well trained in fighting ourselves."

"Not all of us are as good as you," Layla said nervously.

"And I'm not the linguist you are. But we're a team."

Jonathan stood from the bed. "We really don't have any choice. We either give them the satchel or go on the offensive."

Layla sighed. "We can't trust them to just let our teachers go. I know that."

The group nodded in the recognition of their growing consensus.

"If we do this, we need a plan," Will said.

Jonathan walked across the room. He returned with his laptop bag.

"What are you doing?" Layla asked.

"Remember that I have the distinction of being the only student at the academy to ever get an out-of-school suspension."

"That's right," Carmen said. "You hacked into the school's server. Did you do that to change a grade?"

"Better," he said. "To get that red-headed junior's cell-phone number."

"Celeste?" Layla laughed. "Why didn't you just ask one of us?"

"Right," he said. "And then the whole school would know I like her."

"How did you do it?" Carmen asked. "And what are you doing now?"

Jonathan removed the cord from the hotel phone and inserted it into the back of the laptop. "I used my uncle's log-on at his job to get into a few databases." He took another cord out of his bag and connected it from his computer back into the phone itself.

"He's at the Department of Transportation, right?" Layla asked.

"Yeah," Jonathan said, double clicking his way through several screens. "And he's got plenty of toys at his disposal."

"How did you get his log-on?" Carmen asked.

"A lucky guess on his password," he said softly. "It's the nickname my dad used to call him."

"Sorry," Carmen said, putting her hand on his shoulder.

"Those guys are probably going to call back soon to tell us where to bring the satchel," Jonathan said. "And when they do, I'm going to get some information off that call."

The phone rang.

"That's them," Jonathan said. "Layla, answer it and try to keep the guy on the line as long as you can."

"Why me?"

"He had an accent of some kind. Only you have a chance of figuring out where he's from."

She nodded and picked up the receiver. "Yes?"

The students watched as Jonathan furiously typed on his computer.

"*¿Dónde?*" Layla asked.

Jonathan nodded and continued to type.

"*Entiendo. Pero, ¿dónde, exactamente? ¿Y cuándo?*"

She pulled the receiver from her ear. "They just hung up."

"Don't hang up yourself!" Jonathan shouted. "There are still packets of info that fly back and forth." He continued typing and then lifted his hands from the keyboard, smiling.

"What is it?" Carmen asked.

"I've got their phone number and a location." He clicked to reveal a map. "That call was placed from a cell just a mile north from here."

"They're asking us to drop the satchel in a trash barrel on the north side of the Coliseum in exactly two hours," Layla said.

"Where was he from?" Carmen asked.

"He was pretending to have a Castilian accent, but he's actually Latin American."

"So who could these people be?" Will asked. "Cubans?"

"I said Latin American. Not Caribbean."

"Sorry, Miss Linguist," he chuckled.

"Listen," Carmen interrupted. "I guess all we can do is hope that our teachers are being held where the call was placed from. But if they're planning to pick up that satchel in two hours, we have to move."

"You're right," Will said. "Are we really going to do this thing?"

Each one nodded in turn.

"Every operation needs a leader," Carmen said. "I nominate our Senior Class president."

"I concur," Jonathan said.

"Ditto," Layla added.

"Thanks for your vote of confidence," Will said. "I think."

"Alright, leader. What do we do about the guards in the hall and downstairs?" Jonathan asked.

Will looked up in thought. "Here's the plan. When we step out of this room, Layla will explain to the guard in her best Italian that we are going to the lobby for snacks. But when we get down there, we will walk casually out of the hotel and then run to the right and lose the guards stationed down there."

"And what if the police talk about losing us on their radios and the kidnappers hear about it?" Jonathan asked. "Wouldn't that broadcast the fact that we aren't going to the drop-off point in two hours as instructed?"

"Possibly," Carmen said. "But not necessarily. Maybe we left early just to make sure we could find the place. I mean, we had to leave anyway, if we were going to deliver the satchel."

"It's all suspicious," Jonathan said. "But it's a risk we'll have to take."

"What's our plan when we get to where the call was made?" Carmen asked.

"One crazy scheme at a time," Will replied. "I'm making this up as I go."

They all nodded in agreement.

"Let's do this thing," he said.

****

Their escape from the hotel had gone exactly as planned. It was just after midnight and the group was walking along a dimly-lit boulevard lined with tall apartment buildings.

"We turn right at the next corner," Jonathan said. "From there it's three more blocks. Remember, all I have is a location based on the closest cell tower."

"Understood," Will said.

"Is anyone else's heart about to explode out of their chest?" Layla asked.

"I think that's a unanimous feeling," Carmen said. "Six hours ago we were sightseeing in the Forum. Now, our teachers have been kidnapped and we're on our way to try and rescue them. Take that, St. Benet's Academy!"

"No more talking," Will said, feeling uncomfortable at giving an order he felt was necessary.

The group complied and walked in silence until they approached the area of the caller.

"Well?" Will asked softly.

Jonathan pointed forward. "It's that tall apartment building."

Their eyes all locked on a seven-story structure with separate sets of apartments on the front and back of the building.

"So they could be in any one of those?" Layla asked.

"Here's where I would be open to ideas, team," Will said.

"I got the location off the cell tower," Jonathan said. "But it's accurate down to about fifty feet. From the range of the signal, it has to have come from an apartment on the back alley side of the building. Past that, I have no further information."

"Think, people," Will said. "There's always a way."

Carmen raised her hand.

"Yes, Miss Mattila?" Will said, smiling. "Thank you for raising your hand and not speaking out of turn."

"Sorry," she said. "Instinct. We have the number of the phone that called us. The kidnappers are probably keeping the apartment lights off while they wait."

"Why do you think?" Will asked.

"I would," she answered. "Whenever you're doing something illegal or clandestine, you try to reduce your visibility."

"You're probably right," he said. "Later on you can tell us all about your illegal and clandestine activities."

"So we call that phone from one of our cells. They don't know we have their number, since they called our landline at the hotel. They're going to look at their phone to see who's calling them."

"And maybe turn a light on in the process," Jonathan said. "It's as good a plan as any."

Will turned toward the group. "Alright, people, listen carefully. We are going to set this in motion and fast. After I finish talking, we will proceed, without any further words, to the back alley. I will place a call to that phone from my cell. We will all be watching the building for any possible sign of the apartment where that phone might be ringing. If we're lucky, and we get a location, we will enter the building and immediately storm that spot. I'm assuming a locked front door of a regular apartment can be compromised by you,

Jonathan, running against it and hitting it with all your force. Carmen, as the best fighter in this group, you will be the first through the opened door. Your only directive is to disable anyone you can. The rest of us will enter as follows. I am after Carmen, then Layla. Jonathan, you come in as you are able, but depending on the strength of that door, we may not be able to count on you."

They all nodded.

"We have no back up coming, so all we can do is defeat the enemy and rescue our teachers. That's if they're even in there."

"Permission to speak," Carmen said.

"Yes."

"I love you all," she said, her eyes filling with tears.

Will smiled. "Alright, let's go."

The other students followed him to the back alley behind the building. The group spread out into the shadows, their eyes scanning the darkened wall of windows. Will took out his cell and gave it to Jonathan, who entered the number and handed the phone back.

"On three, I place the call. One...two...three."

He pressed the button and lowered the phone, training his eyes across the building with the rest of the group. Everyone saw a single light suddenly appear in the corner apartment on the fourth story. Will closed his phone.

He raised his hand with four fingers and presented it for confirmation of the floor. They all nodded in silence.

Walking closely beside the building, they returned to the main street. The students entered the lobby single file, in the order of their planned assault. On their right was a wall of mailboxes. Passing an elevator on their left, they started up a set of stairs. A rush of adrenaline surged through each of them as they bounded up the steps and arrived at their destination.

Jonathan leaned out of the stairwell. Looking down a hallway dimly lit by a single ceiling lamp, he saw the door of the target apartment. He scanned the floor for obstacles and saw none. Turning around, he spied Carmen directly behind him. She smiled with sad eyes. Will was behind Carmen and held up his open hand. He began closing his fingers one by one, signaling for the assault to begin.

Jonathan turned back and stepped out into the hall. He mentally counted down the final three seconds. On the mark, he began a sprint. He could hear Carmen following closely behind. Knowing that the entire group depended on him getting through that door, he somehow found even more speed. Jonathan came at the door faster than he had ever moved and at the last instant turned his shoulder into it.

Carmen saw the door explode open. Jonathan fell stunned to the ground just inside the apartment. She leapt over him and into the darkened room. Silhouetted against the city lights seeping through curtains on the window, she saw a human form. Carmen heard, not saw, a kick coming toward her and barely dodged it. Punching forward, she struck her target squarely in the face and followed with two quick jabs to the stomach.

Will ran into the apartment. In the faint light, he made out the blackness of a hallway leading straight ahead from the first room. He thrust himself into that darkness and immediately took a sharp punch to his stomach. Doubling over, he shot his fist up in the direction from which he had been struck. He felt his blow drive into the assailant's chin.

Layla followed quickly behind and joined the fray, sending another sharp fist into Will's now off-balance opponent.

Carmen turned and saw Jonathan getting up from the floor. Sounds of a commotion in the next room told her that Will and Layla were in a fight. She made a rapid scan of the area to see if her opponent had dropped a useful weapon. Seeing nothing, she raced to follow her friends.

Just as she entered the hallway, all the lights in the apartment went on. The students squinted in pain as their eyes adjusted.

"Well done, students," Dr. Valquist said, stepping out of a bedroom.

Carmen sunk into a defensive stance. "Get down, sir. We're here to rescue you!"

An athletic whistle blew from the front room. "Stand down!" a familiar voice called out.

"What's going on?" Will asked.

"Stand down, all of you," Mr. Cole said, stepping into the hallway.

"I see that our pupils have passed their final exam," Miss Maple said, emerging from yet another bedroom.

Jonathan stumbled into the hallway himself. "Someone needs to explain what in the hell is happening here."

Will and Layla's opponent stood up slowly from the floor, rubbing his jaw. "You've trained these lads and lasses awfully well, Nick," the man mumbled in a thick Scottish brogue. "MI-6 assassins aren't supposed to get beat up by a couple of teenagers."

"Thanks," Mr. Cole said. "My protégée got the better of me as well."

"MI-6?" Will said loudly. "Please, Dr. Valquist. What's going on?"

He looked at his students and smiled. "This will require more explanation than I can give standing in a hallway in Rome. So let's go to England."

Chapter Three

Within minutes, the group was in a white van, speeding through Rome. Out the windows, the students saw the red and blue lights of a police escort dancing on the darkened buildings racing by. After twenty minutes of travel, they came into a section of the international airport reserved for private planes. The students saw a Lear jet emerge out of the darkness as they drove onto the tarmac.

"Is this our ride?" Jonathan asked.

"Yes," Dr. Valquist answered. "And I regret that I will not be able to answer any of your many questions until we are at a certain facility south of London. Please enjoy the accommodations and be patient. I really do understand how frustrating all of this must be to you."

"Well, especially because it's starting to look like we aren't going to explore Rome," Layla said.

"Sorry about that. But with any luck, you'll be back soon."

"Would it be safe to assume that you're still with the NSA?" Carmen asked.

Dr. Valquist raised an eyebrow. "Let's see, in light of you finding a classified document in my satchel, learning that one of my associates is with MI-6, and now the fact that we're about to get on a jet to fly to London, that would indeed be a safe assumption. But I'm not saying that's the truth."

"Good Lord!" Carmen exclaimed. "Okay, I can wait."

For three hours, the students sat in comfortable confusion as their jet sped toward London. Upon arrival, they piled into another van.

"We'll be there soon," Miss Maple said.

"Are you with MI-6 as well?" Will asked her.

"No," she said, smiling. "I'm an agent at GCHQ."

"What's that?" Jonathan asked.

"Government Communications Headquarters," she replied. "It's the British equivalent of the NSA."

"How come she can talk about this stuff with Will and you can't answer my questions?" Carmen asked.

"Simple," Dr. Valquist answered. "The Brits have their own rules."

"NSA'ers are notoriously serious about security, Carmen," Miss Maple explained.

"Ah ha! So he is with the NSA!"

"I never said that," Miss Maple countered. "It's just a statement of fact, based on my observations. It doesn't necessarily have any connection to the rest of the conversation."

"Alright, alright," she said. "I get it."

The vehicle sped down a highway surrounded by thickly forested hills. They turned off onto a single lane of gravel road. Following miles more of travel, they approached a tall gray iron gate, manned by four guards in black jumpsuits holding assault rifles. The guards stepped aside and waved the vehicle through.

The horizon was just beginning to glow with orange as they drove up a tree-lined lane toward a massive tan stone mansion.

"It's good to be home again," Miss Maple said.

"You lived here?" Carmen asked.

"Kind of. This is home base for the mission."

"What is your mission, or can't you tell us that?"

Miss Maple laughed. "As you'll soon find out, it's really *our* mission. My role is done. Yours has just begun."

"First, we need to get these kids cleaned up," Dr. Valquist said. "The attendants inside will show you all to your rooms and give you what you need, including clean clothes."

"How do they know our sizes?" Carmen asked.

Dr. Valquist smiled. "Oh, they know, Miss Mattila. Rest up for an hour and meet us in the main dining room. At breakfast, everything will be explained."

"It's about time!" Jonathan said.

The students were led to separate quarters on the second floor of the estate.

Carmen looked in amazement at the lavish furnishings in her room. Rich blue and white velvet wallpaper seemed to glow on the walls all around her. As she walked into her bathroom, she gasped at the brightness of the space, the walls all mirrored and the fixtures plated with gold. An elegant green dress clung to a hanger on the wall. She lifted it and let it gently fall through her fingers.

"You *are* in my size! I hope I get to keep you," she whispered.

Jonathan threw himself onto the bed in his room and closed his eyes. He almost felt sleep beginning to seep into his brain, but he shook it off. "I sure wish you were here, Frank," he said.

Layla entered her room and immediately had stripped off all her clothes. Soon she was soaking in a hot shower. "*Laa 'afham*," she whispered. "*No entiendo. Non intellego.* I don't understand what's happening."

Will sat down on the bed in his room. He took a deep breath and made the sign of the cross. "My Lord Jesus, please give me strength."

An hour later, the students had washed up and were seated around a long banquet table, covered with a bright white table cloth. Silver cutlery lay atop ruby-red napkins. The young men had been provided with black suits and blue ties. Layla wore a bright white dress in the same pattern as Carmen's green.

"Why so formal for breakfast?" Will asked.

Layla looked around the room. Large paintings covered all the sky blue walls. She squinted at one, a purple and pink pastel scene of a pond. "That's a beautiful Monet print," she said.

"Sweetie," Carmen returned. "I think that's the real Monet."

Will pointed at the seats and made a quick count. "I see enough place settings for Dr. Valquist, Miss Maple, and Mr. Cole. But there are three other spots set. Who else will be here?"

"Well, it's got to include Mr. Chen and Miss Grant," Jonathan said. "They're the only people from the school we haven't seen yet."

"I suppose," he said. "And judging from the settings, breakfast should be extraordinary."

They heard muffled voices as people approached from behind a tall mahogany door. It opened and Dr. Valquist emerged, followed by Miss Maple and Mr. Cole.

"*Salvete, discipuli*," Dr. Valquist said. "I hope you're somewhat refreshed. Please rise to greet our special guests who will help explain things to you."

They stood from their seats and saw three figures emerging from the darkened hallway. The first to appear was an old man with scraggly gray hair, wearing a white lab coat which seemed inappropriate for the elegant setting. The second and third figures seemed to the students equally inappropriate merely from the impossibility of their presence in the room.

"Are we really seeing this?" Layla whispered to Carmen.

"We are."

"Mr. President, Mr. Prime Minister," Dr. Valquist said. "I am pleased to introduce you both to the seniors of the Fairfax Classical Academy."

The students stood with mouths agape, trying to make sense of seeing the two dignitaries.

"You're the President!" Carmen blurted.

"I am," he said with a chuckle. "Along with the Prime Minister, I invite you to take your seats. I'm sure you're very hungry after all you've been through in the last day. So let's get our breakfast underway and start explaining this obviously unique situation to you."

The students slowly sat down as they watched the adults take their places. They were a bit surprised to see the old man in the lab coat sit at the head of the table, with the President and Prime Minister on his right and left.

The Prime Minister noticed their attention to this and smiled. "The President insisted I sit at the head of the table since we're in my country. I insisted that he sit there as my honored guest."

"So I said, damn it, I'll sit there if no one else is going to!" the old man said loudly.

Those previously not acquainted with the man learned from his accent that he also was a Brit.

"Let me introduce Dr. Jeremiah Silver," the President said. "He'll be in charge of answering some of the more technical questions you'll have soon."

"Nice to meet you, sir," Will said.

"You must be the science freak they've been telling me about. Oh, what I could have turned you into if they hadn't filled your brain with languages all these years!"

A tone chimed three times.

"No speaking until the attendants have left the room," Dr. Valquist said firmly.

Men in long-tailed tuxedos entered and distributed baskets of frosted cinnamon buns and trays with pats of butter onto the table. Another wave of workers refilled water glasses and left pitchers of various beverages.

"Thank you," the President said.

The attendants nodded and left the room. A single tone sounded for several seconds.

"We're clear to talk," the Prime Minister said. "Mr. President, I'll let you formally swear in your citizens first."

"Thank you," the President returned, standing from his seat. "Carmen, Layla, Jonathan, please stand."

They looked at each other in confusion as they stood from their chairs.

"Please raise your right hand and repeat after me," he said. "I, state your first and last name, do solemnly swear…"

They repeated the words.

"…to uphold and defend the Constitution of the United States of America…against all enemies foreign and domestic…so help me God."

The students repeated his words and looked at him in puzzlement.

"I now formally grant you clearance for all intelligence information at or below the level of Ultra Secret." He smiled and faced the Prime Minister. "Your turn, my friend."

The President sat down, followed by the American students.

"Carmen," Dr. Valquist said. "I can tell you now, I'm still with the NSA."

She laughed. "Thanks. I figured as much."

"Please stand and raise your right hand, Will," the Prime Minister said, rising from his chair.

Will stood and faced the Prime Minister.

"Repeat after me. I, state your full name, do swear that I will be faithful and bear true allegiance to her Majesty Queen Elizabeth, her heirs and successors, according to law. So help me God."

Will repeated the words seriously.

"And I now formally grant you clearance for all intelligence information at or below the level of Ultra Secret," the Prime Minister said. He sat down, followed by Will.

"Now we're ready to get started," Dr. Valquist said. "I'll inform you of an additional fact of what has just happened here. In the event that you ever share any information at the Ultra Secret level with someone not cleared to hear it, you will serve the rest of your life in strict solitary confinement. That's the reason for the triple tone. Nothing we say can be heard by the people that work here. They're all cleared for Top Secret. Ultra Secret is something altogether different." He turned to each of them with a genuine smile on this face. "Is that clear and agreed upon before we continue?"

The students were stunned.

"That's pretty heavy, Dr. Valquist," Will said.

"And quite necessary," the President said. "You'll understand just how serious all this is as you learn more."

A tone sounded three times.

"No talking," the Prime Minister said.

The attendants returned and set a fruit salad in front of each person.

"I love fruit salad!" Layla exclaimed. She looked around and noticed that the no-talking rule was apparently absolute. Her face cringed as she silently mouthed 'sorry' to the President. He smiled kindly and nodded.

The attendants left the room. A few moments after the door closed, a single tone sounded again.

"Dr. Silver," the Prime Minister said. "Would you start things off by explaining how all this began?"

"Certainly, sir," he said, picking up his fork and stuffing several pieces of melon into his mouth. "The year was 1981," he said through his food. "I was working on a project for MI-6. It doesn't even matter what it was, some silly energy saving thing or what not. You have to remember that we had just been through an Oil Embargo. Anyway, I discovered a time machine."

"A time machine," Will said.

"That's right, young man," he said. "Or, to be more accurate, I discovered the mathematical and scientific principles behind the construction of a functional time machine. Making the damn thing was going to be the trickier part."

"Dr. Silver's discovery was certainly the most significant advancement in the history of science ever achieved," the Prime Minister said. "And our government immediately recognized the potential for disaster if this knowledge were ever misused. This required the creation of a new level of secret classification, which we termed Ultra Secret."

"So who knows about this?" Carmen asked.

"Current and former Presidents and Prime Ministers and the people in this room," Dr. Silver said.

The President sipped from a glass of orange juice he had poured. "It's a tragedy that the greatest breakthrough in human history didn't get this poor man the Nobel Prize he deserved."

"Ah, that's the breaks," Dr. Silver said. "The thing was, while I discovered the theory behind all this, the cost of constructing the time machine itself wasn't even the issue. The issue was the fuel. The time machine runs, so to speak, on a particular enormously expensive isotope of plutonium. I knew immediately that the British government could never afford to do this on our own."

"Prime Minister Thatcher approached President Reagan and informed him of the breakthrough," the Prime Minister said. "She asked the United States to become a full partner in the project."

"President Reagan agreed and the two governments conducted the first and only ever test of the technology," the President said.

"The overall cost of running just that one test was such a drain on the economies of the United States and Britain that it only worsened the recessions of the early 80's," Dr. Silver said. "We knew that was the only test we could ever run until we had some operational use of the technology."

"If I may," Jonathan said. "We're in a global economic meltdown right now. Can we take that to mean that you all recently again spent half the world's GDP on producing more time machine fuel?"

The President chuckled. "Quite right, Jonathan. But we wouldn't have done that if we didn't have a very serious reason."

"I have to back up now a little bit to explain our operation," Dr. Silver said. "Have any of you ever heard of Planet X?"

"Yeah," Will said. "That's a planet believed to exist based on some gravitational anomalies with the outer planets. But no one's ever seen it."

"Exactly right," Dr. Silver said. "Back in the 1960's, the damn thing passed right in front of a star. A US government astronomer saw that and was able to establish its size."

"Now, I'm assuming all this that we're hearing is somehow connected," Layla said. "The time machine, Planet X, and, I suppose, four high school students suddenly being whisked away to a private dinner with the President and Prime Minister."

"It pulls together pretty fast from here," the President said.

Dr. Silver sipped from his water glass. "What it all means, kids, is that..."

Three tones sounded.

"Bloody Hell!" Will said.

The Prime Minister looked at him in horror at his use of this British expletive.

"Sorry," he mouthed in silence.

They waited as the attendants brought in the main course—steak and scrambled eggs. Water glasses were checked and refilled. Salad plates were whisked away. Finally, the attendants left the room. The single tone sounded.

"That was the longest five minutes of my life!" Jonathan said.

"Let me try to sum it all up into one sentence," Dr. Silver said. "We need you four to go back in time to ancient Rome to get us information so we can keep Planet X from destroying the earth in a collision which will happen next year." He picked up his fork. "*Bon appétit!*"

Will looked across the table at Jonathan. The two erupted in laughter.

"You know," Jonathan said. "Sure, I'm sitting having breakfast with the President, which is pretty crazy as it is. But what you just said is insane."

"We're keeping this upcoming calamity Ultra Secret for obvious reasons," the President said. "But Planet X will hit the earth in about a year unless we change its course."

"Don't we have missiles that can destroy it before that happens?" Carmen asked.

"No," the President said. "We're talking about an entire planet here. In fact, Planet X is about three times the size of the earth."

"Alright," Jonathan said. "Now that we're cleared for Ultra Secret, can't you tell us about a certain alien spacecraft that crashed in Nevada and is held at Area 51? Didn't we learn anything from that which can help us?"

"Never happened," the President replied. "It really was just an Air Force weather balloon."

"Damn it!" Jonathan said. "I really wanted that to be true. What about Bigfoot?"

"Now they're real," the President said. "But they can't help us out here."

"What it comes down to," Dr. Silver continued, "is that we will have exactly one shot at hitting Planet X with just about every nuke the US and Britain have. If we hit it on the correct side, we will divert its course enough that when it arrives in a year it won't hit the earth."

"Sounds like a plan," Jonathan said. "So what's the problem?"

"The information we have on Planet X is enough to confirm the collision with Earth," the Prime Minister said. "But it isn't enough to guarantee hitting it in the right spot to deflect it."

"You see, we've only got two data points on its movement," Dr. Silver said. "That first one in the 60's confirmed its existence, but the scientist who saw it didn't even record the exact time of day of his sighting."

"Which makes it virtually worthless for tracking purposes," Will said.

"The second sighting was back in 2006," Dr. Silver said. "Based on that information, we know that Planet X is coming our way and, because of its massive size, a near miss will still kill all life on this planet. If it doesn't directly hit us, we'll be thrown from our current orbit."

"And life on earth won't survive that," Layla noted.

"So why does our going back in time to ancient Rome change all that?" Carmen asked.

Dr. Silver smiled. "Based on the trajectory we do know, we can confirm that Planet X made a relatively close pass by the earth back in the year 48 BC. It wasn't close enough to cause any problems, but it should have been visible to people. We assume that it was seen and information about its appearance may be housed in the Bibliotheca Ulpia in Rome."

"That's why we studied it so much," Miss Maple said.

"Someone has to go back in time to check out a book from a library?" Layla asked.

Dr. Silver nodded. "If we can get any information about the sighting of Planet X in 48 BC, what part of the sky it was seen in or even a specific day it was visible, we will be able to use that as the third data point to very accurately fix the trajectory and location of Planet X."

"And have much better odds of changing that trajectory with a massive missile strike," the President said.

"I just hope the Russians aren't sitting on alien technology they got from the Siberian Tunguska crash," Jonathan said.

"That really was just a comet," the Prime Minister said.

"Damn it!" Jonathan said. "The Ultra Secret world is boring!"

"Planet X and a trip back in time aren't enough excitement for you?" Mr. Cole said, chuckling.

"After the news of Planet X's arrival was digested, we realized that we finally had an operational use for the time machine," Dr. Silver said. "I proposed then that we locate the best classical language scholar we had in the intelligence community and send that individual back to get the information we needed."

"And that's where I was brought in," Dr. Valquist said. "I was working as a linguist at the NSA when they cleared me for Ultra Secret and offered me this mission."

"You told us you were former NSA," Will said. "Wasn't that a potential security breach?"

"We decided to make my former status a part of my cover," Dr. Valquist said.

"Kind of like Poe's *Purloined Letter*," the President said.

"But you never thought I was a former SEAL and current CIA operative, did you?" Mr. Cole asked.

"And you never suspected that I was GCHQ," Miss Maple said.

"Is the whole school staffed with spies?" Carmen asked.

"No," Miss Maple said. "Mr. Chen and Miss Grant are uncleared civilians. They know nothing about the school's true mission."

"But our bus driver Juan is a CIA operative like me," Mr. Cole said. "We always figured the bus ride was a place we needed eyes and ears on the mission."

"Anyway," Dr. Valquist continued, "I informed Dr. Silver and the then president and prime minister that the chance of one individual pulling off the mission was remote at best. I suggested, since we had some years before the missile strike would have to happen, that we train up new operatives for this task. I thought that the best chance at success would be to send back a team of agents who had some years dedicated to mastering the language skills they would need, know the culture of ancient Rome intimately, and be trained in the usual fighting skills of the time. And, for legal reasons, we even had everything timed so you would all have turned eighteen just before we would send you on the mission."

The students looked at each other, soaking in the implications of what he had said.

"So the Fairfax Classical Academy was a secret front created to train the four of us for this mission," Carmen said.

"What about the lower grades?" Layla asked. "Are any of them going as well?"

"No," Dr. Valquist said. "Continuing to add students each year was just part of the front. Otherwise, the four of you would have become suspicious about our unique academy."

"Granted," Will said. "But, do our parents know about any of this?"

"Your parents are all intelligence officers who volunteered your involvement when they were told that a matter of world survival depended on it," the President said. "But they aren't cleared for Ultra Secret. So all they know right now is that you four will be taking part in a critically important mission. They know nothing of the time machine."

"Wait," Layla said. "My parents are not CIA agents. They're teachers."

"Your parents are NSA agents," Dr. Valquist said. "In fact, I once had a cubicle right next to your mother's. She's a brilliant linguist of Spanish, Arabic, Persian, and, curiously, Dutch. And their jobs as teachers are a part of the cover they took to keep you from knowing about all that was going on."

"And my parents?" Will asked.

"MI-5," Miss Maple replied. "Their jobs at the British embassy in Washington are a cover for them."

"Are we really nobility or is that part of the cover?" he asked.

"Your father really is *Lord* Stanhope," the Prime Minister said. "Royals and nobles have a long tradition within the military and the secret services."

"What about my mom and dad?" Carmen asked.

"NRO, actually," Mr. Cole said. "That's the National Reconnaissance Office, tasked with maintaining our network of surveillance satellites."

"So my mom's not a gourmet chef and my dad's not an insurance salesman?"

"For the time being, they are," the President said. "But they were both rocket propulsion scientists. Your Mom's actually turned out to be so good at cooking that she wants to get her *Cordon Bleu*. And we'll pay for that. It's the least we could do for her."

Jonathan picked up his glass of water and took a drink. "And here's where I find out that my parents didn't really die in a car accident, isn't it?" He looked at his plate and all could see his eyes flooding with tears.

"Jonathan..." Dr. Valquist started.

"I'll take this," the President said softly. "Jonathan, in the first year of this project, we let all the parents keep doing their real jobs. They were in what we call 'soft cover', meaning that they told you different things but they were still doing classified work."

"What were they really?"

"Your mom and dad were the best covert CIA agents we had for Afghanistan. They spoke Pashto and Urdu both."

"I thought they were on a second honeymoon in Europe, but they were really in Afghanistan?"

"And they were killed by a roadside bomb there. You need to know that your parents did very important work to help stabilize that country before they died. Their names are inscribed on a secret memorial at CIA headquarters."

"It's going to take me a while to process that," Jonathan said.

"I understand," the President responded.

"After what happened, we put all your parents into hard cover in their current jobs," Dr. Valquist said.

"Does my uncle know about any of this?" Jonathan asked.

"No, he doesn't," the President said.

Jonathan nodded, looking up at the ceiling, tears now streaming down his cheeks.

The conversation was again suspended by the arrival of a chocolate mousse.

"That brings us almost to the present," Dr. Valquist said. "We decided about a year ago to test your operational readiness with a completely unanticipated crisis. The mock kidnapping was a way to see how you would function as a team. And so I am happy to tell the President and Prime Minister that Operation Classical Academy has been a success. We have at this table four fine young men and women who are, in fact, this planet's only hope of survival. They are ready to perform this mission with greater competence than I ever could have. And I have complete confidence in them."

The President finished his dessert and wiped his mouth with the red cloth napkin. "In the end, we can't force you to do this mission," he said. "Much of what has happened to you over the last four years is quite unfair. Your high school years were, without you knowing it, a complete lie. But this was all done because of a firm belief that only four people such as yourselves, trained in your youth, could do what needed to be done to save humankind. On behalf of the Prime Minister, I am asking you now to accept the mission we have described." He stood from the table, followed by the other adults. "We're going to give you all some time to sort through what we've said."

The adults left the room.

The four young people picked at their desserts and looked at each other in some silence. It was finally broken by Layla putting her head in her hands and beginning to cry. Carmen, sitting next to her, rubbed her back.

"It's okay, sweetie," she whispered.

"This is just all too much," Layla whispered.

"I know," Will said seriously. "We've basically just had our lives taken away from us. Not just our future lives, but our past as well. It was all a lie."

Jonathan scoffed. "You all learned that your boring parents are actually spies," he said. "But now I don't know what to think of mine."

"You should be proud of them," Carmen said.

"Well I'm not!" Jonathan shouted, his face turning red. "I'm mad as hell at them! Instead of flying around the world as secret agents, why didn't they stay home and raise their son?"

"Jonathan…" Will started.

"No one can tell me how to feel about this, okay? I cried and cried for them when I thought they died in an accident. And now I picture them running around in some desert somewhere and I don't know what to think anymore."

"Alright," Will said. "So what are we going to do here, people?"

"Well, what choice do we really have?" Carmen asked. "It's kind of hard to tell the President and Prime Minister that you don't want to save the planet from destruction."

Layla rubbed her eyes. "I know."

"We have to all be in this together," Will said. "I'm in."

"Me too," Layla said.

"Me three," Carmen said.

"You with us, Jonathan?" Will asked.

"Of course," he said. "But I don't know what use I'll be. We won't likely need to hack any computer networks in Ancient Rome."

"I bet we'll need you for other talents," Will said. "Every operation needs a leader. Because of the particular nature of this one, I nominate Layla, the best linguist in our group."

"No," she said. "I'm not a leader. I'll put my talents to use however the group needs them. But instead I nominate Carmen, the best fighter in the group."

"Agreed," Jonathan said.

"No," Carmen said. "It's obvious that Will is the natural leader of our class."

"Agreed again," Jonathan said.

"It does have to be you," Layla added.

"But we're doing this as a real team," Will said. "Carmen, I officially put you in charge of any matter related to the security of this mission. Layla, you are designated as the official linguist."

"And me?" Jonathan asked.

"I don't know yet," Will said. "For the time being, how about you just tell me whenever you think I'm completely off my rocker."

The students stood from the table and formed a group hug.

"Here are some words I never imagined would come from my mouth," Layla said. "Let's tell the President and Prime Minister that we accept this mission."

Chapter Four

The Prime Minister and President gladly received news of the students' acceptance of the mission and left the estate to return to their duties. The students were given the remainder of that day for leisure, but were told they would receive a mission briefing from Dr. Valquist later at dinner.

After brief walks on the grounds, however, all the students felt the lack of the previous night's sleep and napped the whole afternoon in their respective rooms.

Jonathan was the first one back to the banquet hall. He found the table fully set over a new white table cloth. The moment he sat down, an attendant in a long tailed black tuxedo entered.

"What can I bring you, sir?" the man asked.

"Ah, just a cup of coffee for now," Jonathan answered, rubbing the sleep out of his eyes.

"Right away." The man retreated to the kitchen.

Will appeared through the main doors and sat down beside Jonathan. "Wow," he said. "Given everything that happened over the last two days, I'm amazed at how well I just slept."

"That's because you haven't slept at all since our first plane ride across the Atlantic," Jonathan noted. "And that was before we foiled a mock kidnapping and met the President and Prime Minister while learning we were actually being trained as secret agents to save the entire world but didn't know it."

"You see, that part should have kept me awake. But it didn't."

The attendant emerged with a coffee service for Jonathan. Will requested the same.

They heard more people descending from the upper level of the house. Carmen and Layla entered the banquet hall, followed by Dr. Valquist. The attendants covered the table with abundant dinner options. Plates of steak, chicken breast, and pork ribs were followed by platters of French fries, salads, and vegetables.

"Let me brief you all now on what was learned in the test mission back in 1982," Dr. Valquist said, buttering a roll. "It has implications for how you will plan and conduct the current mission."

"First off," Carmen said. "Is there any idea of when our mission is supposed to start?"

He nodded. "Good question. Our nations already launched our missiles at Planet X three years ago."

"Didn't the Russians and others notice this massive missile launch?" Jonathan asked. "They must have wondered what was going on."

Dr. Valquist smiled. "They sure did. And our official response to them was that we did it for the sake of all humanity. Various countries asked for more information on what was happening and we told them that we could not share anything further."

"So when we get the information about exactly where Planet X is, what happens then?" Layla asked.

"The missiles are approaching the point where we will want to redirect them. The information you supply will let us focus the course of the missiles for optimal impact, which should save the earth."

"But when does our mission begin?" Carmen asked desperately.

"One week from today," Dr. Valquist replied.

As the students helped themselves to food, Dr. Valquist continued the briefing.

"As we told you, the US and UK governments conducted just one test of the time machine to learn some important facts about this technology. The time machine itself is a five by five meter room, surrounded by various nuclear components. When activated, it sends everything in that little room back to the chosen time, depending on the exact tuning of the isotopes. I don't understand all this myself. But the important thing is that you will appear back in time in the same place where the machine is built."

"In other words, you can't chose *where* you get sent back to," Jonathan said.

"That's right," Dr. Valquist replied. "But you also can't choose exactly *when* you want to go back to. The nature of the time continuum is that there are specific moments in the past to which you can go."

"So the 'when' of our time travel mission has limited options?" Will asked.

"Yes," Dr. Valquist replied. "One slot is in the year AD 235."

"Oh snap!" Carmen said. "Right in the middle of the Time of Troubles!"

The group all nodded, knowing the chaos that had infected the Roman Empire for a hundred year period in the time she referred to. For a whole century not a single Roman emperor had died of natural causes. The empire fell apart in a series of civil wars, plagues, and foreign invasions.

"What other options do we have?" Jonathan asked.

"AD 157 is another," Dr. Valquist said. "The only other slots are before Planet X passed by the Earth in 48 BC."

"So AD 157 is really our only option," Jonathan said.

"It's a fine year to go," Layla said. "Emperor Antoninus Pius was in one of the longest and most peaceful reigns in history."

"And you all knew that already," Carmen noted. "That's why Miss Maple made us experts in that time period for the last four years."

Dr. Valquist nodded. "Let's get back to the test mission and what was learned from it. The government decided on the least distant time slot available, only thirty years in the past."

"How come?" Will said. "Didn't they want to see everything the machine was capable of?"

"Sending someone back thirty years is just as mind-boggling as three thousand," Jonathan said. "And probably better for a test run of the technology."

"I see your point."

"That's exactly right," Dr. Valquist said. "If you send someone back into an uncertain place, you might not get valuable information from the test. The location selected, in fact, was the summer estate of the emeritus director of MI-6. The idea was to send the agent back to a place where he could have a good chance of being safe for one month."

"Why one month?" Carmen asked.

"Dr. Silver's calculations indicated that the area where things were sent back in time would, after almost exactly one month, become a time portal again and return anything on that spot to the present time. It works sort of like a rubber band. You can send things back in time by pulling it and letting go."

"But the laws of physics require a snap back eventually," Layla said.

"Precisely. So Mr. Breakwater, the MI-6 agent selected for the mission, was given the task of convincing the MI-6 director in the past that he was an MI-6 agent from the future on a mission to test this technology."

"Where was this summer estate?" Will asked.

"You're sitting in it. And the first prototype time machine is still in a storeroom downstairs. We'll go look at it later."

"So what did they learn in that test that concerns our mission now?" Jonathan asked.

"Well, first off, the machine worked. And Agent Breakwater reported only mild nausea immediately after the time travel. You're going to all have access to his diaries and the full report on the experiment, but I'll tell you the highlights. When MI-6 approached the emeritus director about using his summer estate for the test, he started to laugh."

"How come?" Carmen asked.

"He said that he had always known a time machine would be discovered and they would ask to use his house."

"How in the world could he have known all that?" Layla asked.

Will nodded. "Because Mr. Breakwater told him it would happen."

"You're right, Will."

"But how could he have told him that when he hadn't been sent back in time yet?" Carmen asked.

"Don't you see?" Will said. "Because it had already happened."

"I'm very confused by all this," Jonathan said.

"Let me try to explain," Dr. Valquist began. "We believe, based on this experiment, that the past, present, and future are all part of a fixed continuum. Someone going back into the past from the future can't change the past because they were already there. Whatever they did in the past already happened."

"So that means everything is predestined?" Carmen asked.

"Not necessarily," Will said. "Just because my past actions are now unchangeable doesn't mean I didn't freely chose to make them. So actions I go back in time to do, even though they're in the past and have already happened, can still be my decision."

"This is getting way beyond my pay grade," Jonathan said. "By the way, *am* I on a government pay grade?"

"You are," Valquist answered. "And you all make way more than me. An HR person will yet talk to each of you about your various benefits. Don't forget to take advantage of the government matching funds on your retirement contributions."

"So the return trip worked as well?" Carmen asked.

"It did. The time window reopened exactly when Dr. Silver predicted it would. Mr. Breakwater even brought things with him from the past that weren't with him on his trip back in time."

"And those stayed in the future?" Will asked. "I might have expected those to last only one month before getting sucked back into the past."

"Nope, they stayed. And several objects he brought to the past but didn't bring to the storeroom for the return trip stayed in the past."

"So the things that move back and forth in time don't matter," Carmen said. "It's the place itself. I think I'm figuring this all out."

"And this means that if someone goes back in time and isn't on that spot a month later, they'll be stuck in the past forever?" Jonathan asked.

"It would seem so," Dr. Valquist replied.

"What if something went back in time and appeared somewhere with an object in the way?" Layla asked. "I mean, if you appeared in the middle of a wall, that wouldn't do you any good."

"Right," Valquist said. "And the store room in the basement was selected because the emeritus director was able to confirm that it was completely empty during the intended time slot."

"So we actually don't know what would happen if you appeared in the same place as an existing object," she said.

"We don't," Valquist said.

Layla shook her head. "That's a serious concern for us because we can't be sure what was on a particular spot in AD 157."

"We know that," Dr. Valquist said. "But we have a spot selected already that we're fairly confident was clear of any objects."

"Somewhere in Rome, I hope," Carmen said. "I mean, once we get there, we can find the information and hang out for a month while we wait for our ride home."

Will shook his head. "This is an Ultra Secret gadget we're talking about here. There's no way our governments are going to risk setting it up on some other country's soil."

"That's right," Dr. Valquist said. "Your entry point has to be somewhere on the British Isles."

"Are you crazy?" Carmen asked. "We're supposed to get from Britannia to Rome and back in one month? There's no way!"

"The only other option is to use a point in America, and then we truly are in the realm of impossibility," Dr. Valquist said.

"But the world is at stake here," Carmen said. "For the sake of a successful mission, can't our governments get some ally closer to Rome in on this plan somehow?"

"Look," he said. "I do see your point, but the decision on this has already been made by the President and Prime Minister."

"What about this Mr. Breakwater," Jonathan said. "Can we meet him?"

"Unfortunately Agent Breakwater died a few years back."

"What did he die of?" Will asked seriously.

"It was cancer."

"Any possibility that he caught this cancer because of his exposure to radiation in the time travel experiment?" Carmen asked.

"Dr. Silver doesn't think so," Dr. Valquist replied. "I mean, the guy was a chain smoker as well. In fact, Dr. Silver was none too thrilled when he learned that Breakwater had brought two hundred cartons of a discontinued brand of cigarette back from 1952. I can't say one hundred percent that time travel is safe, but there's no reason to believe it's a dangerous process."

"Whoa," Jonathan said. "In other words the only living creature that went back in time in that experiment was Breakwater?"

"In retrospect," Valquist stated, "that was a colossal oversight."

"Yeah, I mean all they had to do was send back a cage full of mice with him. Then they would have had more data on possible negative side effects."

"If I tell you right now, that this mission may cause you to catch cancer and die about twenty years from now, will you decide you aren't going to do it?"

They looked at each other and smiled knowingly.

"No, we're still in," Will said. "And, like you said, it may not have been the time machine that gave him cancer."

"So what's our plan?" Carmen asked. "How do we get from England to Rome and back in one month?"

"If my memory serves me correctly," Jonathan said, "the boat ride from Britannia to Gaul is just a matter of hours."

Carmen smiled. "That's right, you are a sailing expert. And you said you had nothing to contribute."

"After that, we'll have to use the *Cursus Publicus*," Layla said. "And that's why we studied it so much. You and Miss Maple already knew it was the only way."

"We've done some advance calculations," Dr. Valquist said. "It's about one thousand two hundred miles. A typical horse can do fifty miles a day. But if you make ninety miles a day, you can get there and back in almost exactly a month."

"Horses can go faster for shorter periods of time," Carmen said. "We know that's how the *Cursus* worked. Curriers swapped out their horses a few times each day. And that makes ninety or even a hundred miles feasible for a day of travel. But that's not really very good on those animals."

"There's no other way we'll make it to Rome and back in a month," Layla said.

Carmen nodded sadly. "I know it."

"Thinking out loud here," Will said. "The fact is, it's possible but not probable for us to get there and back in a month. But getting to Rome itself in a month is certainly doable. In the event that we find the information about Planet X, is there any way we could bury it in a pre-arranged spot so that it could be recovered in our time?"

Dr. Valquist smiled. "I knew one of you would think of this. Yes, indeed. And we've already selected a spot near Rome for you to bury the info. You'll be briefed on it later."

"What kind of equipment are we going to take on this mission?" Jonathan asked. "I mean, the ancient world is dangerous, so we should go back there packing, right?"

Dr. Valquist shook his head. "This has been discussed as well. There is a belief that time travel technology in the wrong hands will make nuclear weapons look like toys in comparison. Nothing is allowed to go back in time which, if lost back there and then discovered later, would be evidence that someone has the ability to travel in time. We'll give you perishable things, like matches, a flint, and period-style clothing. But obviously no guns."

"I see the point here," Carmen said. "If archeologists find a modern pistol in a dig somewhere in Rome and the whole world now knows that someone must have gone back in time, it could lead other nations to invest in time travel research."

"I really would like to have a device that could tell us when that time window opens again," Will said. "Just so we know where we're at in the mission."

"It's not going to be allowed," Dr. Valquist replied.

"What if it were made to self-destruct when the time was up?" Layla asked. "That way no trace of it would be left."

Dr. Valquist crunched his eyebrows. "That's a very good idea," he said. "I'll look into the possibility."

"How long are we gone in *this* time?" Carmen asked.

"When you return, you'll be coming back into virtually the same instant you left."

"So it's agreed we have to use the *Cursus Publicus*," Layla said. "To do that we need the official document that allowed such travel."

"Called a *diploma*," Dr. Valquist noted.

"It would sure be nice if we could get our hands on one of those," Will said. "How could we get one once we're there?"

Dr. Valquist smiled. "We do have a few of them preserved from ancient times. Between the CIA and MI-6, I'll bet we can make you a convincing forgery."

"It's dangerous, though," Layla said. "The punishment for fraudulently using the *Cursus Publicus* was death."

"Well, it's that or we have to try and walk across Europe," Carmen said.

"Then we have no choice," Layla said.

Dr. Valquist stood from the table. "You've got a good grasp of how this works and what you're up against. Starting tomorrow morning, you'll spend the next seven days in physical training and studying the mission in further detail. I'll tell the President and Prime Minister that the mission is a go in one week."

"Will they be there?" Layla asked.

"They wouldn't miss it for the world."

Chapter Five

"One more lap!" Mr. Cole bellowed. "Imagine you have only a minute to make it to the extraction point!"

The students increased their speed as they raced past him and rounded the first curve of the 400 meter track. What had started as a spring shower turned into a downpour. They were dressed in gray woolen tunics, typical of the period they were entering. Their clothing had soaked in the rain and weighed them down.

Carmen took the lead, followed by Will.

"Anyone over a minute is doing another one!" he shouted from the center of the track.

They reached the straightaway on the other side, with Layla beginning to trail.

"Miss Ramzy, you are in serious danger of repeating this exercise!"

They rounded the final curve. Carmen flew across the line. Will, then Jonathan, and finally Layla. Mr. Cole blew the whistle.

"59 seconds, Miss Ramzy," he shouted. "That's cutting it awfully close!"

"What do you expect with me running in these stupid sandals?" she shouted back.

The students walked with their hands on their hips, struggling to pull the humid air into their lungs.

"I can't take it anymore," Will said. "He's working us too hard."

"Are you forgetting that we go to ancient Rome tomorrow?" Jonathan asked. "This has been his last week to get us ready."

"I don't mind the physical training," Carmen said. "It's the long sessions of Dr. Valquist speaking rapid Latin to us."

"Don't forget evenings with Miss Maple on ancient Roman culture," Layla added.

Jonathan chuckled. "What I hate is the Roman period food they're making us eat. That salty fish sauce *garum* makes me want to hurl."

"I thought we'd learned so much in the last four years," Will said. "I wish they'd told us we were secret agents a few years ago so we could have had more than a week to get ready."

"That's just the way these things work out," Mr. Cole said, approaching the group. "I used to get dropped in enemy territory after a one hour briefing. Count yourselves lucky to have a week."

A chime sounded. Mr. Cole lifted his cell phone from his pocket and looked at the screen. "Alright, the team is expected back at the main house for a mission briefing in one hour." He looked over the group. "Listen, kids, you're not working out tomorrow. So you're done with me."

"You won't be seeing us off?" Carmen asked.

"I'll be at dinner tonight, but not at the actual site tomorrow. But while I have you all here, away from the crowd, I just wanted to tell you..." Mr. Cole's lower lip began to quiver and his eyes suddenly welled with tears.

The group was stunned to see any emotion from the rock of a man they had trained under for years.

"I am so proud of each and every one of you," he managed through a whisper. "Helping to prepare you all for this mission has been the greatest privilege of my life."

Will embraced him. "Thank you, coach."

One by one, they hugged him. He wiped his eyes and nodded.

"Alright, enough of these water works. Go get showered up. Dr. Valquist will be waiting for you in the conference room."

****

"I hope this doesn't last too long," Jonathan said, arriving at the room. "I'm starving."

"I bet they have a terrific final meal planned for us," Carmen said.

Will laughed. "Final meal? I don't like the sound of that!"

"You know what I mean."

Dr. Valquist entered the room and sat at the head of the long table. "*Salvete, discipuli,*" he said. "*Quid agitis?*"

"*Multum bene,*" Layla said. "Mr. Cole has gotten us into fine shape."

"This is the final briefing I've got for you before tomorrow," he started, taking a remote out of his pocket and pointing it at a massive flat screen TV on the other side of the room. A map of Europe appeared. "We've been through the mission several times in detail. We're going to go through it now just once more, with you telling me what you're doing, when, and how."

"*Sic*," Will said.

"Tell me where you start," he said.

Carmen raised her hand. "Not far from the coast, MI-6 has built a facility over a granite crag we are reasonably confident was unoccupied in ancient times."

Dr. Valquist clicked the remote and brought up a picture of a simple white building set against an artist's representation of the same spot in the past. A Roman road lay yards off a slow incline leading up to the massive granite slab atop the hill.

"The machine will send us back in time and we will arrive on August 16, *Anno Domini* 157," she added. "Several hours before sunrise."

"Continue, Jonathan."

"Our first order of business will be to find transport across the channel at a village six kilometers from our insertion point. We will pay for passage across the channel and arrive in the port city of Gesoriacum, modern day Boulogne, France."

"*Bene*. Will."

"In Gesoriacum we'll buy horses and enter the *Cursus Publicus* system. We will be taking the Via

Agrippa which runs north to south through Gaul. Our goal will be to average ninety miles a day by swapping out our horses regularly at the network of *mansiones* and *mutationes*. Replacement horses and other supplies are free to people holding an imperial diploma."

"Describe these facilities."

"A *mansio*, Latin for inn, will be a large complex and will have a full dining room, guest bedrooms, and a well-stocked stable. A *mutatio*, a hostel, will be a smaller version of the same. We can expect to find at least a *mutatio* every ten miles on our route. *Mansiones* are spread out more widely, but we should be able to plan our day around sleeping in one every night."

Dr. Valquist clicked the console. A picture of a leather unrolled scroll densely packed with writing appeared. "What do we have here?"

"That's our *diploma*," Carmen answered. "Without it, our mission is over before it starts."

He clicked the console again. A photo of a crude Roman map covered with little pictures of houses appeared. "And this?"

"That's the *Tabula Peutingeriana*," Jonathan said. "It's a detailed description of the routes and available *mansiones* on the roads of the *Cursus*. That particular map dates back to the late Empire. So it wouldn't help us much. But we're hoping to find something like it once we're there."

A close-up shot of Gaul now appeared on the screen. "What's the itinerary, Layla?"

"Gesoriacum to Durocortorum, modern day Reims," she started. "On to Augustodunum, now called Autun. Then to Lugdunum, modern day Lyon."

"That's where the Emperor Claudius was born!" Carmen interrupted. "I wrote a paper on him for Miss Maple's class once."

Dr. Valquist chuckled. "*Multum bene*. Then where?"

Carmen nodded. "Just south of Lugdunum we will take a road eastward through the Alps, then a road heading south, and come into Italy at Genua."

"Take us home, Jonathan."

"Genua to Pisae, Pisae to Rome," he answered. "At ninety miles daily, the trip should take thirteen days. Two days in Rome to take care of business and we reverse the trip to be back at that granite slab in time for the extraction."

"And if we fall behind," Will said, "we've discussed skipping a night of sleep and just riding through."

"*Sic*," Dr. Valquist said. "But that would hold enough danger that it should be used only in an emergency. Will, describe your mission in Rome."

An artist's depiction of the Roman Forum appeared on the screen, focusing in on two buildings facing each other across a courtyard with the towering Column of Trajan between them.

"We assume that the Bibliotheca Ulpia, founded by Trajan forty years before our arrival, will have a section on Astronomy. We're going to start with the Latin building and try the Greek collection if necessary. They don't just let anyone in there to look at books. We're going to have to somehow talk our way in."

"Or break in, if it comes to it," Carmen added.

"And we hope it doesn't," Dr. Valquist said. "Breaking and entering and then needing to travel by horseback on an official government road for two weeks isn't Plan A."

A photo of scattered columns appeared on the screen. "Here's the site outside the city where you will attempt a burial of any information you get in Rome. You'll bury the info, written on papyrus and sealed in wax-covered clay jars, at points five and ten meters north from these columns, which were already a ruin in AD 157. I'm told the CIA has already been to the site, but what they found is being kept even from me, lest I inadvertently give you information that could create a time paradox."

"Understood," Will said.

"Let's talk about covers," he said. "What's your Roman name, Jonathan?"

"Nennius. And I'm married to Carmen, which is already Latin, so she keeps it as her name."

"Will."

"I am Valerius, married to Layla. She and I will attempt entry into the Library under the cover of a married couple of scientists seeking information on a mysterious planet."

"Your cover, Layla?"

"I'm Aurelia, 'Golden one'," she said smiling.

"And where are you all from, Aurelia?"

"We assume that despite our excellent Latin, we will not come off as natives. And so we had better not pretend otherwise. We need to be from places Romans know about, but which no one's likely visited. I am from Arabia. Valerius and Nennius are from Hibernia, modern day Ireland."

"I'm personally from Northern Hibernia," Will said, grinning.

"And I'm from Ultima Thule," Carmen said. "The mysterious frozen country somewhere in the far north. Nothing else would explain my fair, Finnish complexion and dazzling blonde hair."

"What supplies will you be bringing along, Carmen?"

"We each will have a sack with three changes of clothes and a woolen blanket. The team will have a medical kit for dressing and suturing wounds in case of emergency."

"And you've all gotten everything from tetanus to rabies to mumps and rubella boosters in the last week. Let's talk money," Dr. Valquist stated. "What will you have and what do we know about its worth, Jonathan?"

"We know that Rome was subject to rampant inflation at times. And on a local level prices could fluctuate wildly. The best research tells us that a horse in that time period should cost about 150 *denarii* apiece. We have 1000 silver *denarii* total, as well as an assortment of smaller change in copper pieces to cover the cost of four horses and other expenses, and still have a safe buffer."

"These are actual period coins that were cleaned and polished to look new," Will added. "And they're pretty much all the period *denarii* that were available for purchase on the collectors' market."

"A few museums also don't know that they're now just displaying convincing forgeries." He looked around the table seriously. "What about weapons, Layla?"

"We each have a sword and a dagger that we hope we'll never have to use."

Dr. Valquist nodded and closed his eyes. "I have some things I need to say while I have you all here alone."

"Oh God," Carmen said. "He's gonna make me cry again."

"Just one week ago, you found out that everything you thought was true about your lives was not."

"In retrospect, I feel stupid for not being suspicious," Jonathan said. "I mean why else were we being trained to speak Latin, ride horses, and fight with swords?"

"Don't feel that way, Jonathan," he said. "You could never have guessed the truth behind the school. But all that said, you were unfortunately used in many ways.

You were trained with a set of skills for a mission that you then really could not turn down. And no one has any idea if this plan will really work."

"We wouldn't have any chance of success if it weren't for you, sir," Will said. "No students ever had a better teacher."

"That's the part that actually pains me, Will," he said. "Because from my seat, no teacher ever had a better set of students. And instead I was an undercover agent duping you about the nature of your school. I really am very uncomfortable with the role I played in all this. A part of me knows it had to be done. I mean, the whole world does depend on your mission. But until you are all back here safe and sound, my heart is very heavy." He looked at the table, tears creeping down his face.

"Dr. Valquist, you just told me I shouldn't feel stupid," Jonathan started. "And you're right. But just like we couldn't turn down the mission to save the planet, you couldn't turn down the mission to prepare us."

"You're right," he whispered. "Just know that I could never be prouder of anyone in my life, than I am of each one of you. That's even if I had children of my own."

"There it is," Carmen said, starting to sob.

He stood from the table. "You've got the rest of the day off. Dinner, I hear, will be amazing. Rest up and we have a surprise a little later."

****

After an afternoon of relaxing and even indulging themselves in some video games the staff hooked up to the massive TV, the students were seated at the table in the main dining room.

"Lots of settings here," Jonathan said. "What other dignitaries are we expecting?"

The tall mahogany door opened. Dr. Valquist entered, followed by Miss Maple, and Mr. Cole. The students could hear more people coming down the hallway to the dining room. Will saw two familiar faces come through the door.

"Mum! Dad!" he shouted. He got up from his spot and threw his arms around them.

Carmen's parents entered through the doorway.

"I'm going to cry again!" she shouted and joined them.

"*Yaa 'aynii*!" Layla's mom said loudly, coming into the room, her husband in tow.

"I missed you so much!" Layla exclaimed.

The Prime Minister and President came through the door. Jonathan stood from his chair.

The President walked across the room and put his hand on Jonathan's shoulder. "I know you have an uncle who's been raising you," he said. "But long before I became president, the rule has been to keep knowledge of all this very classified. We just couldn't bring him in."

Jonathan drew in a staccato breath. "I understand, sir." Tears ran down his face.

The President wiped his eyes. "I personally felt that we shouldn't have any parents here if your uncle couldn't be involved."

"No!" Jonathan protested. "I'm happy for my friends. This is good for them."

"I'm just so sorry, young man."

"Thank you."

"Before we begin dinner," Dr. Valquist shouted into the chattering room, "the President and Prime Minister asked me to address you all."

The room slowly fell silent as the families turned toward him.

"Your parents are only cleared for Top Secret, so you can't share any details of what you're doing. But they do know you are leaving tomorrow on a mission that pertains to the very survival of this planet. You'll have plenty of time to talk during and after the meal. We're going to have the parents leave this evening and force these kids to get a good night's sleep."

Dr. Valquist looked about the room seriously. "I know you parents love your children and must be terribly worried about what they are heading out to do. For those of us who have gone on missions in the field—and I know some of you parents have—nothing we have ever done compares to the importance of what your children are about to undertake. And you also should know that nothing we have ever done had the danger they will face. According to your tradition, join me please in a moment of silence. In words of my tradition, I will offer a prayer for them."

Some people folded their hands, others closed their eyes.

"Lord, we are all pilgrims in a foreign land," he said slowly. "Just as you traveled with your disciples, so please now protect mine. Send your Guardians Angels to watch over them. Grant them the strength to carry out their mission, according to your will. *Gloria et Honor Patri et Filio et Spiritui Sancto*," he said, making the sign of the cross. "*In saecula saeculorum*. Forever and ever, unto Ages of Ages, Amen."

"Amen," people murmured.

The President and Prime Minister took their usual seats. Dr. Silver was about to sit again at the front of the table, but saw Jonathan sitting alone listening to Carmen's parents telling her something. He got up and walked over to him.

"Young man," he said. "The President and the Prime Minister would like you to join them for dinner."

Jonathan smiled. "Thank you." He walked up and sat at the head of the table.

The group ate their meal in a room filled with laughter and conversation. At the end of the evening, everyone present, even the world leaders, hugged everyone else with tears of joy and sorrow abounding.

Chapter Six

The students sat in a cramped briefing room at the MI-6 facility built to house the time machine. They were dressed in the rough gray tunics they had trained in for the previous week. The nerves of knowing what they were about to do were building by the second. A door opened and Dr. Valquist, Dr. Silver, and the two heads of state appeared outside.

"Everything's ready," Dr. Silver said. "Now that I've charged up the machine, we do need to hit the start button within about fifteen minutes. There are a lot of things I thought about telling you in this moment, but they just don't seem to make any sense now. Good luck. That's all."

As they filed out of the room, the Prime Minister stepped forward and shook each of their hands. "A grateful world that can never know what you are doing will forever owe you a debt for even trying this."

"Thank you, Mr. Prime Minister," Carmen said.

The heads of state stepped back and let Dr. Valquist forward. "It's all up to you four now," he said. "God bless you and your mission."

"*Gratias, Magister*," Will whispered. "Thank you for everything."

"I have one final gift for you," the President said softly. "The techies just put together the item you asked to bring along." He reached into his coat pocket and produced a black tablet computer no larger than his hand.

"It's your time piece," Dr. Valquist said.

Will took the item from the President. "How does it work?"

"The moment you arrive in the past, it will automatically begin a countdown toward the time of the extraction."

"It also has a type of GPS which reads off the earth's own gravitational field," the Prime Minister said. "In the bottom right-hand corner it will display the time left until the extraction. The main screen is a map of Europe showing you exactly where you are and where you should be based on an average of ninety miles a day. Just make sure that, if you do miss the window, you're far away from that thing."

"Because it's designed to blow up so big that no trace of it will be left," Dr. Silver said. "That will happen ten seconds after the extraction. And it goes without saying that you sure as hell shouldn't bring it back with you."

"Understood," Will said.

"Let's do this thing," Jonathan declared.

They all walked down a short corridor and entered a bright and spacious room with wires and pipes flying every direction off the ceiling. In the center of the space stood a square structure with an open portal.

"Enter the chamber," Dr. Silver said. "Once you're in there I need to run a few diagnostics before I send you back."

One by one, the students stepped through the hatch and into the five by five meter enclosure within the machine. They saw their bags of supplies already lying on the floor. In the darkness of the chamber, they could not see one another, but they grasped each other's hands in reassurance.

"Closing the hatch," Dr. Silver said.

The door slid automatically shut.

The students felt a momentary change in air pressure on their eardrums as the chamber sealed. For a matter of seconds that seemed like minutes, they stood in the darkness waiting for word that their mission would begin.

"Everything's ready," Dr. Silver said to the President and Prime Minister. "On your word, I will send them back."

The two men looked at each other momentarily and each nodded.

Dr. Silver pressed a button to open the intercom to the chamber.

"I want each of you to take a deep breath and then exhale it."

They did as instructed, feeling just a slight alleviation from their rising nerves.

"Mission commencing in five, four, three..."

Layla squeezed Will's hand.

"...two, one." He touched the computer screen.

A deafening hum blasted the students' ears. They felt an electrifying tingle sweep the skin of their bodies, followed by a sensation of falling.

They stood together, suddenly aware that the air felt very cool around them. As their eyes adjusted to their surroundings, the blackness of the chamber slowly turned into a dark night. They stood atop the granite ridge and could make out the hill sloping down beneath them.

"Oh my God," Carmen gasped. "We're here."

Will turned about, looking at the others. "Is everyone alright?"

"I guess so," Layla said. "A little queasy is all. What does the screen say, Will?"

He looked at the console. "Twenty-nine days, twenty-one hours and forty-two minutes. How are you, Jonathan?"

"I've felt better," he said.

"Welcome to AD 157, everyone," Carmen said. "Shall we move?"

Each picked up their bag and walked down the hill from the granite ridge. A few minutes later, they came to a Roman road. They started walking in the direction of a guard post which their briefing said would be close to this point. In the distance they saw flames flickering just beside the road.

"That's a Roman sentry up ahead," Will said. "Everyone remember that we are in an empire at peace.

There is nothing suspicious about merchants traveling, even in the middle of the night."

"We'll follow your lead," Layla said.

Will smiled. "*Amo, amas, amat,*" he chimed. "Get your Latin ready."

The group continued toward the sentry point. Several oil-burning lamps were set on poles around a tent next to the road. A soldier who had been facing the other direction turned in response to the sound of their approach.

"*Salvete!*" the man called out. "State your business."

"*Salve,*" Will responded. "We are merchants heading to Gaul."

"You are on a public road," the soldier said. "Remember that you must give right of way to any military group or a diploma carrier."

Will considered whether to mention that they had one, but decided it was unnecessary.

"Understood, soldier," he replied.

"Where are you from?" the Roman asked. "I have not heard an accent like yours before."

"*Ego sum de Hibernia,*" Will said.

"*Quoque ego sum de Hibernia,*" Jonathan added.

"*Ego sum de Thule,*" Carmen offered nervously.

"*Et sum de Arabia,*" Layla said. "We are a group of merchants who make yearly rounds in the empire to sell items from our nations of origin."

"You speak much better than your friends," the soldier said, smiling at her. "*Quid est nomen tuum*?"

"*Nomen meum est* Aurelia," she replied.

"Well named indeed, since your beauty matches the brilliance of the precious metal."

Layla blushed and smiled.

"Good Lord," Jonathan whispered to Carmen. "Our first native turns out to be a flirt."

"Thank you for your compliment," she said. "We will be back in this area next week. I would love to show you some of my goods at that time."

Will turned to her, startled.

"I will look forward to giving them my special attention," the guard said, smiling. "Ask for Brutus Agrippa at the central guard station."

"Will do, soldier," she giggled.

"Well, we must be going," Will said. "We want to make it to the town of Grappina by day break."

"Stay on the road and beware of bandits," the guard said. "There is always a danger at this hour."

"*Gratias*," Jonathan said. "We will be careful."

The group walked past the checkpoint and started down the road.

"*Vale, Brute*!" Layla shouted, turning around. She saw him wave back to her.

"That was actually fun," she said, catching up to Will.

"I don't think we should make a habit of engaging in unnecessary conversations on this mission," he said. "That's how we could get ourselves into trouble."

"I disagree," Carmen said. "I think that the more natural we feel the easier it will be to go about the business of our cover normally."

"Remember, we are an empire at peace," Layla said, imitating his voice. "There's nothing suspicious about merchants travelling."

"Even at night," Jonathan added.

"Alright, I get it," Will said. "Let's just be careful."

The group walked what they thought was about a mile down the well constructed Roman road.

"When you think about the thousands of miles of this stuff they laid down all over Europe," Jonathan said, "it's a bigger engineering feat than the Great Wall of China."

"But walking these cobblestones isn't fun," Will said. "When we get to Gaul, we'll buy ourselves some horses and ride the rest of the way."

The whole group heard the sound of a twig break loudly somewhere off the road.

"Code Red," Will stated in a moderate volume. "We are on the X."

"No way off this X by just continuing," Carmen declared. "Those are probably bandits who will take what they want off us unless we stop them."

"We are in Hydra formation, people," Will shouted.

The students took up a defensive configuration they had practiced a hundred times with Mr. Cole. They formed a Y-shaped grouping, with Layla standing beside the bags in the center, and the rest in three directions three yards away from her.

"Speak for us, Layla," Will said. "I want them to believe you are the leader and we are your guards."

She nodded. "Show yourselves," Layla shouted. "We will negotiate with you for passage."

A long silence followed.

"You will leave with your lives, nothing more," a voice finally said from the darkness somewhere ahead.

They saw a tall man emerge from the shadows. He stood thirty feet away down the road.

"I have twenty men, all with swords surrounding you," the man said. "You leave all your bags here and walk back toward the town. We will not follow you."

"*Non*," Layla said. "My best against your best. If she wins, we continue. If your man wins, you have everything and we are all your slaves."

"She?" Carmen whispered. "So it's me you're talking about?"

"We need to field our best."

"This is a lot of confidence you're putting in me," she whispered.

"It's well placed," Will said.

"Did you say *she*?" the man asked.

"*Sic*," Layla said. "You are apparently afraid to send your best man against my woman?"

The man laughed. "He's afraid of no one. Are you talking about this scraggly thing with the white hair?"

Carmen stepped away from the group, slouching a bit to seem even smaller. She nodded.

"I don't even need to send my best fighter against this thing," the man shouted.

"Then maybe you want to fight her yourself," Layla said. "But the deal stays the same. She wins and we proceed."

"I have not agreed to this deal," the man said. "Why should I not just order my men to kill you all and take all your things?"

"Good question," she shouted back. "Why haven't you ordered them to do that? It's either because you don't really have twenty men or because you're afraid your best man can't beat my girl. Maybe both."

"Marcus, come here," the man shouted.

A moment later, a muscle-bound man even taller than the tall man stepped out of the shadows from the left side of the road.

"This is my champion," he said. "I give you one last chance to drop your things and run back to town."

Carmen walked down the road a few steps. "I was expecting someone bigger," she said. "I forget, do we yet have the maxim, '*The bigger they are the harder they fall*'?"

"From a '*David and Goliath*' standpoint, we do," Will said. "But the quote itself still waits a few centuries."

"Marcus is not afraid of woman," the large man said. "Master, agree to this deal. I want to teach her a lesson."

"All I can ask for is your word of honor," Layla said. "And I don't know what that's worth. So I hereby tell each of your soldiers that all of us can fight. If you decide not to honor the deal, think that through after you see my little girl in action."

"Kill her," the leader said.

Marcus started down the road, drawing a large sword from a sheath at his side.

Carmen unhooked the belt about her waist and tossed her sword to Will. "I'm going to travel light," she said, pulling a dagger from a sheath tied to her ankle.

She walked a few feet down the road and took up a defensive position. As Marcus continued toward her, the group saw three other figures slowly emerge from the darkness, trying to get a better view of what was about to happen.

"That's the whole group," Jonathan said softly. "If we have to, we can take them."

Marcus lifted his sword into the air and began now to sprint down the road toward Carmen, screaming as he went. She stayed in the center of the road, stepping carefully toward him. As he pulled his blade down swiftly, she just stepped aside of his attack. The sword crashed upon the cobblestones. Carmen shot her hand out and buried the dagger in the man's chest. She pulled it out and again assumed a defensive stance, watching her enemy closely.

He staggered backwards, gurgled a faint cry, and then dropped to his knees. His sword slowly slipped from his hand and clanked upon the cobblestones. He looked up at Carmen in a combination of surprise and sadness. Only in that instant did she realize what had just happened.

She crouched beside him and gritted her teeth. "Why did you make me do that!" she screamed.

The man's eyes fluttered and he fell backwards onto the street.

"Attack them!" the leader of the bandit group shouted, drawing his own sword and rushing toward Carmen.

Will saw Carmen slowly stand from the fallen body beside her. Her hand opened and the dagger fell from her fingers onto the street. Will began to run in her direction, but knew he could not reach her before the bandit leader arrived at her position. The students watched in shock as Carmen stood motionless before the rapid approach of the man.

"Get out of there!" Jonathan screamed.

The man shouted as he pulled his sword back to sweep it through Carmen. She suddenly leaped into the air and shot her foot into his face. The bandit went limp and slid unconscious beneath her as she landed back on the street. She turned around and saw Will arrive, sword drawn.

"Get away from us," Will shouted into the shadows. "You've lost this fight." He put the tip of his sword blade against the unconscious leader's chest. "Carmen, are you alright?"

"I don't know," she whispered coldly.

"Are you hurt?"

"I just killed a man, Will."

The three men who had stood watching the events drew closer.

"We will honor your deal," one of them said. "Do with that man as you wish." They retreated back into the darkness.

Will spotted a coin purse on the man's belt. He reached down and snatched it away. "This is the least you can give us," he said to the still unconscious man.

"What do we do about this guy?" Jonathan asked.

"Nothing," Will replied. "He doesn't even deserve death from us." He looked up at the group. "Let's get going. These bandits might be the tip of the iceberg."

The group continued down the road without a word for at least an hour. Layla once tried to put her hand on her friend's shoulder in silent comfort, but she brushed her away. They finally arrived at a point where their study had suggested they should expect footpaths leaving the main road and heading south for the shore.

"The channel's about an hour away, directly south from this road," Jonathan said. "It's still a long time until sunrise. I think we've earned a little break."

"Alright," Will said. "I'll stay on guard if anyone wants to get a little sleep."

"No," Carmen returned quickly. "I can't sleep anyway. I'm on guard."

The group broke out their packs and laid down on a grassy expanse just off the main road. Carmen unfolded her blanket, but just sat looking down the road.

"Do you blame me for what happened?" Layla asked her.

"No," Carmen replied. "Given everything we knew, it was as good a plan as any."

"But was there something else we could have done? Something that...didn't..."

Carmen turned to her, her eyes surging with tears. "Ever since we learned about this mission, I have known I would eventually be put into a fight. Chances are, given the way things have started out, I'm going to kill again before we get home. Being the best fighter in the group back at that gym—that was just fun. But now..." She convulsed, putting her face in her hands. "I just don't know what I'm going to become here."

Layla slid over and embraced her friend. "You're Carmen Mattila. You're the president of the Chess Club at the Fairfax Classical Academy. And you are my friend."

Carmen grieved in Layla's arms. Will and Jonathan lay on their blankets, eyes closed but weeping with her.

Chapter Seven

When the faintest orange hint of the coming dawn crept upon the horizon, Carmen gently nudged the other members of the group. She had let them sleep for three hours.

"Let's head for the shore, people," she said. "I want to sleep tomorrow night somewhere in Gaul."

They quickly repacked their belongings and started single file down a footpath. As the students reached the top of a tall hill, the glistening waters of the English Channel rolled into the distance.

Their descent toward the water went more quickly than they expected, as the path kept a gentle decline the entire way. After a half an hour, they arrived at an area of cottages along the shore.

"It's not exactly a village," Will said. "But I'll bet there's a fisherman here who would like to make some extra money."

They walked to the front door of a small structure with white plastered walls and a brown thatched roof. "I don't remember what the protocols are in ancient Rome," Will said. "Do we knock on the door?"

"There's something you need to remember," Layla said. "This little community is probably all Britons. They may not know much Latin at all."

Will nodded and knocked at the wooden door. "*Salve*? Is anyone home?"

They saw an old woman appear from behind the house, carrying a basket of bread. She spoke to them in a language they did not understand.

"Dr. Valquist should have given us a rudimentary Gaelic lesson some year," Layla said.

"*Nos sumus Romani*," Jonathan said, pointing at the group.

She looked at them fiercely and entered the house, slamming the door behind her.

"Remember that not all Britons are huge fans of the invasion of their land by *us Romans* just a hundred years ago," Carmen said.

"I could sure go for some of that bread she had," Jonathan said. "We were planning to eat at some point during this month, right?"

"Let's go to the shore," Will said. "Some fisherman here must know even a little Latin."

They continued down the row of cottages and arrived at a large break between the buildings that seemed to serve as a route to the sea itself. As they walked down the path, they saw the soil turn to sand. The damp sea air felt several degrees cooler as they reached a small harbor. A dozen boats of varying sizes were tied up along a weathered wooden pier stretching the length of the curving shore. Men on some of the vessels were tying ropes and working on nets.

"*Salvete!*" Will shouted. "*Aliquis hic est qui dicit Latine?*"

A man on the pier motioned with his hand for the group to approach.

"We have a nibble," Jonathan said.

"*Salve, mi amice*," Will offered, leading the group toward the man. "We are looking for passage to Gaul. Do you know someone who could help us?"

"Why he, you not go big city?" the man responded in ungrammatical Latin.

"We are in a hurry," Will said. "Do you have a boat that can make this trip?"

The man pointed toward the largest vessel on the pier, a thirty foot flat bottomed boat with a single mast.

"I not go that far except sometimes," the man said. "Money for this?"

"That thing is pure oak," Jonathan whispered to Will. "That's a very nice boat."

"Tell me a price," Will said.

The man raised an eyebrow in thought. "No, you to tell me price!"

Will chuckled. "All of us together, *duo denarii*."

The group nodded, knowing that the offer was adequately generous.

"*Duo denarii* each person," the fisherman returned.

Will shook his head. "Impossible. *Tres denarii* and that is my last offer."

"*Quattuor denarii*."

Will shook his head. "You heard my last offer."

The fisherman laughed. "*Sic, tres denarii.* We go soon." The man jumped onto his boat and started to adjust the ropes.

"Where can we get food?" Jonathan asked.

"You pay money for food?" the fisherman asked.

"*Sic, certe.*"

The man shouted loudly in Gaelic toward the cottages. "Food coming," he then said.

After a few minutes, the group heard someone coming down the path toward the shore. Holding a basket full of bread, dried fish, and a large bottle was the old woman they had first encountered.

"It's Miss Sunshine of the Welcoming Committee," Jonathan chimed.

"Bread, fish, wine is one *denarius*," the fisherman said.

Will reached into a pouch he was holding and gave the fisherman three *denarii* and several bronze coins. "This is a generous payment for the trip and the basket, my good man."

The fisherman looked at the coins and nodded. "Enjoy food. We go when ready."

"Let's eat, people," Will said, taking the basket from the woman.

"My good man," Layla said. "How do you say *gratias* in your language?"

The fisherman looked at her curiously. "Why you to ask this?"

"Because I want to say it."

"It is *diolch*."

"*Diolch*," Layla said to the woman with a smile.

The whole group thanked her as they passed the food around.

The old woman smiled at them and nodded, clearly taken aback by the gesture.

"Now, none of us is twenty-one," Will said. "And we'll try to buy skins of potable water when possible. But we're going to be drinking wine on this trip at almost every meal. So..."

"Let's be careful!" the group said in unison.

"Do I say that too much?" Will asked.

"Eat some food," Carmen said, handing him a loaf of bread.

"Thanks." He ripped some meat off the side of a fish and made a little sandwich. "How are you doing?" he asked her.

"I'm alright," Carmen said, looking at him seriously. "I know this is just the beginning."

"Be honest with me," he started. "You can do that again if the mission requires it?"

She nodded slowly. "I will do what we have to do so we get this job done and go home. But how about you?"

"Me?"

"Was letting the leader live a good idea?"

Will ate from his food and scratched his head. "Killing him while he lay unconscious didn't seem right."

"I agree," Carmen said. "But you had the luxury of contemplation this time. Next time you might not be so lucky."

"You're right. All of us will be tested in ways we never imagined."

She took a deep drink from the bottle as it made its way around and handed it to Will. "*In vino veritas.*"

He nodded and sipped from the bottle.

After the group had finished eating, they stood and stretched their limbs.

"We're ready to go, my good man," Will said.

"Come aboard, one of you and then one of you," the man said.

They carefully stepped from the pier and down into the boat.

"How long will this trip take?" Jonathan asked.

"Wind is good today," he answered. "You there before middle of the day."

"Just in time for lunch," Layla said. "Can we eat something different?"

Jonathan laughed. "I think we won't have a truly good meal until we're back in England, in our time."

"A month without Mexican food?" Carmen asked. "They owe us some hardship pay bonuses."

The fisherman untied the boat from its moorings and hoisted the single large sail. Jonathan helped him adjust the tension on the ropes to achieve maximum wind resistance.

"Nice job you do," the fisherman said. "Where you learn to run a boat?"

"I learned to sail from my father."

Within minutes, the boat was picking up speed and moving steadily through the sea. They sat in silence, watching the waves in tired contemplation of their mission. After two hours, they could already see the distant shore of the province of Gaul.

"Philosophical question," Will said. "Will we be able to say we were in France when this is all over? I mean, that's the same place as modern-day France, but there are several political upheavals that have to happen before it actually becomes *France*."

Layla laughed and patted him on the back. "I think when you tell people about the countries you've visited, you should tell them, 'Yes, I've been to France, but that was a long time ago'."

After another hour, the group could make out the features of the approaching shore. "They'll speak Latin in Gaul?" Jonathan asked.

"I hope two centuries of occupation at least makes it more common," Layla said.

"I go to harbor you see," the fisherman said, pressing against the rudder to turn the ship slightly. "That is Gesoriacum."

As a port became visible, Jonathan and the fisherman lowered the sail half way, slowing the boat. Several minutes later, they drifted into the Port of

Gesoriacum. A man standing on the dock threw a rope onto the boat.

"*Gratias*," Jonathan said, catching the rope and tying it to a post on the bow.

"*Nihil est*," the man on shore replied.

"*Gratias Deo*," Layla said. "They speak Latin here!"

"*Deo*?" the man asked. "Do you not mean 'gods'?"

In a moment of nervous silence, the whole group realized a potential danger. While the reign of Antoninus Pius did not include the organized persecutions against Christians that previous emperors had carried out, stating Monotheism out loud was still not advised.

"*Gratias* to all the gods," Layla said. "I am so happy to meet people who speak Latin. Not too many of them in Britannia."

He nodded. "People here mostly speak Gaelic and Latin. You'll find older people in small villages that you can't talk to, but you'll have no problems."

They stepped out of the boat and started off the dock. Will stopped and gave the fisherman five more *denarii*.

"*Gratias*, *Domine*," the fisherman said. "We not agreed. Why you to do this?"

"What I have given you is just part of the price of our return trip. But I don't know when that will be exactly. Can you please plan on being right in this spot and waiting for us, starting in about twenty-five days?"

"Seas are bad that time," he said. "I no fish anyway. How long I wait?"

"Be here twenty-five days from now. If we do not come after four more days, we won't be coming. And the money I just gave you is yours to keep."

"And if you come?"

"I give you another ten *denarii*."

"We have agreement," the fisherman said. "Gods bless you in your journey."

"*Diolch*," Will said. He nodded and went down the dock after the others.

"I overheard that," Carmen said. "That's a lot of cash."

Will laughed. "So far I haven't spent any of our own money. This has all been from the pouch I stole off that bandit."

"Nicely played."

"It's time to stop walking," Jonathan said. "I say we buy ourselves some horses and start using this valuable diploma."

"I'm going to get an ulcer worrying about that thing," Layla said. "People get executed for abusing a legitimate diploma for travel on the *Cursus Publicus*. If anyone finds out we have a forgery, it's curtains for us."

"The thing looks official enough," Will said. "Beside, you know we don't have a choice. We are standing on the northern shore of Gaul. To have half a chance of getting home we will need to average ninety miles a day. We're not going to do that on foot."

"I know, I know," she said. "I just hate it, that's all."

"Well, get used to it, because we are going to be presenting our diploma by the end of this day."

"Don't worry," Jonathan said. "If we get into any trouble, you'll be in charge of trying to talk our way out of it."

"*Multas gratias!*" she said.

Will approached a Roman soldier he saw standing guard at a sentry post just off the dock. "*Salve*," he said. "Would you be so kind as to direct me to a place to purchase horses for the travel of my party?"

"There is a stable in the second quadrant of the city," the man said, turning and pointing south. "Go five streets and then turn to your right."

"*Gratias ago tibi*," Will said, nodding.

They started in the direction the soldier had indicated.

"Do you suppose other Romans use sentries as the Empire's information booth?" Carmen asked.

"It's just that they're everywhere," Jonathan said. "And so polite!"

As they neared the fifth street and took their turn, a shift in the wind let them smell the stables long before they heard the whinny of a horse.

"Wow," Jonathan said. "I hope we're not smelling that for the next month."

"Now, we need some high quality horses to match the prestige of our Imperial Diploma," Will said. "This is not going to come cheap."

"How much bandit money do we still have?" Carmen asked.

"Two *denarii*," he said. "How much did we expect a nice horse to cost again?" Will asked.

"About a hundred and fifty," Layla said. "A little more might not be out of the question. So let's plan on spending up to eight hundred for the four of us. That will be on the high end."

"Thanks for the bargaining parameters," Will said. "And that will still leave us plenty of money for our lodgings in Rome. But maybe you should conduct the transaction. You're quicker in your comprehension. I'm always worried I'll misunderstand a number."

"Alright," she said. "Give me the money bag."

Layla led the group toward the stable area. A Roman man wearing a toga was giving orders to several people wearing rough tunics.

"Those are slaves, aren't they?" Jonathan asked.

"Yes," Layla replied.

"This is so sad," he said.

"Especially because you're about to see me talk to the man as if there's nothing wrong."

"I know."

"*Salutationes tibi*," Layla said, approaching the man. "We are merchants on our way to Rome. And we would like to buy four of your better horses."

The Roman man turned and scanned the assembled students. "*Nomen meum est* Marcus Gracchus. *Quis es tu*? And where do you all come from?" he asked kindly.

"*Ego sum* Aurelia," she replied. "We come from many parts of the world. I myself come from Arabia."

"Your accent doesn't exactly sound like others from Arabia whom I have met."

"That is because my father was from North Africa and I think I talk like him."

The man looked at her curiously. "I have several friends from North Africa. You don't sound much like them either."

"That is because my mother was originally from Illyria," she said, hoping he had never met someone from there.

"Such a wonderfully diverse world. What price do you have in mind?"

"I was thinking a hundred and ten *denarii* for each horse," she said, wanting to leave some bargaining room. "And I need the animals to come ready to go, with bits, bridles, and riding pads."

"My lady," he started. "I do not mean to insult you, but I am sorry to say that in these parts that price is nowhere close to the going rate for a decent riding horse."

She nodded. "So what is the going rate?"

He looked at the whole group again. "For nice horses, I will give you four at a rate of two hundred and seventy each."

"Two hundred and seventy?" she said in actual surprise. "I will not pay that kind of price for a horse. Thank you, but I will inquire elsewhere."

"You are welcome to try," he said. "But you should know two things. First, I own all the horse dealerships in Gesoriacum. And my prices are uniform at all my stables. Second, I am not quoting you an unreasonably high price for a good horse."

"Excuse me a moment, sir," she said. "I need to discuss matters with my partners."

She turned away and pulled the others along with her.

"Could we have just been wrong about what horses cost?" Jonathan asked.

"I guess," Layla said. "There might have been some pestilence in this area that drove down supply." She looked at Will seriously. "We're going to need to spend a lot of money here."

"I know," he said. "This isn't your fault. Two hundred and seventy each is more money than we have. Try to at least get him down to two hundred and fifty. We're going to have to do something about getting more money, but that's not today's problem."

She nodded. "I'll see what I can do."

Layla returned to the Roman. "Good sir, I'm ashamed to admit this to you, but I have been misled by a man back in Britannia about what horses cost here in Gaul. I can go as high as two hundred and thirty *denarii*, but I dare not spend more."

"I am so sorry, my lady," he said. "You are still not close to what a good horse is valued at in this area. Two hundred and sixty is possible, and I have customers coming this afternoon to buy half my stock at that price."

She looked into his eyes seriously. "Two hundred and fifty."

He nodded slowly. "You are robbing me. I should summon the centurion. But I accept your price. Two hundred and fifty *denarii* each for four horses."

She handed him the money. "One of my partners will select four from your stock."

Carmen stepped forward.

"Right this way, young lady," he said.

A short time later, the students were climbing onto their horses outside the stable.

"They're nice," Will said. "Expensive, but nice. We have exactly two *denarii* to our name. And I've already promised ten more for our trip home."

"Any ideas for how we'll make more money?" Jonathan asked.

"Something will come along," he said.

Carmen came to the front of the group on her animal. "Things are going fine," she said. "It's the afternoon of our second day in 157 and we are on horses in Gaul. By night we will make it to a place where we will sleep in actual beds."

"And eat more than bread and fish," Jonathan said.

"Then let's ride, people!" Will shouted.

They started down the road toward the sentry checkpoint at the edge of the city. A soldier on guard held up his hand.

"I've got to hold you here for a bit," the man said. "A cavalry detachment will be heading down this road in a little while. Can't risk having you in their way."

"It's time, people," Will said.

"I'm going to throw up," Layla whispered.

Will reached into his satchel. "We hold a diploma from Gnaeus Julius Verus, Governor of Britannia, authorizing our use of the *Cursus Publicus*."

"Let me see the document," the soldier said.

Will handed it to him. He held it away from his body, clearly needing corrective lenses which would not be invented for several more centuries. The soldier nodded.

"Sorry to trouble you, sir," the soldier said. "You are free to go. Please do allow any military group to pass, though."

"*Certe*," Will said.

The soldier lifted the bar blocking entry to the road and the group filed past him. Soon their horses were moving at a fast riding speed.

"He wasn't as cute as my soldier back in Britannia," Layla noted.

"And did you notice the conversation between him and Will?" Carmen said. "Absolutely no magic there."

"Very funny, ladies."

The group rode fast for several hours. Dark green forests crowded upon the road, interspersed with brief patches of cultivated fields. They arrived at a *mansio* of the *Cursus* when the sun was getting low in the sky.

"We dare not go much farther today," Carmen said.

"I agree." Will looked at the console. "Obviously we didn't hit ninety miles. Tomorrow we need to meet that mark."

"Every inch of my body is sore," Jonathan said. "When do actual saddles become common historically?"

"They're already being used in some places," Carmen said. "But when we get to Rome and you see Trajan's Column, you'll notice the Emperor himself is depicted as riding on a pad just like we're on."

"We should get accustomed to this after a few more days," Layla offered. "I hope."

They rode toward a sentry posted at a gate in a wooden wall circling several buildings.

"Diploma carriers only past this point," the guard said.

Will produced their document. "Here you go."

The guard studied it even less than the sentry at the city and handed it back. "*Bene venti,*" he said. "As you enter through the gate, you'll find the stables on both sides of the road leading to the main building. These are beautiful animals. But you've run them pretty hard today. You'll want different horses tomorrow. But where'd you get these?"

"At the stable of Marcus Gracchus back in Gesoriacum," Layla said. "And they cost a good amount. Will we be able to replace them with animals of such quality?"

"Why did you buy them?" the soldier asked. "Graccus' stable is part of the *Cursus*. Your diploma would have gotten them for you for free."

Will put his face in his hands. "We have got to relax and start asking more questions in ancient Rome," he whispered.

"Thank you for the information," Layla said, giggling.

"Let's drop off our rides and get something to eat!" Jonathan said.

Just through the gate, long brick buildings stretched on each side of a gravel road. The smell and sound of horses surged through the air.

Slaves approached them as they continued down the road. "We'll take care of the horses from here, sirs," one of them said.

"*Gratias ago tibi*," Jonathan said, descending from his animal.

"No need to thank me," another slave said. "That's our job here."

"Where we come from, people say '*gratias*'," Layla offered.

"Courtesy to a slave?" the first one said. "What strange place do you come from?"

"The guard probably told you," the second slave said. "Just ahead you'll find the main building. They'll give you rooms for the night and get you fed."

"*Gratias*," Layla said.

The slave laughed. "I just can't get used to that."

Free of their horses, the group saw a large building ahead of them. They had studied the basic layout of a *mansio* in Miss Maple's class. It was a two story brick structure surrounding an open-air inner court with a pool collecting rain water. Just outside the inner court on the ground level were the kitchen, storerooms, and some larger bedrooms. The second story, reached by staircases on each wing, housed further rows of bedrooms for guests at the *mansio*.

They entered the atrium and squinted in the relative darkness of the space. Heat and the smell of various foods swept through the air from their right, indicating the location of the kitchen.

"Will you be needing rooms?" a man in a toga asked.

"*Sic*," Will said. "*Tu es mansionarius?*" Will already knew the man must be the official in charge of the *mansio*, but wanted to introduce his group with all possible courtesies.

"*Ego sum*," the man said, with a smile. "I will have the slaves prepare rooms for you on the second level. Dinner will be served shortly in the main dining room off the inner court. And let me know if there is anything else you need."

"*Gratias*," Jonathan said. "Do you happen to have a guide to the *Cursus Publicus*?"

"*Sic*," the man said. "I've got only one copy left here of a map listing all the *mansiones* in Gaul and Italy. It will cost you two *denarii*."

Will cringed.

"We really could use that thing," Carmen whispered. "Even just from a security standpoint."

"I know," he sighed. "We'll take it, sir." Will handed the last two *denarii* of the group to the *mansionarius*.

"I'll go get you your map." The *mansionarius* clapped his hands. "*Servi*! *Cubicula*!"

A slave-girl in a rude gown appeared. "I'll show you all to your rooms, sirs," she said.

They followed her down a darkened hall and then up a flight of stairs. She showed them all to individual rooms. Each one held a rough woolen mat on the floor. A pitcher of water, a wash basin, and a pot for bathroom matters sat in the corner.

"This will be fine," Will said.

"As *Dominus* told you, dinner will be served soon," the slave-girl said, heading back down the stairs.

"While we're alone up here," Carmen started, "I want to talk through a few security issues."

"Good," Will said.

"First off, Layla, I don't mean to nitpick, but your use of the singular word *God* back at the shore looked like it could be a dangerous thing to play with."

"Don't worry," Layla said. "I realized it immediately. It won't happen again. I'll be the perfect pagan in all my speech from here on out."

"Can I raise an issue?" Will asked.

"Sure."

"I can understand that being under cover makes us play a certain role. So I'll say things like '*Gratias omnibus deis*' because that's just using the language. But I'm a practicing member of the Church of England. And there are things I am *not* going to do."

"Such as?"

"I won't make an actual sacrifice to the Roman gods. Christians died in this time period because they wouldn't do that. And so I can't do it either."

"I understand," Carmen said. "No one's going to be asked to violate their conscience. But as security officer, I just want to see if we can avoid getting into situations where we draw attention to ourselves. And, I'm sorry to say, that includes saying '*gratias*' to slaves."

"I'm really not liking this," Jonathan said.

"I'm not either," Carmen said hotly. "But we're on a mission to save the future world, not enlighten the past."

"I agree," Will stated. "We're all on the same side. Okay, a few ground rules. Carmen's right, no more 'thanks' to slaves. As leader of the group, I'm making that a rule for us to follow. No overt language about being a monotheist, but obviously we also don't need to go to a temple and sacrifice an animal just to fit in. Everybody happy?"

They all nodded.

Carmen hugged Jonathan. "I'm sorry if I seemed mad at you. We need to get through this together."

"I know," he whispered.

"Alright," she said, breaking the embrace. "As security officer, I am declaring how we get through this time. We are never all asleep. We will take shifts as an awake guard at all times. For regular sleep patterns, we will keep the same schedule nightly. I will start, then Layla, Will, and Jonathan. You hold guard for two hours and then you wake your relief and go to sleep yourself. This is in place until further notice."

"Understood," Jonathan said.

"I think we're doing as well as can be expected," Will said. "Except for losing all our money, that is."

"It wasn't your fault," Jonathan said. "We were all there."

"Thanks. Let's get some food and then rest up."

The group went back down the stairs and found a table laid out with assorted plates of food. The *mansionarius* handed Will a booklet of sewn leather pages. When he unfolded it, the students saw that it was in the style of the *Tabula Peutingeriana* they had studied.

"This will be an enormous help," Jonathan said. "We'll at least have an idea of whether there's a *mansio* close enough to press forward for the day. We can't make ninety miles daily without that knowledge."

The dining hall was a large room punctuated with columns wrapped in green garlands. Oil-burning lamps on the walls and tables softened the space with an orange glow. Other guests at the inn had already helped themselves to food and were reclining on couches circling a central table. The students took positions at available spots.

"*Salvete, iuvenes*," a round and bald Roman patrician said to them, kissing the cheek of the woman beside him. "*Sum* Marcus. *Et haec est uxor mea* Lavinia. Where are you all heading to?"

"*Sum* Nennius," Jonathan replied, settling on the couch and reaching to take an apple off the table. "We are merchants on our way to Rome."

A slave handed Jonathan a glass of wine. He took it and looked up at the woman sadly.

"What types of goods do you deal in?" the man's wife asked, cuddling up against her husband. "Anything I would like?"

"*Sum* Aurelia," Layla said. "We sold our stock back in Britannia. We are on our way back to Egypt to pick up another shipment."

"I've never heard of merchants going such distances," the man said. "Usually Egyptian merchants take things to Rome. Roman merchants take things to Gaul. Others buy them and perhaps go to Britannia."

"*Nomen meum est* Valerius," Will said. "We try to keep our prices low for our customers by handling all the shipments."

"That makes sense," Lavinia said. "As travel becomes safer and faster in the realm of the empire, we'll probably see more of that. So who's married to whom?"

The students looked at each other nervously. They knew their cover stories, but they had not yet lived them in a mission setting.

"*Ego sum* Carmen," she said, leaning over to kiss Jonathan on the cheek. "This one's mine."

"You're a lovely couple," the woman said, smiling.

Layla swallowed hard, knowing that she was expected to explain the group further.

"Valerius here is my husband," she said, awkwardly rubbing his shoulder.

"Really?" the Roman man asked. "It doesn't look that way."

"Why do you say that?" Will asked.

"I've been married forty years, young man," he said. "I've seen couples in love. I've seen married couples who simply hate each other. You two are not really married."

"Let's show them how it's done, *mi Marcule!*" Lavinia said in a suddenly raspy voice.

The students watched in a combination of surprise and fascination as the older couple began to make out on the couch.

"Awkward," Jonathan said.

Will looked at Layla. "We didn't pull this off."

"This is a problem," she whispered. "You and I are supposed to talk our way into the library under that cover."

"Right. And if we don't pull it off there, we're finished."

"More wine!" Marcus said, coming up for air.

After another hour of dining, drinking, and watching Marcus and Lavinia kiss and grope, the group rose from their dinner couches.

"You guys all go upstairs and get some sleep," Carmen said, lingering at the table and pouring another glass of wine. "I'll wake Layla in a few hours to relieve me on the watch."

The other three headed up to the second level of the building and went into their quarters. For several long minutes, the entire group heard Marcus and his wife finish what they had started down at dinner.

Sleep did not find Will. He played the evening over and over in his mind. A simple tipsy couple at a *mansio* knew they were not really married. A librarian in Rome would be even harder to fool.

The plan for Will and Layla to jointly enter the library was sound. Between Layla's linguistic abilities and Will's knowledge of Astronomy, the two of them held the best chance for success in the library. But the culture of this time truly demanded them to be a married couple. There was no other credible connection for them to claim. She was dark skinned, he was fair. They obviously weren't siblings. The married couple cover just made sense. Except, he now knew, they had not pulled it off. And Will couldn't understand what had gone wrong.

A few hours of such tormented thoughts and Will heard a light knock on the door next to his. It was

Carmen waking up Layla for her watch shift. He heard Carmen giggle a little louder than he thought was appropriate for the hour. And then came the creaking sounds of Layla leaving her room and taking a position near the stairs.

Will heard Carmen seem to dive into her bed. A few moments later, silence again had fallen upon the floor. He tossed and turned for another hour and finally knew he had to speak with Layla. He gently pushed his door open and stepped into the dark hallway.

"You have another hour," Layla whispered.

"I know," he returned softly. Will stepped slowly toward her.

"We're off to a rough start, huh?"

"We've got an uphill battle to even get to Rome," he said.

"And then, if we make it, it all comes down to you and me."

Will nodded. "There's no other cover that makes sense."

"That's true," she whispered. "But if being married to me is something you don't think you can fake, maybe we need to think of another plan."

Will's eyes had now adjusted enough that he could see her well, bathed in the light of the moon creeping from the center courtyard.

"*I have to let her know*," he thought.

A sudden snap rang through the air.

Layla shot out her left hand to rest on Will's shoulder. He dared not make the slightest movement, fearing she would withdraw from him.

"The building settling," she whispered, not moving her hand.

They each felt energy surging between them.

"I— I can imagine being married to you," he said. "I've been doing it for years."

Her eyes flooded with tears. She withdrew her hand and his face fell. But she had lifted both hands, reached behind his head, and pulled him into a deep kiss.

They lingered, pressing ever closer. Her hands and his began to explore each other. And then they fell into a tight embrace.

"Layla," he whispered into her ear.

"*Te amo*," she whispered back.

"*Quoque te amo*," he sighed. "*Multos annos te amavi*."

For a long while they held each other tightly, their cheeks mingling joyful tears. She began to smile broadly, feeling his body respond.

He stepped back. "Layla, I..."

She laughed. "Will, it's okay."

"I'm..."

She took his right hand in hers. Pressing open the door of her room with her back, she pulled him inside. Will's heart pounded within his chest as he followed her. They collapsed onto the bedding on the floor. He was upon her, their instincts releasing movements as they explored an ever deeper kiss.

Layla began to pull the fabric of Will's tunic upward.

Will suddenly got to his knees and put his hands on his forehead. "Oh, Layla," he gasped. "Forgive me."

"What is it?" she asked frantically.

"If you understood how badly I want you in this moment..."

"I'm yours, Will."

He sat back. "Please know, you are the most gorgeous creature on the planet, in this or any time."

"What's wrong?" she whispered.

"I didn't want to do this till I'm married."

Layla slowly sat up. She reached out and took his hands into hers. "That's fine," she said softly. "Just know that I'm yours. I mean my heart and I mean my soul. Everything that I am."

He leaned forward and kissed her. "And I'm yours, Layla."

They sat in silence a long while.

She finally began to giggle. "And now we have a very different problem."

Will looked toward the rafters of the ceiling, which he could barely make out in the darkness. "I suppose we have to tell Jonathan and Carmen."

"I'm going to have a hard time keeping my hands off you," she said. "So, yes we will."

"I'm the leader of a highly trained espionage team on a mission to save the world," he said, looking into her eyes.

She understood his point. "This doesn't change that. You give me any order you feel is necessary and I will carry it out."

"That's the problem," Will said. "Am I going to second guess sending you into danger if the team requires it?"

She shook her head. "No, you won't, Will. You better not. The world is counting on us. There's more at stake here than..."

He pressed his lips against hers. After a long and lingering kiss, he sat back again and caressed her cheeks with his fingertips. "*Te amo*, Layla."

"*Et te amo*," she said. "*In saecula saeculorum.*"

Chapter Eight

Will had let Jonathan sleep through his time on the watch. He awoke the group when the sunlight through the open ceiling poured brightly into the center court. They grabbed several loaves of bread and some dried fruit off a table on the ground floor and received their new horses for the journey.

The group sat upon their steeds and looked out upon the expanse of road ahead.

"Before we head out," Will started, "there's something that needs to be said."

"I suppose you're talking about you and Layla hooking up last night," Carmen said.

What?" Layla asked.

"Awfully thin walls in that *mansio*," Jonathan said.

"What?" Will returned.

"You two came pretty close," Carmen said. "But Will wants to save it for marriage."

Jonathan laughed out loud. "You love each other forever. Blah, blah, blah."

"This is a complication," Layla said. "But we're committed to the principle that our relationship does not affect the mission."

Carmen pulled her horse alongside Layla's and put her hand on her friend's shoulder. "Having watched you two in love for four years without you voicing it, I'm just so relieved you've finally brought this thing to light."

"We know our mission," Will said. "We've got a month ahead of us. We're racing to Rome and back. And I can't imagine doing this with anyone else but *all* three of you."

Jonathan smiled. "Appreciated. And don't be afraid to kick our butts when you need to. You're the leader and I wouldn't want your job for anything."

"*Gratias*," Will chuckled. "I think."

"*Sic*," Layla added. "We're never going to make it if we don't stay on a straight and narrow path here. And only a leader can make that happen."

Will nodded. "I get it. But at the same time, don't be afraid to tell *me* when you think I've completely screwed up."

"Done," Carmen giggled.

"Let's ride, people," Will said, snapping the reins of his horse. "It's more than another day to Durocortorum. And we'll still be in the north of Gaul when we get there."

After a long day of fast riding, switching out their horses twice, they arrived at yet another *mansio*. The students quickly settled into a routine. Carmen was the horse expert, and so she went and selected the animals for the following morning's travel. Layla, the master linguist, conducted the conversations with the staff of the *mansio*.

After depositing their things in their bedrooms, the four were once again resting downstairs and awaiting the dinner which would soon arrive. They were sprawled out on the couches ringing the large circular table at the center of the dining area. As they feasted on appetizers of olives and various cheeses, slaves refilled their wine glasses.

Carmen drained her glass while the slave was still pouring others. "More please," she said.

The slave emptied what was left in her pitcher and headed back to the kitchen for a refill. Several more guests at the *mansio* began to descend from the upper level.

"Time to practice our covers again," Jonathan said.

"How's my hubby?" Carmen asked, pouring the rest of her cup into her mouth.

"*Multum bene,*" he replied. "But let's play like we have a contentious marriage tonight."

She laughed. "Understood. This will be fun."

The several new guests took places at the couches surrounding the central table.

"*Salvete,*" a togaed man said, reaching to take an olive. "*Nomen meum est* Rufus."

"*Sum* Nennius," Jonathan said. "*Et haec femina est uxor mea.*" He put his arm around Carmen and kissed her on the cheek.

She pushed him away. "After what you did last week, you think I'm going to forgive you that easy?!"

Rufus laughed loudly. "Sorry, my good man. I guess you have some repairs to perform."

"*Et haec femina est uxor mea,*" Will said, leaning over and kissing Layla.

She smiled and purred.

Rufus laughed. "Lovers, obviously. But married, you two are not."

Will looked at him, startled. "What do you mean?"

"I don't know," the man returned. "You look like engaged maybe. Hot for each other, certainly. But you're not married yet, right? I mean, lots of people say they're married to make travel issues easier."

Will looked into Layla's eyes. "We still have a serious problem," he whispered.

"*Vinum!*" Carmen shouted, trying to change the subject.

A slave appeared with a new and full pitcher.

"Keep this glass full," she said.

Will and Layla rested back into dinner mode, hoping that the matter would be dropped.

"So what's your real story?" the guest asked.

"We really are married," Layla said sternly.

"No," he said. "You really aren't. But it's not my business. So enjoy your dinner."

Will and Layla locked eyes again, both filled with deep concern.

"What did we do different from Marcus and his wife yesterday?" Layla whispered.

"What are we doing different from Jonathan and Carmen right now?" Will asked. "No one's questioning their story."

"*Te adoro*," Layla said. "You know that you have standing permission to take me, body and soul to your room tonight."

He smiled. "I know it. And I'm having a really hard time preserving my resolve."

****

Early the next day, they passed through the city of Durocortorum. The sights and sounds of people bargaining in the forum, surrounded by white marble temples, was a welcome respite from the boredom of riding on a road through the country. After several more hours of travel, a third evening was spent at another comfortable *mansio*. In conversations with other guests, the students were particularly focusing in on the character of vowels, which Dr. Valquist had told them made up most of any distinctive accent. Four more days brought them to Augustodunum, where they stayed at an inn just beyond the city before pressing forward toward Lugdunum. After only a week of practicing the vowels they were hearing other Latin speakers use, the students were no longer getting questions from curious guests about where they came from. But Will and Layla did regularly experience challenges to their cover story.

****

"Are we reaching Lugdunum today?" Carmen asked, looking into a bright sky.

The team moved steadily down the cobblestone road, the shadows of trees slapping their eyes with darkness and light.

Will studied the device. "Not a chance. We are officially behind schedule by more than a full day. It's just turned out that ninety miles isn't as easy in practice as we had hoped."

"I have a plan," Carmen said. "What if we got fresh horses sometime near sundown and then just continued through the night?"

"Some of us need our beauty sleep," Layla said.

"You're gorgeous, sweetie," Carmen replied. "Especially now that you're flush half the day from Will's kisses. But seriously, we get to the morning and again we change horses. Obviously tomorrow would be a drag. And we can even knock off early, maybe stopping at the best *mansio* we find about twoish in the afternoon. But if we do this from time to time, we'll actually be earning extra days on our trip. You never know when we'll need them."

"What say you, Jonathan?" Will asked.

"I don't like it. This was supposed to be an emergency measure. The risk of bandits and our compromised condition if we're tired the following day just isn't worth it."

"Noted," Will said.

"Being behind a day will become an emergency eventually if we don't solve it," Carmen said. "Just because there were bandits in Britannia doesn't mean they're everywhere in Gaul."

"I would have thought you would want to avoid even a slim chance of a fight," Jonathan countered.

She took a drink from a water skin. "I've shown what I can do to them, haven't I?"

"Enough, people," Will said. "Let me think."

They rode in silence for a few more minutes.

"I've decided the plan has more pros than cons," Will finally said. "At the end of this day, we will be on the lookout for a *mansio* or *mutatio* to change horses, get supplies, and then we press forward tonight."

"Ugh," Layla said. "I guess it's going to be a long next twenty-four hours."

With the sun low enough in the sky that red tones were splashed upon the clouds, the students spotted a large *mansio* just off the road ahead.

"This one looks awesome!" Layla exclaimed. "Can't we postpone this plan by even a day?"

"No," Will said. "We stick to plans that are made."

They traded out their horses. Layla and Jonathan went into the inn and came back with a full stock of food and drink skins.

"Stretch your limbs, people," Will said. "This won't be fun. And by the time we get in beds tomorrow night you'll be awfully sore. But we are on a mission to save the planet, remember."

Carmen took a deep drink off a skin.

"Give me some water," Jonathan said, holding out his hand.

"Just a sec." She stepped to her horse and pulled a skin out of a sack. "I don't want your germs. So this one's all yours."

"Geez," he said, taking it from her. "Are we in middle school?"

"Saddle up, people," Will said, jumping up to mount his ride. "We've got a long night and day ahead of us."

They set out into the dusk.

****

Will gazed at the sky above. "Look at all those stars, people. That's a rare sight in our time."

"No lights and no smog to blot it out," Layla said. "It's kind of romantic."

Jonathan raised an eyebrow. "I wish there were even the sliver of a moon in that sky so we weren't riding almost blind. We're going to be here for another three weeks. Can't we plan these overnights for more light next time?"

"You make a good point," Will replied. "Obviously we're committed tonight, but we can wait until a fuller moon to buy some more days."

"Good."

Layla's horse neighed in alarm.

"What is it, girl?" she asked, rubbing her animal's neck.

A group of shadows appeared on the road ahead of them.

"Whoa," Jonathan said, pulling back on his reins.

"Code Red," Will said loudly.

They brought all their horses to a stop.

"Speak for us, Layla," Will said.

"You're all doing fine now," she said. "Does it always have to be me?"

Will sighed. "I guess not. What's your business?" he shouted down the road.

For a lingering moment there was no movement or sound. Then the group heard the clopping of hoofs on the road ahead. One of the shadows came into view before them as a uniformed and armored rider.

"Soldier," Will shouted. "We are holding an imperial diploma. Please stand down to let us pass through."

"You should not have called him 'soldier'," Layla whispered. "He's a centurion. That's an insult."

"Oh, great," Carmen said loudly. "So it was a good idea to make Will speak instead of you, right?"

"The Empire does not pay us enough to just protect these roads," the centurion shouted back. "We take some payment for passage. The cost at this spot is only *duo denarii*. Hand it over and you can be on your way."

Will huffed. "If we had that much money, I would just pay this."

"But we don't have the 'toll', do we?" Carmen said.

"You know we don't."

Carmen took a drink off a skin. "And so, give me my orders, Will."

"Can anyone see how many are in their party?" Will asked.

"I think it's three other riders," Jonathan replied.

"I concur," Layla added.

"We can assume they're all fully armed with swords and spears," Carmen said. "I would say that the best army fighters have been promoted up through the ranks and aren't hanging around on the road in the middle of the night to extort travelers. These aren't simple bandits, but we can take them."

"Not all of us can fight like you, Carm," he said. "Our best plan here is still to make an unexpected show of force and even the odds."

She nodded. "By 'unexpected', you mean, of course, a little blonde girl killing her opponent."

Will swallowed. "I hate this, Carm. But I have to do what I think is right."

"I understand," she scoffed. "And unlike Layla, I'm going to follow my orders instead of asking my boyfriend for special treatment."

"Propose single combat with our best," Will said to Layla.

Layla turned to Carmen. "Sweetie…"

"Shut up."

Layla hung her head a moment. "Is your best fighter afraid to face our champion?" she shouted down the road. "Because here she comes."

Carmen flapped the reins of her horse and proceeded slowly down the road.

"Send your best!" the centurion shouted. "What are we supposed to do to this woman? Ravage her?"

"Why don't you try that and see what happens!" Carmen shouted, dismounting and pulling the long blade of her sword out of the sheath at her side.

The spokesman of the other group pulled the reins and faded into the shadows. Another shadow emerged. A taller rider stopped his horse and dismounted.

"I have never killed a woman," the man shouted. "Do I have the right to enjoy her first?" he asked, turning back toward his leader.

"Do whatever you want with her," the first man called out.

Carmen looked back at her group. "Don't they know that this kind of talk will only make me not show them mercy?"

The man charged, lifting his sword high in the air.

Carmen stepped steadily forward, watching his approach.

He slammed his sword down. Carmen jumped to the right and swung her blade as she flew by her opponent. She sliced along his shoulder and landed on the other side of him.

"By Hercules!" he screamed, grabbing his arm and spinning around. "You'll pay for that."

He stepped forward and pulled his arm back. A rapid thrust of his weapon raced directly at Carmen.

She dropped to the ground, hearing the blade sing through the air above her. Spinning on the cobblestones, she drew her sword against the man's calf. She then stood quickly, buried the blade into his side, and quickly twirled the other direction. Carmen landed on her feet and took a defensive stance.

The soldier dropped to his knees, grabbing choppy breaths as he felt spasms of pain gripping his body. He weakly tugged at the sword still planted in his ribs.

"What are you?" he gasped.

Carmen stood straight and walked toward him.

"I'm a girl," she sputtered.

She drew her sword from the man and then swung it through his neck. The soldier's head dropped from his shoulders and rolled backwards toward his allies in the darkness.

"Let's get out of here!" a voice screamed from within the shadows.

The students heard the sounds of hooves scrambling into the distance.

"You called it right," Jonathan said softly. "This act will never get old. Every fighter will be sure they can beat her."

"And no one can," Will noted. "I just worry about what this is doing to her."

Carmen knelt down and searched the body.

"Not a penny on him!" she shouted. "But his sword is nicer than mine, so I'm keeping it." She walked slowly back to the others, wiping the blood off her original sword against her tunic. She sheathed the weapons and hopped atop her animal.

"Let's be on our way," she said, reaching into a pouch draped over her horse. She pulled out a skin and took a deep drink. "We've got a lot of miles to cover."

Chapter Nine

The growing orange in the eastern horizon snuffed out the stars one by one. The air was teeming with bats as a single avian chirp rang into the morning. As if relieved of their duties, the bats vanished, replaced by song birds exploring a new day.

"I'm not terribly tired," Layla announced. "And I'm a bit surprised about it."

"We will be tonight," Carmen said. "Whose bright idea was this, anyway?"

The group laughed.

Will took out the device and examined the screen. "If it's any consolation, our night trek bought us a lot of time. It seems to me that the slaves always had food ready before we woke up, so I think we can stop for some breakfast at the next place we see."

"A pizzeria would sure be a very welcome sight right about now," Jonathan said. "I miss modern food so much."

The sun had climbed to mid-morning when they saw the gates of Lugdunum in the distance ahead.

"That city is roughly half way to Rome," Jonathan noted. "And we're doing fine, my friends."

Just outside the city gates, they spotted a *mansio*.

"At this point we'll make this place our breakfast and lunch stop for the day," Will said. "So eat well and rest. We'll spend an hour here."

"*Garum* and dried bread never sounded so good," Layla said.

They checked in their horses at the stable and selected new animals for the next leg of the journey. Entering the main building, they saw a bustling hall lined with soldiers.

"I don't think there's anywhere to recline, sirs," a slave said, carrying a tray of sausages to a nearby table. "I'll give you some food while you stand, if you'd like."

"We would like that..." Will said, checking himself from saying '*gratias*'.

The slave nodded and disappeared back into the kitchen.

"Where are your manners, you dogs!" a centurion shouted, getting up from one of the couches. "Don't you see that there are women standing in the room?" He grabbed one of the soldiers by the arms and pulled him into the air. He tossed the man aside and turned to Carmen.

"Please, my lady, be our guest," he said.

Other soldiers scrambled off couches and offered a place to Layla.

"Thank you, Centurion," Carmen said, reclining and taking a glass of wine. "It is good to know that traditional manners are still alive up here in Gaul."

He nodded courteously and found a place beside another table.

The slave returned with more platters and set them in front of Carmen and Layla. Will and Jonathan stood beside them and reached over to eat their breakfast.

"Attention!" the Centurion shouted and bolted from his place. The other soldiers fell immediately silent and stood as well. Carmen and Layla alone were still reclined in the room. They turned around and saw a tall man wearing a silvery polished breastplate standing in the doorway. A deep blue cape hung from his shoulders.

"As you were, men," he spoke in a deep and gruff voice.

The soldiers returned to their places but continued their speaking in hushed tones.

"What's his rank?" Will whispered.

"He's a *legatus*," Layla returned. "The general of an entire legion."

The man walked slowly toward the young people, studying them, as he turned his head side to side. "You just rode through the night." It was a statement, not a question.

"*Sic*," Will replied. "We are merchants travelling with an imperial diploma."

He nodded, staring at Carmen. "I want to talk to the group of you, but not here. Follow me out of the room." He turned and walked quickly through the doorway.

The students looked at each other, fear flooding them as they imagined the worst.

"Someone is on to us," Layla whispered. "I'm going to be sick."

"We don't know anything right now," Jonathan said. "Let's go see what he wants."

"We need a plan, Will," Carmen said. "What do we do in the worst case scenario?"

"For now, just be ready to follow any order I give," he said. "Obviously we aren't here to be captured and executed. They'll kill us trying to escape before we let that happen."

They exchanged nods. Will lead the group out of the hall and into the courtyard in front of the *mansio*. The general was standing in the middle of the grass-covered space, his hands behind his back.

"You wanted to speak with us, General?" Will asked.

"I know it was your group that killed a soldier last night down the road."

Will opened his mouth and took a deep breath. He slowly released it and then nodded. "General, we were attacked by a group of soldiers that were extorting money from people passing on this road. It was illegal."

"I know what it was," the man said. "And I don't tolerate it in my ranks."

"How did you find out about this, if we might ask?" Layla said.

"I'd gotten reports of the extortion ring and so I did a spot check on the barracks in the middle of the night.

When we found four men missing from a unit, I knew I'd found the culprits."

"We only killed one," Will said.

"And I was waiting at the barracks when the other three tried to sneak back in. I made it clear to them that telling me everything that happened was the only way for them to avoid the sword this morning."

"So what did they say?" Carmen asked.

"That a white-haired young woman, I presume you from their description, had bested the champion swordsman of their unit. And they fled in fear that they were next."

"Not to be disrespectful, General," Will interrupted. "But we still need to eat something and continue on our journey as soon as possible. Do you need anything further from us?"

"*Sic*," the General said. "I want to hire you."

"Hire us?" Jonathan asked. "For what?"

"You've obviously proven your ability to fight. I need bodyguards to transport my father down to Massilia so he can board a ship to Asia Minor."

"Excuse me, General," Will said. "But, well, you're a general. Do you not have soldiers much more equipped for such a task than us?"

"I have my reasons and you knowing them is not part of this agreement."

Will looked at the others. Through their eyes, all voiced both concern and the awareness that this could be the money-making venture they needed to finish the trip.

"What is your price?" Will asked.

"One hundred *denarii* for the group," he said.

"This was not the route we were going to take on our way to Rome," Will said. "It had been our intention to travel through the *Alpes Cottiae*. Would it be possible for your father to board his ship at Genua?"

The General thought a moment and then shook his head. "The ship that will take him to Smyrna is already organized. He can't be figuring out alternatives in Genua when he gets there. Two hundred *denarii* to take him to Massilia."

"Please, sir, let me consult with my colleagues for a moment."

"*Certe*," the man said, nodding.

Will stepped back and walked a few paces away. The others crowded around him.

"This only adds about a hundred miles to our trip," Layla said.

"We make up the time by doing what we did last night," Carmen added. "We need this money desperately. When we get to Rome, we're going to have to pay for our lodging, our food, our drink..."

"Not to mention the money we promised that Celt who's supposed to be waiting for us back in Gesoriacum," Jonathan noted.

"We aren't going to make ninety miles a day with the general's father in tow," Will said. "But I don't think we have much of a choice. This is kind of a Godsend for us. From Massilia we take the coastal road to Genua."

"With the mountains in the Alps, this route may not even be much longer in terms of time," Carmen said.

"Alright," Layla said. "Let's do it."

They turned back to the officer and approached him.

"We accept the offer, General," Will said. "When will your father be ready to leave?"

"You eat your meal and rest a few hours. Be at the south gate of Lugdunum at about the sixth hour and we will meet you there. He'll have a horse and be ready to join your group."

Will smiled. "And you'll have our payment."

The general smiled. "*Sic, certe.*"

****

The students sat on their steeds just outside the south gate of the city. Each time they heard a horse or wagon about to exit, they were expecting to see the general and their mystery guest.

"What time is it?" Layla asked.

Will looked at the device. "It's half past the sixth hour—or 'noon', as we call it back home," he said. "But remember that no one else on the planet has a clock as accurate as ours, so he probably doesn't even know he's late."

Two horses filed out from the gate. From atop one of them, the general craned his neck around, looking for the students.

"There they are," Jonathan said.

The two rode toward the young people. "Thank you for being prompt," the general stated. He held out a sack to Will. "Go ahead and count it before you leave."

"No offense," Will said, opening the cloth bag and looking inside. He reached in and flipped through the coins, counting silently as he moved his lips. A minute later, he looked up. "It's all there. *Gratias*, General."

The officer brought his horse up next to the other man. "Be well, Father," he said, before then kissing the man on both cheeks. He took the man's right hand, lifted it to his lips, and kissed it as well.

The other man put his hand on the general's head. "Be well, my son," he said. "I will see you next Spring." With his hand still on the general's head, the man leaned over and whispered something.

The general nodded and closed his eyes. He then snapped the reins of his horse and turned back into the city.

The students looked at the man.

"I'm Valerius," Will said.

"Pleased to meet you, Valerius," he said. "I am Irenaeus."

"Aurelia."

"I'm Carmen."

"Ladies," the man said softly, tipping his head to them.

"And I'm Nennius."

"I am so thankful that we found people like yourselves to take me to my ship," Irenaeus said. "I was told you are in a hurry so, please, let us be on our way. If ever I am not traveling fast enough, let me know. I am the one indebted to you."

"Not really," Will said with a chuckle. "Your son paid us well. The only thing you do need to know is that, in the event that we face any trouble on the journey, I want you just to stay out of the way. We will be able to deal with anything that happens, but we can't be worried about what you might do."

"I certainly won't be involved," he said.

Will studied the man and his gear. "Sir, do you have a sword with you?"

"No," he replied. "I don't know how to use one anyway, so I don't want to carry one."

"I would have thought your son would know that a sword even as a prop is a good idea," Jonathon said.

"You can have my old sword," Carmen said. She held the sheathed weapon in the gap between them. "Here, tie that around your waist."

The man looked down. "I won't carry a sword."

"This doesn't matter," Will said. "Let's get going."

The group started onto the road and reached a fast but comfortable speed, forming a loose column behind Will.

They had traveled hours before Will suddenly realized their guest might not have been accustomed to the pace. He slowed his animal, allowing Carmen to take the lead as he drifted to the middle of the group where Irenaeus was riding.

"How are you doing?" he asked the man.

"I'm well, thank you," Irenaeus replied.

"Have you done much riding?" Layla asked from ahead of their position.

"Very little, and I admit that this will cause me some pain before we arrive in Massilia."

"It'll be very bad only on the first day," Will said. "After three or four more days we'll reach the destination. You'll feel better by then."

Irenaeus chuckled. "And then I deal with seasickness."

"What do you for a living, sir?" Jonathan asked from the rear.

"I'm..." the man paused as if considering his words.

"I mean, were you a military man like your son?" Will asked.

"No," he answered. "I'm a writer."

Layla searched her memory for any recognition of his name within her studies. Something told her that the name did seem vaguely familiar. "What type of writing?" she asked.

"Philosophical works," he replied.

"That explains it. A part of me thinks that I did recognize your name, but since I don't care for philosophy, I don't think I've ever read anything you wrote."

He looked at her seriously. "You've really heard of me?"

She looked at him curiously, wondering if this discussion compromised their dabbling in the past. At last she decided it was harmless. "I really have."

He smiled. "And what do you all do?"

"We're merchants," Will said.

"How do you happen to have an imperial diploma to use the *mansiones* and *mutationes*?"

"Our particular wares have been purchased by a member of the imperial family," Jonathan said. "We think that someone there wants to make a birthday present out of it, so that's why we are kind of in a hurry."

"Then why would you even agree to go out of your way to take me to Massilia?" he asked.

"We need the money," Will stated. "We've already been paid for the goods we transport, but we're always willing to earn more."

"Fair enough," he said.

"Please let me know if you get tired and want to take a break," Will said. "We'll be continuing for about another four hours before we stay at a *mansio* our map says is coming up."

"Thank you, young man," Irenaeus said. "You've gone out of your way to make me comfortable. May God bless you."

Will nodded. As he rode back toward the front of the line, he raised an eyebrow as he thought about the curious guest.

"God?" Carmen whispered.

****

The entire group reclined around a large table and sipped at glasses of wine following a lavish meal.

"Pressing forward to this place was so worth it," Carmen said, refilling her glass and taking a deep swallow. "Have we had lamb prepared like that before?"

"I don't think so," Layla said. "Did you enjoy your meal, Irenaeus?"

"*Sic, gratias,*" he said, a tone of sadness in his voice.

"Is something wrong, sir?" Jonathan asked.

The man looked at him and smiled. "No. I'm sorry. It's just that I'm already missing my family back in Lugdunum."

"Who's in Smyrna?" Carmen asked.

"My parents were born there, so I have family still in the area."

"That explains your Greek name," Layla said. "You speak Greek too?" she asked in that language.

"Of course," he replied in kind. "You speak well. Where are you from that you also know some Greek?"

The others followed a conversation they understood well enough but also knew that only Layla was competent to pull off.

"I'm from Arabia, but we had a Greek slave in the house for a while when I was growing up. I never learned it very well."

"You're being too hard on yourself," he said. "You told me earlier that you don't like philosophy. What writers do you like?"

"Vergil, obviously. Otherwise, I rather enjoy Livy."

"The legends of ancient Rome, before she became the ruler of the world," he said. "In Greek or Latin have you ever read any of the works of the Jews?"

"Yes," she said. "I've read them in Greek. Are they translated into Latin…" She caught herself before adding "in this time."

"Only pieces," he said. "It's a very different view of the universe, isn't it?"

"Yes," she replied softly, suddenly wondering why the conversation had gone here.

"I'm so sorry," Irenaeus said in Latin to all. "This first day of travel has taken a lot out of me. I am going to go upstairs and get to sleep early. Please wake me whenever we need to be on our way."

"*Nox bona*," Will said.

Irenaeus nodded and headed down the hall toward the stairs.

"Shouldn't one of us stand guard up there for him?" Jonathan asked.

"I don't think it's necessary here at a large *mansio*," Will said. "We've just been hired to transport him."

"Why do we keep a guard for ourselves every night then?" Layla asked.

"Well, that's more because we're actually special agents from the future," Carmen said.

The students laughed.

"God, that will never stop being funny," Layla said.

Jonathan raised a finger. "Speaking of which, did you notice that Irenaeus said 'May God bless you' earlier?"

"It stood out," Will replied. "But maybe only because we're being careful not to say it in front of others."

"Vergil called Jupiter the 'Omnipotent Father' in the *Aeneid*," Layla said. "And the guy was clearly still a polytheist."

"Whatever," Will said. "I think we should all get to sleep early tonight. When we finally see our guest off in Massilia, we need to start pulling those all nighters immediately. I don't want to be making them up on the way back from Rome."

"You're right," Carmen said, refilling her glass with wine. "Cheers, my friends. As always, I'm on first guard."

****

The next day was dragging into a later afternoon. The group had decided to pass a *mutatio* that looked sub-par to make it to a *mansio* their map had just ten miles farther down the road. As they approached the spot where they should have found it, the sun was already falling beneath the trees on the horizon, throwing jagged shadows upon them. On the left of the cobblestone road, they saw the burnt hull of what must once have been a *mansio*.

"Damn it!" Jonathan said. "What happened here?"

"Looks like a fire destroyed the place," Will said. "And it wasn't long enough ago that they've changed the maps."

Carmen rode up beside him. "Code Red," she whispered. "That run-down *mutatio* we saw would make anyone want to travel on. So someone destroyed this place to lay the trap we are now officially in."

"What are you saying?" he asked.

"We're on the X. Right now."

Will nodded.

"People, we made a mistake today. We've never backtracked before, but we're returning to the *mutatio* we saw back there."

"Someone doesn't think so," Jonathan said, pointing down the road from which they had come.

The group turned and saw two horses at a distance.

"The trap is sprung," Carmen said, nodding forward.

Down the road past the former *mansio*, they saw three more riders.

"Calm down, people," Will said. "Let's assume the worst. We are on the X and there's no way off. We're outnumbered five to four."

"Only Carmen has fought," Jonathan said. "But we were all trained to do it."

"I don't want to hurt anyone," Layla said, her voice choking.

"Let them get close," Carmen said. "And go ahead and propose the surprise offer. After I've done my bit, it'll be four against four. But I think you're all going to get in the fight after that."

"What's going on?" Irenaeus asked. "What do these people want?"

"They want the two hundred *denarii* your son gave us," Jonathan said. "And they're not going to take them without a fight."

"Listen," Irenaeus said. "If we surrender all our money to them, I'll be able to give you your money back when we get to Massilia."

"Sorry, sir," Will said. "That's not a sure thing for us. And we didn't come this route to hope we could find money somewhere else."

"I just don't want anyone to die over me."

"It's not over you," Carmen said. "It's over money. It always is."

"The root of all evil..." Irenaeus whispered.

The riders approached their group on both sides and stopped twenty yards away.

"They're dressed in chainmail, but they're just common bandits," Carmen said, studying them. "At least this time it's not wicked well-trained soldiers."

"What does that mean?" Irenaeus asked.

"It means after I kill the one who will be sure he can beat me, we can easily take the rest."

"I hate this," Irenaeus said.

"I do too," she whispered back.

"Get off your horse, Carm," Will said. "Nennius, Aurelia, turn your horses to face the other two. You're on them if this turns into a fight. Carmen and I will take this side."

They complied as Carmen jumped off her horse.

"Your best against my best!" Will shouted. "If my girl conquers your fighter, you let us go on our way."

The bandits began first to chuckle and then laughed heartily as they saw Carmen seeming to walk nervously back and forth across the road.

Murmurs of conversation rolled on both sides of them and finally a man from the group of three hopped off his horse and walked confidently toward Carmen.

"You are pretty," he said, spinning his sword around over his head. "It will be a shame to cut that beautiful face away from such a beautiful body."

"They're making me do this," she said to him in a feigned sob. "Please don't hurt me."

The man looked at her in puzzlement. "You are not their best?"

"I don't even know how to fight," she said, looking down. She placed the tip of her sword carefully on the road and turned it until she saw the reflection of the bandit on the blade. "Can't you please just take our money and let us go?"

The bandit looked Carmen up and down, smiling. "No. I see something else here I want to take. I'm not going to hurt you. At least not with my sword."

He began walking forward, lowering his weapon as he approached her.

She saw him in the reflection on her blade and counted down his arrival within the range of her widest sweep.

"You are sweet," he said, lunging toward her.

Carmen lifted her sword and swung it around. The weapon whistled a high tone as it flew in front of the man. The tip of the blade sliced through his wind pipe.

The bandit raised his hands to his neck for just a moment and then collapsed backward.

Carmen turned to Will. "Here it comes."

A roar sounded from both sides, as the other bandits charged.

"Incoming!" Will screamed. "Aurelia, Nennius, advance! Carmen, you're with me."

Jonathan snapped the reins, sending his beast hurtling toward an enemy already in a full gallop. He drew his sword from its sheath and leaned forward, accelerating to top speed. The lead bandit began to slow, suddenly unsure how to face such an attack. Jonathan was on him. He rode past, using the force of his arm and the speed of the horse to bring the edge of his sword crashing against the opponent's armored chest. The blow echoed through the air and knocked the man off his horse. Directly behind him, the second thief swung at Jonathan. He ducked down just as the blade swept over him.

Layla was following closely behind and kicked the second man in the face just as his sword flew over Jonathan. He joined his compatriot on the ground beside their horses.

Doubling back, Jonathan and Layla jumped off their steeds and held swords over the two wounded and groaning men.

Will charged toward the two bandits on the other side. His horse jumped over the body of the bandit Carmen had slain as she leaped back onto her animal.

"Split formation," he yelled back to her.

"Affirmative," she shouted, and kicked the sides of her horse to match his speed.

The two raced directly at the oncoming enemy. Just before reaching their position, Will and Carmen split off from the center, riding now along the edge of the road. They passed on each side of the bandits. who weakly swung their swords, missing Carmen and Will entirely.

The instant they were past their opponents, the two students brought their horses to a stop and pulled the reins to turn them around. They kicked and snapped the reins to return to a full gallop.

The two bandits in confusion slowed their horses and looked back just in time to see Carmen and Will already on their position from behind. They were still in the middle of getting their animals to turn around when the two students had arrived, each one cleanly thrusting their swords through their marks. The two bandits slid from their horses and fell lifeless to the ground.

"Report!" Will shouted in the direction of Jonathan and Layla.

"We've got two prisoners here!" he replied. "One's wounded. One's just stunned."

Will and Carmen rode toward the others. Irenaeus still sat on his horse, his face in his hands.

"No more killing," he said through staggered breaths. "Please."

"It's over," Will said. "Just stay here. We'll be right back."

They continued to Jonathan and Layla's position.

The bandit Layla had kicked was now sitting upright on the road. The other one was breathing rapidly, holding the wound in his side.

"How bad is it?" Carmen asked.

"I sliced him pretty good," Jonathan said. "It got through that chainmail, but I don't know what it looks like under there."

"We're going to try and help your friend," Layla said.

"He's not my friend," the man hissed back, getting up and beginning to run down the road.

"Let him go," Will said. "He doesn't matter anymore."

"Settle down," Carmen said, crouching beside the injured bandit and lifting up the layer of chain mail. She grabbed the linen tunic underneath and ripped it open, revealing a four inch gash along the man's ribs. "You're lucky," she said. "If this had been any lower, we would be looking at everything inside you." Carmen looked up at the others. "He won't live if we don't sew this wound closed."

Will nodded. "I know we practiced this on fetal pigs during the briefings. But who wants to actually attempt this?"

"I'll do it."

They turned to see Irenaeus standing a few yards away, his face wet with tears.

"Get the medical kit, Nennius," Will ordered.

Jonathan stepped to his horse and opened one of the satchels draped over the animal. He pulled out a small black bag.

"You've actually done this?" he asked, handing it to Irenaeus.

189

"Yes. Hold him down." Irenaeus threaded the needle with the surgical thread. "I've never seen a needle this nice. What alloy is this?"

"The latest invention from Egypt," Will said. "And probably designed to rust to nothing in two years," he whispered to Layla.

Jonathan and Carmen pressed their hands down on the man's arms. They watched closely as Irenaeus carefully guided the needle through the wound on one end and pulled the thread through. The man struggled for just a moment and then passed out. Irenaeus tied several knots in the end of the thread and then brought the needle back through. He repeated the operation, slowly sealing the gaping wound as he went.

"That's beautiful work," Will said. "Nennius and Carmen, you have the best view. Watch this closely. You're our doctors now if we need to do this ourselves."

Irenaeus finished the sutures and reached into a little bag hanging from his belt. He pulled out a small vial and opened the lid. Holding it over the wound, he drizzled oil across the length of the sutures. Very slowly, he rubbed his hand along the wound. Jonathan saw that he closed his eyes and was mouthing words.

"Some spell or blessing in your religion?" he asked.

Irenaeus continued for a few more moments and then opened his eyes. He looked at Jonathan and smiled. "Something like that."

"Can he travel?" Will asked.

"It would be good if he could stay off a horse for several more hours," Irenaeus said. "The night will bring healing."

"Even the walls of the burned-out *mansio* will be a nice shelter," Carmen said.

"Make camp, people," Will ordered.

****

The group sat around a blazing fire in the center of what had once been the *mansio*. Despite his serious wound and with hands tied behind his back, the bandit slept deeply.

Will looked up and saw sparks from the fire flying into the sky, borne aloft by the heat of the flames, and seeming to reach for the sliver of moon peering through the night.

"So you were a doctor?" Jonathan asked Irenaeus.

"I once worked with one in Lugdunum," he answered. "But that wasn't my path."

"What was your calling?" Layla asked.

Carmen drank from a wineskin. "There's something funny here," she said. "That officer was way too old to be your son."

"Don't pry," Will whispered to her.

"It's alright, Valerius," Irenaeus said. "We've all been through a lot today and I'm tired of avoiding the truth."

"You mean tired of telling lies?" Carmen asked.

"I've not told a single one," he replied. "And to do that I've been so careful in everything I've said that I fear I have misled you four."

Layla laughed. "My God, you are a philosopher."

"God?"

She looked at him and raised an eyebrow.

"Who are all of you?" he asked.

"We've told you," Will replied. "We're a group of merchants from various places who are on an imperial mission to..."

"No," Irenaeus interrupted. "You're not."

They looked at him in silence, waiting for him to go on.

"You speak excellent Latin, all of you. Especially Aurelia. And your Greek, Aurelia, is also terrific. But in everything you all say, I detect a hint of...book learning."

"What do you mean?" Jonathan asked.

"Merchants learn languages on the go. They learn how to just make certain mistakes and not care. You all speak a bit slowly, very carefully, and don't make any grammatical errors at all."

The students looked back and forth between each other.

"Alright," Layla said. "But Carmen has a point. A lot of your story doesn't add up either. Why is a Roman officer kissing the hand of a man we've figured out isn't really his father? Why is a Roman general dropping down two hundred *denarii* to have a group of strangers transport his so-called father to a ship instead of having his own guards do it?"

Irenaeus nodded. "You all deserve the truth. The fact is, he was being careful to avoid having his soldiers know about his connection to me. And that's because he knows that the next emperor may not be as enlightened as his majesty Antoninus."

"Enlightened about what?" Carmen asked.

"Religious liberty. I'm a Christian priest."

The students' jaws all simultaneously dropped and then raised slowly as all the clues suddenly made sense.

"Was that the 'Sacrament of Healing' you performed earlier?" Jonathan inquired.

"The 'Anointing of the Sick' is what we call it." Irenaeus looked at them all and smiled. "Your turn. A group of people who speak Latin like they've been trained for a mission. I know what you are."

"Really?" Will said. "Let's hear it."

"You're angels."

The students burst into uproarious laughter.

"That we are not," Jonathan said. "Try again."

"No," Irenaeus stated firmly. "Because I'm right. An angel is a messenger of God. You're here, and I don't understand why, for a reason so important that I feel as if the entire world depends on it."

The students fell suddenly silent.

"Interesting," Irenaeus said. "My words certainly caught your attention."

Will swallowed and cleared his throat. "Irenaeus, we actually can't tell you everything about ourselves. And we will have to leave it at that."

"But I apparently was on the mark about the importance of your mission. I understand that you can't tell me everything. But let me try to tell you what I think could be the explanation of what you four are doing."

Carmen chuckled. "You are a delight, Irenaeus. You'll never come close, but give it a try."

He nodded and smiled sweetly. "I love languages," he started. "That's what first made me think something was strange about all of you. As I said, your Latin is extraordinary. Better than anyone I have ever met that wasn't raised speaking it."

"You honor us," Layla said.

"I speak Greek and Latin. I've picked up some Gaelic and even some Hebrew. So I know how hard it is to learn a foreign language."

"Indeed it is," Jonathan said. "More for me than for Layla, I mean, Aurelia."

"Layla," Irenaeus said. "That's the Hebrew word for *night*. I guess that's her real name. But you, Nennius, speak well enough yourself. What form of the word '*rex*' do you use for the object in the plural?"

Jonathan looked up for a split second. "*Reges.*"

"Well done, Nennius. But you learned that in a book, didn't you?"

"At first."

"Really?" Irenaeus chuckled. "But such books don't exist."

The students said nothing in reply.

"Cicero wrote a grammar for Etruscan," Irenaeus said. "No one speaks it today, but you can study it as a dead language."

Carmen squinted at him. "Your point?"

"Layla, Aurelia, when was the last big persecution of Christians?"

"Under Domitian," she said.

"When's the next one?"

Layla looked at him in surprise.

"You are all here on a mission to save the world," Irenaeus continued. "That much you've already admitted by your reaction to my statement. Everything taken all together leads to a seemingly impossible conclusion. It's not where you're from. It's when. You must come from a time in the future when Latin is no longer spoken. So you learned it from books. You seem to know current events as if they were history lessons. As for how you got here, I'm certain that's beyond my capacity for understanding."

The students were silent again, looking at each other in bewilderment and sadness.

"Remember what Dr. Silver said," Carmen began. "The past already happened. We can't change it. So we can talk about this."

"I have an idea," Jonathan said. "Irenaeus, can you promise to keep everything we tell you under the seal of the Confessional?"

Irenaeus looked at him curiously. "I don't know what that is."

"The private confessional as we know it only developed later, in Ireland," Will said.

"Alright, Irenaeus, will you just promise to never tell another living soul what we share with you?" Carmen asked.

"I promise," he said. "But why do you now want to tell me things that you were afraid to share before?"

"Because I think we need to," Will said. "We are all so tired and scared. We're adults in this world but still children in our own and…"

Irenaeus put his hand on Will's shoulder. "I understand. I will never tell anyone what you need to say."

"Can I do it?" Carmen asked excitedly.

Will nodded.

"We come from the year 2013," she started.

"When is that?"

"Oh, right. That would be…" She looked up to perform a mental calculation and then sighed. "Help me, math people."

"2766 *Ab Urbe Condita*," Will quickly responded.

"In our time the year is calculated from the birth of Jesus," Jonathan said.

"Really? That would imply Christians being in charge of things."

"They are," Carmen said. "Well, they were. Still are mostly, but not as much as before."

Irenaeus nodded. "I have wondered what would happen if we ever succeeded in our mission and became a majority. And I have suspected that our human sinfulness would make us do no better than the Romans."

"We are here," she continued, "on a mission to get some information that our time needs to prevent the destruction of the planet."

He looked up in thought. "My faith teaches that the world will one day end. If you don't succeed, it may be that this end is supposed to happen."

"We're going to try to stop that from happening," Will said. "If this destruction isn't God's will, then our mission needs to succeed. Look, Father, I'm an Anglican Christian myself. Practicing."

"What's an Anglican?"

"How to explain that to you?" he said. "In our time the Christians have divided into several groups. The Catholics in the west and the Orthodox in the east divided in our year 1054. The Anglicans are Christians who broke away from the Catholics about five hundred years after that."

Irenaeus looked down sadly. "You could have told me that Christians in your time are still persecuted and dying for their faith every day," he said. "Nothing could have broken my heart more than to learn that the Church will be divided."

"There are movements to repair that damage," Will said. "So we are going to try and stop the destruction of the world from happening."

"Then God bless you," Irenaeus said.

"Do you want to know when the next persecution is?" Layla asked seriously.

"No. It's enough that I have deduced one is coming. In whatever time God has willed us to live—and in your cases more than one—may we be worthy of them."

"Amen," Will said.

The students recounted to Irenaeus the entire story of their school, their cover stories and mission, and their trip up to the point in which they had met him.

"So, it's really going to be a race for you to return to your own time," Irenaeus said. "Taking me to Massilia wasn't your best plan."

"But necessary, as you know," Jonathan replied.

"It really all just hinges on getting access to that library," Will said.

Irenaeus shook his head and sighed. "I'm a scholar who has dreamt about entering places like that. Access is very restricted. I know many people who have tried to convince the guardians they deserved to research there. Very few succeed."

"They're not going to believe our cover story," Will said. "We need to be thinking of a back-up plan. A break-in may still be necessary."

"Fruitless," Irenaeus stated. "You'll never find the information you're looking for without inside help. Why won't they accept your cover story?"

"I don't understand it," Will said. "But several times now people have told us they could tell we weren't really married."

Irenaeus curled his eyebrows in confusion. "I can see you two share an attraction."

"We're…" Layla paused. "There aren't words in Latin for this. Um, we're not engaged. But we're in a relationship."

"Kind of engaged to be engaged," Irenaeus offered.

Layla laughed. "I suppose."

Irenaeus nodded. "So, despite being in a relationship, people know you are lying when you say you're married."

"But yet they seem to believe me and Jonathan," Carmen said. "And we're not even a couple."

"Interesting," Irenaeus said. "Will, you're the problem, I can see. You simply can't convincingly lie. At least not about the woman you so obviously love."

"And so, that's why we may very well not get into that library," Will said. "A husband and wife team may have a chance. But if they detect a lie, we're done."

"Quite right." Irenaeus smiled. "You're forgetting the obvious solution here."

"And what's that?" he asked.

"Get married."

"What?!" Layla gasped.

"If you were actually married, you wouldn't be lying."

"But we're only eighteen years old," she said.

"Surely you know people marry long before that in this time," Irenaeus replied.

"Not in ours," Jonathan said.

"Help us think up other alternate plans," Carmen said. "Who were these friends who failed to get into the library? Did they learn anything about the security of the place in the process?"

Will and Layla locked eyes. At first they communicated confusion and fear. Then each softened into a smile.

"I still think a break-in isn't impossible," Jonathan said.

"The Forum in Rome has a sizable military detachment stationed everywhere," Irenaeus said. "The library has armed guards inside and out. Once you get there, you'll see that…"

"Layla, will you marry me?" Will blurted.

All conversation stopped.

"What?" she whispered.

"Marry me."

"You're serious?"

He took her hand. "I have loved you for years."

"This is insane."

"It would be just as insane if we waited until after college," he said.

"We're too young," she protested.

"This is our life. Right here. Right now. We could have been killed in that fight today. I want to die your husband, not your boyfriend."

"This isn't happening," Jonathan said.

"This is so romantic!" Carmen giggled.

Layla's eyes were filled with tears. She smiled. "I will marry you."

Will and Layla met in a kiss.

"Not to rain on anyone's parade," Jonathan said, "but aren't there a lot of weird legal issues around this?"

"How does one get married in this time, Irenaeus?" Carmen asked.

"Members of my church use the Roman ceremony, without the sacrifice to Jupiter, of course."

Will sat back, still holding Layla's hand. "You're a priest. You can marry us, right?"

"Do priests do that in your time?"

"Yes."

"Interesting. Then I suppose I can. I usually just bless the couple after they say the vows."

"Well, that's how it's done in our time too," Carmen said.

"But would we actually be legally married?" Layla asked.

"We would be validly and sacramentally married," Will said. "I don't care about its civil force back in our time."

"You would be legally married here," Irenaeus said. "That's really all that matters, right?"

"Can we do this right now?" Layla asked.

"My bishop tells us priests that we cannot bless a relationship unless it is a legal and binding union. We use the rules that governed the old marriage form known as a *coemptio*. You two will be pledging equal ownership of property."

Jonathan laughed. "The new couple will jointly own two horses and six tunics."

"And a *coemptio* requires five witnesses," Irenaeus noted. "We don't have them right now."

"Layla, then you'll marry me tomorrow night at the nicest *mansio* we can find?"

She kissed him again. "*Sic.*"

****

The following morning the team broke camp quickly and continued their journey. After an hour of travel, they handed the injured bandit over to a guard at a check point. Irenaeus told the young man that he would be praying for him.

An uneventful day of continued riding found the group spying a *mansio* at a distance down the road just as the sun approached the horizon.

"That's a nice one," Jonathan said, bring his horse up alongside Will. The group was spaced out enough that their conversation was private.

"I'm beyond happy," he said. "I'm getting married tonight to the love of my life. But I also feel like the mission is flying out of control."

"How are we on days?" Jonathan asked.

"Three behind now."

"We can easily make that up by skipping some sleep."

"Have you noticed Carmen's drinking too much?"

Jonathan nodded. "Kind of hard to miss it. We're all drinking more than we ever did in the past. I mean, wine at every meal."

"But she's sneaking it other times. I've seen it. And she's just drinking way too much overall."

"I know. But she's been through more than all of us on this trip."

"I don't like it. I don't like what I've made her do. I don't like what she's doing…"

"Until it's a crisis, I don't think this should be addressed."

"I agree. Listen, Jonathan. I need a best man tonight. Will you accept?"

Jonathan laughed out loud. "Father Irenaeus is performing the ceremony. I guess I'm the only other guy available."

Will looked at him seriously. "If we were back home and I had the world to choose from, I would be asking you to be my best man."

Jonathan saw truth in his eyes. "*Sum honoratus, mi amice.*"

The two girls were at the end of the group.

"How do you feel?" Carmen asked.

"I'm marrying the man I've loved since the moment I first saw him, almost four years ago."

Carmen nodded. "It took a trip back in time to save the planet from destruction for him to finally wake up."

"But the fact is, our relationship has become a liability to our mission. You were mad as hell at me that night I told him to speak to the centurion on the road. And you were right. He went along with my suggestion because we're together. And it was almost a disaster."

"How will being married help the situation?"

"Well, for starters, I expect he'll have sex with me!"

Carmen laughed out loud. "Undoubtedly. But why will that help the mission?"

"He's a disaster right now. He's the leader of a team trying to save the world and the two of us are just distracting each other badly."

Carmen nodded. "I get it. And, more importantly, you two actually being married will help your chances of getting into that library."

Layla hung her head. "But is the mission really the reason we're doing this?"

Carmen smiled. "It's a mission to save the entire human race. People have married for worse reasons than that."

"I love Will. But what if, after the mission is over, none of this makes any sense?"

The group had arrived in front of the *mansio*.

"Dismount, team," Will said. "Carmen, take the animals to the stable and arrange for tomorrow's rides. Layla and I will secure our lodgings."

"And I'll speak to the staff about setting up for a wedding," Irenaeus said.

****

Night had fallen. The dining hall of this *mansio* was bathed in a dancing yellow light from dozens of oil lamps hanging along the walls. The usual dinner couches were currently empty as the students, Father Irenaeus, and five additional *mansio* patrons stood in a loose assembly near the main door.

A more formal wedding would have featured some musical accompaniment. Instead a solemn silence hung upon the room.

"We are gathered here for a joyous occasion," Irenaeus said. "Valerius and Aurelia are about to speak the ancient Roman vows that join a man and woman in matrimony."

Carmen stood beside Layla. The girls exchanged a glance, in which Carmen winked and smiled.

Jonathan and Will stood across from Irenaeus in the group. Will looked at his friend, who was fixated upon a spot on the ground. Jonathan wiped away tears.

"I'm supposed to be doing that. Are you alright?"

"Yes," Jonathan whispered. "I guess I've just learned that I always cry at weddings."

"And now the moment has come," Irenaeus said. "By our law, these vows, spoken in the presence of five or more witnesses, create a legal and binding marriage." Irenaeus reached out, took the right hands of Will and Layla, and brought them together. "In the presence now of these witnesses, join yourselves in marriage."

Layla looked into Will's eyes and smiled. "*Ubi tu Gaius*," she said. "*Ego Gaia*."

Will's eyes flooded with tears and he broke into a joyful laugh. "*Ubi tu Gaia, ego Gaius*."

"You have joined yourselves in marriage in the presence of these witnesses," Irenaeus said. "And I bless this marriage." He put his right hand on their joined hands. "*Vos benedico in nomine Patris et Filii et Spiritus Sancti*," he whispered, just loud enough for the couple to hear.

"You may kiss the bride," Jonathan said loudly.

Will and Layla met in a deep kiss. The gathered people cheered.

"Bring on the drinks," Carmen said to the slaves waiting in the wings.

Smiles, tears, and wine—all flowed forth. A dinner more sumptuous than usual was paid for by one of the random guests at the *mansio*. The man told Jonathan that someone had paid for his wedding once upon a time, and he had long felt he needed to return that favor to the universe.

The room was soon loud with laughter, conversation, and drink-inspired singing. Jonathan stepped outside into a sky lathered with milky-white stars.

"I overheard that," Irenaeus said, joining him in the quiet. "A favor to the universe. That's kind of what you're all doing here, isn't it?"

Jonathan chuckled. "I guess. You know, we'll probably make Massilia by tomorrow afternoon."

"I hope so," he said. "But the fact is, I like riding on ships even less than riding on a horse." He looked into Jonathan's eyes. "Carmen's in trouble, you know that, right?"

"We do," he said. "And Will and I don't quite know how to handle it."

"You haven't spoken about your family," Irenaeus said. "I feel a deep sadness off of you. What happened?"

"You mean you don't know everything already from your spiritual powers?"

Irenaeus laughed. "I'm a priest, not a prophet. Sometimes, in the power of the Holy Spirit, my people have told me that I spoke words from the future for them. But I don't feel that gift flowing right now."

"My parents died three years ago."

Irenaeus looked at him curiously. "In this time, that's not an uncommon story. And that's also not your problem. People learn how to move on after loss. What's your real struggle?"

"So you are a prophet."

"No," Irenaeus said. "But I sense you have a deep pain you need to somehow sort out."

"What should I do about it?" Jonathan asked.

"Right now? Go back inside and join this wedding party. Tonight is a night of solace. You all have some horrible things in your path. And yes, now I am feeling the charism of prophesy. Rest, Jonathan. You will need it. And you'll figure out along the way what to do about your problem."

He nodded. "Let's go back inside."

The wedding party lasted into the night. There came a point amidst the dining and imbibing when Irenaeus took the young couple aside.

"We have not had time to speak about what your marriage means," he said.

"No, sir," Layla replied.

"It's a mission, as important as the one you're on."

"Tell us, Father," Will said.

"Your job, each of you, is to help the other find salvation."

Layla smiled simply. "That's beautiful."

"This party will continue for a few more hours," Irenaeus said. "You two should leave it now so you can spend some time alone. This is what God wills for you."

Layla looked into Will's eyes. Both found smiles and glistening tears.

Long hours later, the wedding guests, now absent the bride and groom, finally decided their current pitcher of wine must be the last. Yet two more somehow followed it.

Dawn was breaking as the last of the revelers collapsed exhausted onto their bedrolls.

A few hours of sleep saw the students all assembled back in the dining hall for a late breakfast.

"I guess things haven't quite gone as planned," Will said.

Carmen was sipping at a glass of wine left on the table the previous night. "I wouldn't bet against us."

Layla laughed. "I think it's amazing we've gone this far."

Jonathan grinned. "A miracle."

"Take me quickly to Massilia, so you can continue your mission," Irenaeus said. "I know the world depends on it."

****

Later that afternoon, the students stood along a pier beside a boat pointing proudly into the Mediterranean Sea at Massilia.

Jonathan looked out over the choppy waves sending back piercing white flashes from the sun.

"*Thalassa, thalassa*," he whispered to himself.

Irenaeus handed his single large bag to a sailor organizing the passengers' supplies. He turned and walked back to say goodbye to the students. They were spaced far enough apart that he could speak with each separately.

"Thank you, Father," Will said softly. "I think we needed you more than you needed us."

"Lean heavily on God for support with your burden," Irenaeus said, looking off into the distance, as if seeing shards of the future. "When things seem hopeless, pray. It will yet be even darker before your dawn."

He stepped toward Carmen. "I will pray for you more than all the rest," he said. "You have been wounded more than your friends understand."

Carmen looked at him with sparkling eyes. "I'm fine, Father. Really."

Irenaeus raised one eyebrow. "No, you're not. You will lose a battle someday, Carmen. But you won't lose the war."

He stepped to Layla.

"Layla, be not afraid."

"Of what?" she asked.

"You are about to start yet another important mission." Irenaeus smiled. "You'll understand soon."

He came last to Jonathan, who was transfixed in the distant waves.

"Sorry, sir," he said, turning to the priest. "Have a good trip."

"Before it's all over," Irenaeus started, "the whole mission will rest on your shoulders."

Jonathan looked at him and smiled sadly. "I think I've always known I wasn't coming home," he said.

"You won't go back to the home you had," Irenaeus whispered. "But you can build a new one."

The priest stepped back and spoke to the whole assembly. "God bless your mission. I have come to believe that the end of the world in your time is not God's will. And if his will must be done, then your mission must succeed."

"Why do inspirational speeches always get me?" Carmen said, wiping her eyes.

"We'll never see you again," Layla said, wiping back tears. "Have a good life, Irenaeus."

"When you get back to your own time, feel free to talk to me," he said. "I know I'll have fallen asleep in my Lord many years before. But I will still be praying for you."

"God be with you," Will said.

Irenaeus nodded and stepped onto the ship.

The students walked down the pier toward land and got back on their horses. Minutes later they were racing down the coastal road toward Genua.

Chapter Ten

The students rode through that next night and following day. They stopped for a mere nap at a *mutatio* just past Nicaea, modern-day Nice, and again skipped a night's sleep before finally passing Genua. Between Genua and Pisae they spent a terrible night in one of the cheaper *mutationes* they had seen. They left the following morning early, without even waiting for breakfast.

"That wasn't exactly a resort last night, was it?" Jonathan said.

"Somehow that so-called 'bed' was actually worse than some of the times we've slept on the ground," Carmen said.

"Tonight we have to treat ourselves to a *mansio*," Layla said. "Even if it means not pushing things."

Will nodded. "We're still not caught up on time," he said. "But I agree. We can't keep up this pace or we're going to get sick. We stay at the best place we find after four in the afternoon."

Several hours later, the road was lowering into a valley. In the distance, a large white obelisk flashed the sun toward them.

"What is that?" Jonathan asked.

"Oh my God," Layla said. "You know what that is?"

"No," Jonathan said, a bit impatiently. "Hence my question."

"That's a provincial border marker. We're about to enter Italy itself."

"I thought Italy started way back up in the Alps."

"In ancient times the formal border was this far south. Remember, Julius Caesar crossed the Rubicon, which at the time was the border. And that's east of us at about this point."

They rode through the day, passing food around from on horseback. The sun was approaching the horizon when they saw a large villa just off the road, with the tell-tale path and gate of a *mansio* of the *Cursus Publicus*.

"We made good distance today," Will said. "But this is where we stop."

"*Gratias Deo*," Layla exclaimed.

According to routine, they stabled their horses, staked out rooms in the upper level, and then assembled downstairs for their main meal.

"Did you test your beds?" Carmen asked, lifting a glass off the main table. She filled it from a pitcher of wine and settled onto one of the couches.

"Best we've seen yet," Jonathan said, already reclined on a couch next to her. He was popping grapes into his mouth.

"Yeah, we picked a winner," Layla agreed.

Slaves brought out platters of cheeses and meats as the students sampled from a wider variety of food than they had seen previously.

"Is this place like a five star *mansio* or something?" Will asked.

"It might be because we're in Italy now," Jonathan said. "Just a guess."

The students had eaten their fill and were resting. A heavy-set man, who looked to be in his fifties, took a spot by himself at an unoccupied couch.

Carmen refilled her glass and took a deep sip before filling it again.

"Oh, that's what I like to see," the man said. "A woman who knows how to drink."

Carmen laughed. "It's been a long day for us, sir. Where do you come from, if I might ask?"

"These days I'm a merchant and don't come from anywhere," he replied. "I'm back and forth between Gaul and Italy so many times I lose count. My name is Cornelius."

"We are merchants travelling from Britannia. I am called Carmen. Pleased to meet you."

"Carmen, a song. But what of the other lovely young woman in your group?"

"Her name's Aurelia," she answered.

Layla threw a dirty look at Carmen. "Don't talk to him," she whispered in English. "He gives me the creeps."

"Aurelia, the golden one," the man said. "I'd like to polish her metal all over my body."

Will's heart froze. This was officially a bad situation. He felt he had to respond somehow to the inappropriate comment.

"Excuse me, sir!" he shouted. "But you are speaking about my wife!"

The man sat up from his couch and refilled his own wine glass. "Alright," he said. "So what's she going to cost me, this golden piece of yours?"

"Stop it," Carmen slurred. "You can't talk to my friend like that."

"People, to your rooms immediately," Will said. "Go!"

The group got up and walked out of the dining area.

"You don't know what you're missing, Golden Girl!" the man shouted after them.

They ascended the stairs and headed into their chambers.

"I'm on first guard," Will said. "Then Layla, then..."

"I'm supposed to be on first guard!" Carmen protested.

"Well you're not tonight, okay?" Will said angrily. "You won't be ready. You come after Jonathan."

"Whatever," she said and headed into her room.

The three stood in the hallway.

"This has to end," Jonathan said. "She's going to get us in trouble."

Will rubbed his forehead. "Layla, you have to talk to her."

"I'll try," she said. "I just don't know why she's doing this." Layla entered Carmen's room.

"Get some sleep, Jonathan," Will said. "We may not even use her tonight."

"Roger that."

Layla closed the door behind her. She saw Carmen seated on her bed, pouring from a wineskin into a glass.

"When did you bring wine up here?" Layla asked.

"Before dinner," she replied. "I wanted to make sure I'd have some later before I went to sleep."

She sighed and sat down on the bed beside her friend. "Listen, Carm, you really have to stop drinking like this."

She looked at her cup and then drained it. "Oh really, Layla? I really do? I'm sure your husband told you to talk to me. You know, you all don't seem to care that I've killed every enemy you've sent me to face. So where do you get off now telling me I'm drinking too much?"

"I was there too," Layla whispered. "I saw every one of them die."

"But you're not the one who killed them!" Carmen screamed. "So don't you dare say it's the same thing."

"I just want to help you."

"Well maybe I don't need help. Maybe I'm coping with all this the best I can."

"Carmen, you should not have spoken to that man downstairs. He scared me."

She huffed. "I know. But seriously, you know that for as long as I'm around nothing can ever go wrong. I can't lose a fight. You know that, don't you?"

"Just please promise me you'll be more careful, okay?"

"Yes. Don't worry. That won't happen again."

Layla nodded.

"Join me for a nightcap?" Carmen asked.

"No," Layla said, getting up from the bed. "I need to sleep."

"Good night, Layla. Enjoy your husband."

Layla sighed and left the room.

****

Will looked up from his breakfast to see Carmen coming down the stairs from the upper level.

She walked carefully to the table and plopped down on the couch beside him.

"What I wouldn't give for a cup of coffee," she whispered.

"The plant exists in this time period," he said, spooning some fried eggs into his mouth. "Unfortunately no one yet knows what it's good for."

She sat back and motioned for the attendant slave. "*Vinum!*" she shouted.

"You have got to me kidding me," Will said.

A slave arrived and filled a crude cup he had carried along. "Here you are, madam."

"Thank you," Carmen said, lifting and draining half the cup in one large swallow. She closed her eyes and felt the alcohol already beginning to infuse her brain. "Even better than coffee."

"You've got to get yourself together, Carmen. I know that we weren't ready to be drinking every day like this time period requires, but you're losing control."

"And why do you suppose, Will?" she asked. "My count stands at four. How many people have you killed?"

He curled his lips. "One," he said. "Yes, it turns out that your talents have been critical to our survival. But that doesn't mean..."

"Actually, it does, Will. It does mean that I get to deal with this exactly as I see fit, okay?"

His eyes filled with tears. "There are people concerned about you, Carmen. That's all."

She took a deep sip from her cup. "Well, you shouldn't be. I've got things under control."

The sound of creaking wood told them others were descending on the stairs.

"Good morning, everyone," Layla said. She reclined beside Carmen.

Jonathan followed, sitting on the couch next to Will. "I did not have a good night," he said. "Something we ate did not agree with me."

"It didn't bother me," Carmen said.

"That's because your blood has been a disinfectant these days," Jonathan muttered.

"Let's just get this all out in the open," Carmen shouted. "Yes, I am drinking a lot. But my job around here has been to kill whenever the group needs it done. And at the end of the day, I think it's not the end of the world if I get a little numb."

"What about the beginning of the day?" Will asked.

Layla's face curled into anguish. "Carmen, I hate this!"

Carmen glared at her. "I hate all of it! And I'm starting to hate all of you!"

Jonathan and Will locked eyes. Without words they communicated a mutual knowledge that the mission was in jeopardy.

The stairs creaked the imminent arrival of another guest from upstairs. Will rolled his eyes as he saw the previous night's rude Roman appear.

"Food!" Cornelius shouted. "Wine! Now!"

The grizzled Roman sat down at the only other couch in the main dining room. A slave hurriedly put a glass in his hand.

"Sweet nectar of the gods," he said, downing the glass. He looked around the space and focused in on Layla.

"You settled on a price for a roll with this one, yet?" he asked, directing his question at Will but not removing his eyes from Layla's body.

"Sir, we are simple merchants," Will said. "We just want to go about our business."

"I'm talking business!" Cornelius said. "*Tres denarii*. And that's my final offer before I decide to just take her for nothing."

"That does it," Carmen said, getting up from the couch. "You don't say another word to any of us again, you got it?"

Cornelius looked at his empty glass. "A refill!" he shouted, getting up from his own couch.

As he stepped toward Carmen, she had to crane her neck to keep her eyes locked on his. A slave poured wine from a skin into his glass.

Carmen, still holding her glass, raised it to her lips and found it empty. "A refill!" she said.

The same slave stepped back and refilled her cup.

Carmen and Cornelius gulped from their glasses and sized each other up.

"You really don't know what you're doing," he said.

"I could say the same."

"One of us is wrong," he returned.

Each casually finished their drinks and took a step back.

"Let's do this thing," she said.

"I'll let you throw the first punch," he said.

Carmen smiled. "My pleasure."

She sent a swift blow forward and gasped to find it blocked less than half way to its target. Cornelius pounded a fist into her chest, sending her flying backward and crashing onto a table.

"Carmen!" Layla screamed.

"Stay out of this!" she groaned, struggling to turn over and get onto all fours.

Cornelius had followed her and kicked swiftly into Carmen's mouth.

Will bolted forward and threw a punch at the Roman. Cornelius stooped casually down just in time to avoid the blow. His left fist snapped into his opponent's throat.

Will crumbled to the ground, struggling to pull in a breath.

"Damn it!" Jonathan shouted, jumping up.

"You want a piece of this, little man?" Cornelius asked. "I'm pretty sure that the white-haired witch was your group's best fighter. But give me your best shot!"

Layla flew from the couch and landed on top of the Roman. She began wildly kicking and clawing at his face before he threw her back onto the table.

Just as Cornelius heaved Layla backward, Jonathan landed a kick on the man's chest, flipping him over a couch.

Carmen struggled to her feet, holding a mouth gushing blood over her fingers.

Will had managed to seat himself on a couch, still holding the front of his throat and gasping for breath.

Cornelius stood up. He began to laugh loudly. "You all had no idea I could do that. Only, turns out I was a member of the Praetorian Guard once upon a time."

Will stood up. "We're leaving immediately, people."

"Go on! Get out of here!" Cornelius shouted. "And don't you ever let me see you again!"

Will nodded at him without a word and led his team out of the *mansio*.

****

"Don't move, Carm," Jonathan whispered, pressing a needle through the edge of her wound.

Her eyes flooded with tears and they winced, but she made no noise.

Will and Layla stood several yards away by the horses. The team had quickly ridden a mile down the road before stopping to attend to Carmen.

"What's the plan?" Layla asked.

"Well, I have to cut her off. And I don't even know what that's going to look like."

"Especially since all the water in this time is so horrible."

"Almost done," Jonathan said softly, threading again through the wound and gently tugging the thread. He tied a final knot and cut.

"How does it look?" Carmen asked, surprised at how coherent her words were despite the swollen lip.

"Not too bad. Irenaeus taught me well, remember?"

She smiled faintly. "Jonathan, stay here a minute. I need to talk to you."

"Okay," he whispered back.

"While we're away from Layla and Will."

He nodded.

"How did you go on after your mom and dad died?"

He closed his eyes and rubbed his forehead. "At first I was numb. And then there were times when I didn't know how I would continue."

Carmen took a deep breath and released it in staggered sobs. "That first night, I fell asleep for a while when I was supposed to be on guard. In a dream, I saw that bandit I killed."

He looked into her eyes.

"And we were fighting and I killed him all over again."

"It's a terrible thing you've been burdened with, Carm. I do believe that if I have to, I'll kill one of our enemies. But I sure hope I *don't* have to."

"You hit one with a sword that one time."

"He lived. And I'm relieved."

She smiled and winced from pain. "That next morning, when we were about to get on the boat, when I took a drink of wine there, I felt in my brain as if the burden of killing were somehow lighter. I didn't tell anyone, but the next night, even after my guard shift, I snuck a wineskin up to my room."

Jonathan nodded. "Alright."

She looked down. "And I slept that night without seeing him again."

"And so now you're afraid that any night without a drink will be a night you don't want to face."

"I can't live with the thought that I've taken a human life. And I've taken four now."

"I know."

She sighed and looked up into his eyes. "It was a disaster today, huh?"

"Yup."

"And I can't drink anymore."

"No, you can't, Carm."

She pressed tears out of now tightly shut eyes. "I'm afraid I won't be able to stop."

"Carmen, you need to hear something. We came very close today to losing everything. And that was your fault. But we also came close to losing everything on our first night back in this time. And you're the one who saved us. We can't finish this mission without you. You have to find a place of strength."

"Like what?"

"What did you want to become, I mean before you found out that you were a trained intelligence agent slated to save the world?"

She wiped her eyes. "I thought about becoming a doctor."

"Then here's the deal. You need to help get us home so you can do that. That may even mean you'll have to kill again before it's over. But it can't involve drinking.

And then, once you're a doctor, you're going to have to save a hundred lives for every one you've taken."

She sat back. "And that will really make everything alright?"

He leaned forward and put his forehead against hers. "Yes," he whispered. "And the fact that you'll save six billion lives in the process."

"It's a deal," she said. "What are you going to do when we get back?"

He sat on the ground beside her. "I don't know anymore. And I don't intend to think about my future until I'm back in it."

"Fair enough," she said. "I need to tell Will and Layla about my resolution myself. Let me do the talking."

"That's how it should be."

She nodded. "I have to get this over with—right now."

"I'm right behind you."

She jumped to her feet and walked toward the other two.

"Hi, Carmen," Will said nervously.

"Listen," she started. "I'm not going to take another drink on this mission. But I need this to now be a closed topic. No more discussion, okay?"

Will nodded silently.

"You can order me to attack an enemy just like before. I don't know why I lost to that bastard back there. But I believe that I could have beaten him if I were sober."

Layla walked slowly toward Carmen. "I'm so proud of you," she said, wrapping her arms around her friend.

Carmen stepped back. "I need some space right now. I'm very embarrassed by everything that's happened."

"You shouldn't be," Will said.

"But I am. And leave that be, okay?"

He nodded. "Get on your horses, people. We have a lot of miles to cover today."

Chapter Eleven

Their travel down the western coast of Italy went more slowly than expected. Owing to their age, the quality of the roads in Italy was actually a bit worse than in the provinces, such that their animals were not able to trot as fast or for as long. As they continued plodding forward, the mile markers they saw were counting down the distance from their ultimate goal, the city of Rome itself.

"Four!" Layla shouted, as another stone marker passed on their right.

"I'd cheer with you," Will said, "if that weren't also the number of days we're behind schedule."

"We kinda need a fast turnaround," Jonathan said. "So this time, if we're lucky, we'll spend no more time in Rome than we did on our first visit."

"Nothing to add to the conversation, Carm?" Will asked.

She did not look up from a seeming study of the mane on her horse.

"She's alright," Layla whispered. "Just give her more time."

They continued plodding along the road, noticing an increase in the number of stray houses along the road, as well as traffic coming the other way.

As they traveled, they began an incline up a gentle hill. Yellowish-green grass grew tall along both sides of the road, and a breeze whispered kindly as they came over the crest. A new horizon unfolded before them. The distant silhouettes of buildings peeked through a gray haze.

"Is it?" Carmen whispered.

"It is, sweetie," Layla returned.

"There's the three mile marker," Will said softly, still enthralled by the vision of the approaching city.

"Where exactly are these counting down to?" Carmen asked.

The whole group turned to her in smiles, happy that she was continuing to join the conversation.

"Mile marker zero is right in our destination," Will said. "The Roman Forum itself."

"We were there just three weeks ago," Carmen said. "To think, since then, we've flown to England, gone back in time two thousand years, and ridden on horseback across Gaul and Italy to get back here."

"We deserve medals," Jonathan said.

"You're right, we do," Layla agreed. "Let's be honest. What we're doing is the most important thing anyone has ever done before."

"What will happen when we get back?" Jonathan asked.

Let's talk about some of the logistics," Will said. "It's a month for us, but it's an instant for them."

"Then we still have a month and a half of school?" Jonathan asked. "I mean, what happens to the Fairfax Classical Academy?"

"They'll shut it down, of course," Carmen said. "It only existed to get us ready for this mission."

"My little brother Marwan spent his freshman year at the school!" Layla said. "They can't pull the plug on it until the end of June, at least. I mean, all those kids don't have a successfully completed school year? That's unfair."

"It really would be," Carmen said. "I don't want to believe that the governments we are working for would ruin people's lives like that."

"What, you mean like training us for four years to go on a secret mission without telling us?" Jonathan asked.

"This all sucks!" Carmen said angrily. "I never drank before this! You know that! Other kids had beer and stuff at parties, but I never touched it."

"We know," Layla said.

"I'm just so pissed off," Carmen said. "I don't mind the schooling we got. I mean they taught us well. We got into great colleges. But they've robbed us of something so important." She sighed and looked back down at the mane of her horse.

"What did they rob us of?" Will asked her.

She looked back at him fiercely, eyes and cheeks now shining with tears. "Our school!"

"What do you mean, sweetie?" Layla asked.

"We had a graduation scheduled for the middle of June."

"I was looking forward to it," Will said.

"I sure wasn't," Jonathan replied.

The group suddenly fell silent.

"Why not?" Layla finally asked.

"That's just one of those big things that I see all of you with your parents there and I know I— I don't get to have that."

"What about your uncle?" Carmen asked.

"That's the thing. He's always been so careful to never try and replace my dad."

"He stays too distant?" Carmen asked.

Jonathan nodded. "Frank's just such a decent guy. And I've seen situations where women were interested in him and he doesn't go for it, because I know that he sees raising me as his duty to my dad."

"Your uncle and your dad were close, weren't they?" Will asked him.

"They talked every day on the phone. But here's my point. I miss my mom and dad so much. But they're gone. And I just hate how me and my uncle live under the same roof...pretending...like..."

"Pretending like you aren't a family," Carmen offered. "When that's what you've become."

The group continued riding in silence for a while.

"Your turn, Will," Jonathan finally said. "What makes you angry or scared?"

"Fair enough," he said. "I accept that every group needs a leader."

"And you're a natural," Carmen said. "I mean, I'm your muscle, I know that. But I don't want to be in charge of this thing."

"That's just it," Will replied. "Because I don't either. I never have."

"Then why'd you run for class president?" Jonathan asked.

"Of the four of us at the Fairfax Classical Academy?" he asked hotly. "You think that because I'm the class president that I enjoy being in charge of a mission to save the world?"

"You're doing great," Carmen said. "Even during the rescue mission, you took charge and did everything right."

"Yeah, and we rescued our teachers from a fake kidnapping."

"And if we had not?" Layla asked.

Will laughed. "That's an interesting question. They spent four years getting us ready for a mission to save the planet and then they throw this unfair fake crisis at us to see how we perform. Fine. We passed their test. But if we hadn't? I mean, would they have decided to not send us back? I doubt it."

"Will, look forward," Jonathan said. "That's Rome. We've been following your orders for about two weeks. And we've been through some nasty things!"

"Tell me about it," Carmen said.

"But we're about to enter Rome," Layla said. "You got us here. Whether you like it or not, you are the only leader that this group could have had to get this far."

"I don't think that's true."

"Me?" Jonathan said. "I'm not a leader like you. You'll be lying if you say otherwise."

"And me?" Carmen said. "I can fight. But I can also apparently become a drunk and nearly destroy this mission. Imagine me in charge of it."

"Will," Layla whispered. "It doesn't even make sense to talk about me as leader. I'm a linguist. That's my only gift."

Will sighed heavily. "I understand. I was the best leader for this team. I admit it and I know it. But here's something you can't take away from me. Until each and every one of you is safely home in our own time, I am in utter terror for being in charge of this thing. And if, God forbid, I come home and don't bring you all back safely, I will spend the rest of my life in pain and misery."

They nodded, knowing they could say nothing to refute his feelings. They were his and he was entitled to them.

"So I'm a recovering alcoholic dealing with the stress of being a mass murderer," Carmen said. "Will's life is on the line if he doesn't bring us all home from the most dangerous mission in world history. Jonathan's an orphan whose only family won't properly connect with him. That leaves you, Layla. What's your angle?"

She looked at Carmen with a scared glance. She finally nodded and began. "Here's my burden. I've spent four years suspecting that our school held a secret. And it's because my mother told me our Freshman Year that I had a responsibility to become the greatest linguist there ever was."

"You already spoke Spanish and Arabic," Will said. "You were always destined to be the best of us."

"No, my dear," she said. "That gave me an advantage in vocabulary for the first two years. That's it. But my mother made me sit for hours every night and study Latin because, she kept saying, 'You have to be the best'."

"They weren't cleared for Ultra Secret," Jonathan said. "How did she know that Latin would be so critical to this mission?"

"I guess by the nature of our school," Layla answered. "We know now that she's an NSA agent. She figured out enough that she decided to make me the best at our core topic."

"You love your mom," Carmen said. "You guys have a great thing. What is this really about?"

"She believed my Spanish was a bigger advantage than it really was," Layla explained. "And since she knew, I realize now, that this was all about saving the world, she drove me harder than I think she realized."

"How so?" Will asked.

"Carmen would come some Monday morning and talk about getting her nails done with her mom. And I would remember that my mom spend all day that Saturday drilling me on Latin vocabulary."

Carmen smiled gently. "What did you want instead?"

Layla wiped tears from her eyes. "I just wanted a normal life. You don't understand just how far this went. My mother made me recite the first hundred lines of Vergil's *Aeneid* to her from memory just a week before we went to Rome."

"Your mother knew you were going on a dangerous mission and that Latin somehow mattered," Carmen said. "She was doing it to try and protect you. And we would not have gotten this far without you."

"But I'm totally and utterly exhausted," Layla replied. "I want it to be over. When we get back, I don't want to speak or hear or read another word of Latin again in my entire life. And that's my real problem. Because of my training and now these weeks here, I'm very probably the best Latin scholar alive back in our time. But I don't want to do anything with language ever again. And that leaves me with a bit of a crisis. I'm afraid that I don't have any other talents and now I have no idea what I'm supposed to do with the rest of my life."

"Then that confirms it," Jonathan said. "We're all a mess and yet the world is depending on us."

"Again, I wouldn't bet against us," Carmen said. "So let's imagine we somehow get through this nightmare and we're home. What happens then?"

"I say we make some demands!" Jonathan said loudly.

"If we were going to do that, we should have made them before we went on this journey," Layla noted.

"No," Will said. "The President and the Prime Minister are decent men and they are going to do well by us. If we get back..."

"When we get back," Jonathan corrected him.

"When. Yes. When we get back, what do we insist on getting in return for all we did?"

"In return for saving the world," Carmen noted.

"Look," Layla started. "It's going to be Sunday, the day before school should have started again."

"We finish the year!" Carmen insisted. "At least then the younger kids will have a complete school year on transcripts to take elsewhere."

"A graduation ceremony!" Will shouted.

"Yes!" Jonathan agreed. "With *Pomp and Circumstance* and everything."

"Hell, I want the President and Prime Minister to give us our diplomas!" Carmen said.

"I don't," Will said. "I have always imagined walking across a stage and getting my diploma from the hands of Dr. Valquist."

"You're right," she said. "That's the way it has to be."

"But the leaders should still be there!" Jonathan said.

"Settled," Will said. "We will insist on the school year to finish and a full graduation ceremony. What else?"

"A prom!" Layla shouted.

"Yes!" Carmen shrieked. "We've asked for dances before and there have always been excuses why it wouldn't happen."

"The school's too small," Jonathan said.

"It would detract from the learning environment," Will added.

"It's not the school's job to provide a social engagement," Carmen included.

"This is a great idea," Will said. "Jonathan, you will promise to actually call that number of Celeste's that you stole off the school's data base?"

"Let's see," he started. "I get back from a month on a dangerous ultra-secret mission to save the world. Yeah, I think I can get over my fear of girls at this point."

"I like what we've decided here, people," Will said. "As far as I'm concerned, if they are not willing to do these reasonable things for us, then they can't count on our silence about everything that we did."

"Yeah, but they can just make people like us disappear," Jonathan said.

"Do you honestly think that they won't give us what we want?" Layla asked.

"No," Jonathon said. "Let's not even be paranoid about this. We're getting a prom, a full school year, and a graduation simply because we're asking for it."

"Two," Carmen said, noting the mile marker along the road.

Ahead in the distance they saw a stone wall, marking the official border of the city itself.

"So we get back from saving the world," Jonathan said. "What do you all want to do with your lives now? Any changes?"

"I forget," Will said. "Did they say anything about us being paid enough money so we'd never have to work a day in our lives?"

"Again, we forgot to make demands before we left," Layla said.

"Damn. We were so busy worrying about getting ready for the mission that we forgot to plan for the unlikely possibility we might actually come home from it."

Carmen laughed. "I'm betting that getting a full school year, a graduation ceremony, and a prom will be easy. Getting a million dollars will not be the same thing."

"You're right," Layla said. "So, personally, I'm still planning on going to college."

"To study linguistics," Carmen started, "like you said you wanted to a month ago, or to not study linguistics ever again, like you said a few minutes ago?"

Layla chuckled. "I have no idea."

"What about you, Will?" Jonathan asked.

"As you know, I'm accepted at Oxford. But now I've got a wife in the United States, so I guess we'll have to talk about who goes where."

"I'd be happy to go to Oxford with you," Layla said. "But it's a bit selective, right?"

"I'll bet the Prime Minister can make this happen," Jonathan said. "Another item for our demands."

"I've got my plan," Carmen said. "I've told Jonathan already. I'll tell you two now as well. I'm going to become a doctor and make up for all the killing I've had to do on this trip."

"That's noble," Layla said.

"But when I feel like I've paid my debt," she continued, "I may make radical changes again in my life. This whole experience has taught me to just live life and cherish it. Both my own and others."

"You seem to have it figured out," Jonathan said. "Hey listen, I'm only going to chicken out when it comes to calling Celeste. And we all know that. Carmen, do you have a date for the prom yet?"

She laughed. "Not yet, Jonathan," she said. "But if you're asking, I accept."

"Good," he said. "Thank you. That's one less thing for me to be stressing out about right now."

"Layla," Will said seriously. "I will not be so presumptuous as to assume that our marriage automatically settles this matter. You may want to attend that event with a friend. But if you are not already committed, it would be my honor to accompany you to the prom."

Layla smiled. "I accept, Will. Just two weeks ago, going to a prom with you would have been a dream come true for me." She smiled. "It still is."

"I bet Will's going to get a little after the dance," Jonathan said.

"You're not," Carmen chuckled.

As they continued to ride, the city walls stretched toward the sky before them. The wide open gate was a welcoming embrace from the ancient city. It was a sign that this beacon of culture lived free of any worry about attack. The students knew, however, that the Rome they were about to enter, so proudly standing strong on this day, would one day fall.

"The Porta Aemelia," Will declared, as the horses clopped on cobblestones to enter the city itself.

"Let's review the itinerary," Carmen said. "We continue forward until we reach the Tiber river and cross it on the Pons Aemilius."

"Check," Jonathan stated.

"We then head southeast past the Circus Maximus and then veer up to the northeast to a spot which should have inns for us to stay at," Layla added.

"And that will put us in comfortable walking distance tomorrow to go up to the Forum and attempt entrance and use of the Bibliotheca Ulpia," Will concluded.

Jonathan cleared his throat. "Um, we don't talk about what happens if entry to the Bibliotheca proves impossible, right?"

"Not today," Will replied. "I mean, we haven't come two thousand years and a thousand miles to take no for an answer. But, again, one crazy stunt at a time."

"We're making this up as we go," Layla said. "We know."

The streets were busy with pedestrians and other riders. As they continued, they needed to form a single file line, owing to the continuous presence of carts and trash piles along the side of the streets.

"Oh, wow," Jonathan exclaimed. "I was not ready for the smell of this place."

"It's nasty," Carmen said. "Basically their sewer system is the next heavy rain."

They came into a clearing. Before them stretched a stone bridge over the gurgling Tiber River. Lining the banks of that river stood trees, which were otherwise absent from the streets of the city. A cool humidity raced from the moving waters and surged through them.

"That's refreshing," Jonathan said. "Let's enjoy this while it lasts."

They crossed the stone bridge and reached the east bank of the river. As the students continued on their route, they saw the mile-long block of bleachers which surrounded the *Circus Maximus*, Rome's premiere horse racing track and largest sports facility ever built in human history.

"We're not going to get a chance to see anything in there, are we?" Jonathan asked.

"No such luck," Will responded. "And I still feel awful about my mistake with the horses. We could have had enough money to turn down Irenaeus' mission and then we could have spent a few days here in Rome."

"You really wish we hadn't met Irenaeus?" Carmen asked.

He looked up. "No, I suppose not."

"Remember," Layla said. "Everything that we have done actually happened centuries before we were born. There's no point worrying about how things went."

They finally cleared the *Circus Maximus* complex and hit a jumble of small streets crowded with tall apartment buildings.

"We are officially looking for our accommodations," Will said.

As they turned northeast on a narrow street, they saw a line of wooden signs hanging from the fronts of the buildings. A cluster of grapes told customers about where they could buy wine. A goat was advertising a dairy story.

"There's one," Jonathan said, pointing. "A moon should be a symbol for night. And that means somewhere to sleep."

"I'll go see." Layla got off her horse and walked toward the building in question.

The others saw a man in a toga step out of the building at her approach. They watched as she spoke to him, pointing back at the group and gesticulating wildly. The man nodded and smiled.

Layla came back to the others. "I've got us a single room for 100 bronze pieces a day. Food is not included but he says there are plenty of *tabernae* near here to buy a hot meal."

"Sounds good," Will said. "Let's get settled in and then scout out our trip for tomorrow morning into the Forum for the real business we came for."

****

The students walked north from their inn. Their excitement was building as they knew from their previous trip to Rome where they were about to emerge.

"Oh dear," Carmen said, pointing forward. "Look, you can see it already."

The top edge of the Coliseum loomed above the row of crude apartment buildings in their view. They continued forward and cleared the residential area. Before them loomed the fully built and pristine Coliseum.

"Do you realize," Jonathan said, "that we are standing right on the spot where we believed Dr. Valquist and Miss Maple were kidnapped?"

Will looked in each direction and then back at the soaring monument. "You're right. But where's that beautiful Triumphal Arch we saw over there?"

"The Arch of Constantine?" Layla asked. "Um, Constantine won't be born for another hundred and fifty years."

"Oh yeah."

They walked along the Coliseum and found their way to the Via Sacra, which even in their modern times served as the main conduit into the Roman Forum itself.

"Wait a moment here," Carmen said, a view of the Forum sprawling and descending below them. "You remember when we were in Rome, that Dr. Valquist said anyone who could ever again see this sight would be truly blessed."

"He knew where we were going," Will noted.

"But he was right. I mean, look at it!"

The sun gleamed onto the Forum. Each white marble building seemed more brilliant than the next. They walked slowly down the length of the road. The chaotic bustling of merchants surrounded and pressed in on them all about. At the bottom of the hill, they turned and saw the Temple of Castor and Pollux.

"Three columns stand in our time," Jonathan said. "But here is the whole monument. This is unbelievable."

The students slowly turned, even twirled, as they took in the sights and sounds of the fully alive and vibrant Roman Forum.

"He did it," Carmen whispered. "He gave us Rome."

"It's time to head back to our inn," Will said, looking at the light of day fading. "We don't need to hurry, but let's start back."

As they slowly walked back up the Via Sacra, Layla pointed to the Northwest. "There it is," she said. "The Bibliotheca Ulpia. Somewhere in there may lie the information we need to save the world in our future."

The group stopped and looked at the two facing buildings.

"Give me an assessment, Carm," Will said.

She studied the structures, looking at the height of their windows from the outside, the size of the entrances, and the number of guards arrayed about the area.

"Irenaeus was right. No break-in. Impossible. Too many guards in the forum and around the buildings themselves."

"In other words," Jonathan said, "it really does all finally come down to you two and your married couple act. I'll admit I'm relieved that part of your cover story isn't false."

Will smiled, continuing to look at the library. "I don't have any idea what to say or do anymore."

"Irenaeus would offer a prayer," Carmen said.

"He's praying for us," Jonathan added. "And I'll admit that comforts me."

Will turned and pulled the whole team into a hug. "Alright, listen. Let's go back to the inn, people. I want to sleep as much as possible before tomorrow. We've been through a lot. But tomorrow is what the whole mission was for. And I already feel like I'm going to throw up."

Chapter Twelve

Will and Layla walked hand in hand into the coolness of the dawn. Roosters crowed from every direction, but no human sounds yet stirred.

"This is quite a privilege we have," Will said softly. "We walk the streets of ancient Rome like they're ours. But it's all such a miracle."

"I know what you mean," she replied. "Nothing will ever be the same for us, will it?"

He chuckled. "It can't be. But then again, look at Dr. Valquist. We know he was in Iraq. But on a daily basis, he taught us Latin as if that was the most exciting thing in his world. How did he put aside everything he was involved in and hide all that so well?"

"Because he wasn't really hiding," she offered. "He does love those things. So maybe, just maybe, years from now you can be in the middle of your life. You can be concerned with our son being out from school sick and some stress at work and you'll get home and sit down beside me and relax. And you'll realize that for the entire day before that moment, you didn't once think about the fact that when you were eighteen years old we went back in time to ancient Rome and saved the world."

He now laughed loudly. "God, human nature being what it is, you're probably right."

They reached the spot of the kidnapping and looked at the looming Coliseum. Swarms of swallows darted through the structure, coming in and out of view in a light fog that hung over the area.

"It's so beautiful," Layla whispered.

"*Sic. Tu quoque es pulchra.*"

She smiled. "*Multas gratias, mi Amor.*"

They walked across a narrow road, passed by the massive arena, and started down Via Sacra toward the Forum itself. The business center was just starting to wake up, with merchants opening their booths and shops. Layla and Will crossed the main Forum and entered the smaller Forum of Trajan, where the Bibliotheca Ulpia was located.

"There they are," Layla said, looking at the facades of the facing libraries. "Any final thoughts?"

"I know you aren't religious, Layla," he said. "But I want to make a prayer. Irenaeus told me I was supposed to do this."

"That's fine."

He closed his eyes and made the sign of the cross. "Lord God…" He thought of phrases compiled from dozens of prayers he had memorized. Finally, he threw them all aside and just spoke. "My dear Jesus, I'm just so tired. I want to scream. I want to cry. You know everything and so you know what we've been through. Just help us, please. I beg you."

He stopped for a moment and closed his eyes. Warm tears surged down his cheeks. "We're going in there now, Jesus. And the whole world depends on us. I don't know what more to say. Just please help us."

He again made the sign of the cross.

"I'm glad you did that," Layla said.

Will smiled and wrapped his arms around her. "My sweet Layla," he whispered into her ear. "Let's go save the world."

They heard a loud bell clang and watched as the main doors of the Latin library slowly swung open. A slave stepped out and began sweeping the entry way with a crude broom.

"Follow my lead," Layla said. "Obviously, I'm…"

"Making this up as you go," Will said. "And you just might be a leader after all."

She smiled at him. "*Gratias*. Okay, let's see what we can do in there."

They turned toward the library and started up the marble stairs.

"*Salve*," Layla said to the slave. "We are interested in doing research in the library. Do you know to whom we should speak?"

The man looked up for just a second and then pointed inside the library with the shaft of his broom.

Will pressed the massive wooden door farther open and moved aside to allow Layla to enter first. As the two stepped from the morning into the dark atrium of the building, they were momentarily blind until their eyes adjusted to the weak light flickering from oil lamps hanging from the walls at regular intervals.

"Where's the information booth?" Layla whispered.

As they began to see deeper into the halls creeping away from the atrium, they saw shadows of human figures moving down a passage to their left.

"Let's check down there," he said.

They walked confidently, but not too quickly, toward the people. As they approached, they saw two Roman men, one with a long purple stripe on his toga, speaking to one another.

"Excuse me for interrupting, gentlemen," Layla said. "We are scholars who have come to Rome for research. With whom do we speak for permission to explore the library?"

"*Unde venitis?*" the more stately of the two asked.

"*Sum de Arabia.*"

"You speak excellent Latin for a foreigner," the other man noted.

"*Gratias,*" she replied. "*Hic est maritus meus* Valerius. *Ille est de Hibernia.*"

"Pleased to make your acquaintance," Will said.

"*Quoque dicis Latine bene,*" the first man said. "You have a Roman name?"

"I use a Romanized version my own name, which is Will."

"And you, my lady? How are you called?"

"*Ego sum* Aurelia. *Sed nomen meum in lingua Arabica est* Layla."

"What specifically are you wanting to research here?" he asked.

"*Astronomia,*" Will said.

The purple togaed man nodded. "If you two can wait here for just a moment, I will go see Sentius Augurinus, who is in charge of that collection. Now, just to warn you, he will give you an interview on your knowledge of the subject before he would consider taking you up there. And very few people pass his test."

"*Gratias*," Layla said. "You have been very kind."

"Have a seat. I'll be right back."

****

Will and Layla rested on a marble bench waiting for their appointment. The combination of the hard surface and their nerves made them shift their weight and positions almost constantly.

"Jonathan and Carmen are relaxing back at the room," she said. "They don't even know that we've managed to make the entire mission dependent on the next few minutes."

"We have to impress this guy with our knowledge. *Deus nos adiuvet*," he stated. "God help us."

"No singulars, remember?"

"It was intentional. We need all the help we can get right now."

The sound of shuffling sandals announced the arrival of the astronomy dean. An ancient man, wisps of white hair on the sides of an otherwise bald head, walked slowly down the hall. He wore a simple off-white tunic.

Will and Layla stood and bowed politely.

"*Salutationes*," Will started. "Thank you so much for giving us some of your valuable time, sir."

"And greetings to you," the man said in a weak and hoarse voice. "We get plenty of requests to search the books," he said. "But you two were described as unique. A husband and wife from Hibernia and Arabia."

"*Sic*," Layla said. "I apologize that our knowledge of your language is not perfect."

"*Dicis multum bene*," the man returned. "What I'm more interested in is what you know of the stars and the planets. You'll understand, we want to let legitimate scholars do research here, but we can't just let everyone have access to these collections."

"I understand," Will said smiling. "We hope our knowledge is adequate for entrance and then we would be grateful for your assistance in locating specific information we seek."

The dean turned to Layla. "An Arab scholar came here a few years back and told me that your people worship the moon."

"That's true," Layla said. "What did this scholar study here?"

"Nothing. He didn't pass my test."

"I see," Layla said slowly.

"Other peoples believe the sun to be the dominant power," Sentius stated. "This scholar didn't have a good explanation for the difference. What do you say?"

"First off, sir, not everyone in Arabia worships the moon or even many gods and goddesses. We have Jews who live in Arabia and other people, such as myself, who are more philosophically inclined."

"But why the moon?"

Layla smiled. "Speaking as a scholar, sir, I believe that in a terribly hot environment which made travel during the day impossible, the presence of a full moon was such a blessing that it came to be seen as the more kindly light."

"Very interesting," he said. "And the planets? What are they to your people?"

"There are some who see them as gods and goddesses who interact in the celestial realm," she replied. "I believe they are natural objects. Someday, with careful study, we may even figure out what makes them move the way they do."

"What of your people?" the old man asked, turning slowly toward Will. "We know so little of the islands beyond Britannia."

"There are many powerful kingdoms there," he said. "And like others, we study the stars and their movements. We have peoples there that worship them, and others who do not."

"But what do you know of our scientists?" he asked.

"We know that it was the Greeks," Will began, "who proved the world is round and even told us how big it is."

"Describe the experiment," Sentius said. "And who did it."

"The scholar Eratosthenes, by viewing the length of the shadows in wells at the same time in Alexandria and farther south in Luxor, was able to calculate the circumference of the earth."

"Do you agree with him?" the man asked. "There are many who feel that his earth is simply too big."

"I do agree," he answered. "And it means there may even be lands yet to be discovered past the Pillars of Hercules."

"And what else do you know?" he asked.

"We know that a Greek scholar once proposed the radical view that the earth moves around the sun. I believe his name was Aristarchus."

"Ah, so you know about even him!" the man exclaimed in excitement and surprise. "But no one believed that man. After all, isn't the movement of the sun around the earth something we can plainly observe?"

Layla and Will looked at each other. They knew they were doing well in the interview. Will smiled with an idea.

"It could all be from a point of perspective," he said. "The sun would seem to move across your vision if you yourself were spinning around."

"But then we would all fly off the earth!" the man proclaimed.

"If you spin magnets," Layla said, "do they separate?"

"No," Sentius replied. "But we don't know what makes magnets attract to each other."

"Then perhaps we don't yet know what keeps objects attracted to the earth," Will said.

The old man looked at them nodding. "You are certainly scholars," he said. "And you have earned the right to research here. Now, is there something specific you wanted to learn about?"

Will and Layla looked at each other with profound relief.

"Yes, sir," Layla said. "As the two of us have shared our peoples' knowledge, we each learned of stories passed down about a new planet that was seen only once."

"This would have been about two hundred years ago," Will said. "We wanted to find any information about whether astronomers in other places had also seen it and where exactly in the sky they saw it."

The old man rubbed his chin in thought. "That's the kind of thing that might have been put into *The Annals of the Heavens*."

"This is a book?" Will asked.

"Yes. You would not have heard about it because the only copies of it are here in this library and in Alexandria. It was written years ago by someone who travelled to Mesopotamia as part of Emperor Trajan's campaign there. He translated astronomical observations into Latin and compiled them into a dreadfully boring book that no one has ever read."

"Who was this person?" Layla asked.

"Me. And even though I wrote that silly thing decades ago, I almost think there were some peculiar star signs somewhere in that time frame. Come with me, young people. I will take you to the Astronomy wing of our library."

They followed Sentius down a long hallway. The darkened marble walls seemed to ooze cold air at them as they walked. Continuing up a flight of stairs, the three arrived at a large room full of tables covered with heaps of scrolls. The walls all around were lined with shelves stretching to the ceiling, scrolls sticking out every which way.

"Where in the world did I put that book?" he asked.

Will and Layla both felt their hearts sink at the dean's words.

"May I inquire, sir, how the books are organized?" Will asked him nervously.

"Don't worry," he said. "I know where everything is." He looked up and down the walls of one shelf. "Most days, that is."

Layla looked closely at a nearby shelf. She saw labels on the sides of scrolls indicating names of authors and works she had never heard of.

"What a lost treasure," she whispered.

"It's not lost!" Sentius said loudly. "I'll find it in a second."

He stopped his search and looked down at the ground. "What's funny," he started, "is that I remember putting it somewhere and thinking at the time that I was putting it there because I would remember the spot."

"Is there another book that may provide us with information on this mystery planet?" Will asked.

He shook his head. "I don't believe so. I've read every book in this room closely. *The Annals of the Heavens* is the only book that even might contain the information you're after. I only wish I knew where I put it."

"*Deus nos adiuvet,*" Layla whispered.

"Do you know what we need?" Sentius asked.

"A filing system?" Will asked.

"*Vinum!*" He headed for the door. "I'm going to get us three cups and by the time I get back I will have remembered where I put that book."

Layla chuckled as she watched him leave the room. "That could be the first time in my life I have actually heard someone use the future perfect tense in Latin."

Will rolled his eyes. "The world depends on a lost book and you're thinking about grammar? Whether you like it or not, you might just be a linguist."

She smiled. "I know."

They continued their own informal search for several minutes until Sentius returned with a tray, setting it directly atop a pile of scrolls on a table.

"You're sure it's not one of those under the tray?" Layla asked.

"No," he replied. "Those are scrolls local scholars have submitted to be shelved. I haven't even looked at them yet."

He handed Will and Layla each a cup of wine and then loudly slurped from his own. "This is pure Falernian," he said. "Be careful."

Will and Layla sipped their wine and looked at him anxiously.

"Oh, forgive me," he said. "I did remember where the book is." He walked to the complete opposite wall from where he had been searching and pulled a scroll out from between several others. Scrolls tumbled to the floor from the hole he created. Kicking those toward the wall, he began to unroll the work in question.

"Let's take a look," Will said, leading Layla to the man.

He rolled open the scroll on a table and pointed to the first leaf and the title: *The Annals of the Heavens: the collected observations of the skies in the interest of further learning.*

"What a horrible title," Sentius said. "No wonder this book was such a failure. What year exactly did this planet appear?"

Will knew that 753 BC was year one *Ab Urbe Condita* and did the calculation. "In my country we use a different system for years. So this would have been...705 *Ab Urbe Condita*," he said. "The year Gaius

Julius Caesar and Publius Servilius Isauricus were consuls."

"Did you convert that number in your head?" Sentius asked.

"*Sic*," Will replied.

"If this Astronomy thing doesn't work out, there's an opening for a Mathematics dean here."

"As you know, we use arithmetic to chart the stars as well."

The man unrolled the scroll several leaves. "Here we go, 700-710."

They all scanned the page and found several entries for the year 705. Something caught Layla's eye.

"This is interesting," she said, pointing at the scroll. "It says here that on the third day before the Kalends of February, Jupiter was observed out of place in the constellation Orion."

"Look down here," Will said, pressing his finger on a spot lower down the page. "On the Ides of April, the Evening Star was seen in an unexpected spot on the horizon and unexpected for that day."

"Well, there's nothing here about a new planet," the man said. "Just unusual star signs."

"But I think there is," Will declared. "The people who made these observations believed this was Jupiter and the Evening Star based on their brightness. But they admit that these appear in the wrong parts of the sky. What if this is the mystery planet?"

"I see what you're saying," Sentius said. "But where did this planet go?"

"Far away," she said. "But someday it will return."

Will looked at Layla. "We have two solid data points on this thing."

Her eyes misted up. "It's more than enough."

He nodded. "We did it."

The two hugged out of elation at their discovery.

"This planet really means a lot to you two," Sentius said.

"*Sic*," Will said, breaking from the embrace. "Sir, you have been so kind to us. And your book is far more important to the world than you could ever understand. Words cannot express our gratitude."

Layla kissed the old man on the cheek. "*Gratias*," she said kindly.

"I am happy I could help," the man said. "And I'm glad to see young people excited about science. Sometimes I think that the youth these days just don't learn enough and don't respect their elders. You two give me hope for the future."

Will laughed. "People always think the younger generation is ruining the world. And they're always wrong."

The two looked again carefully at the text and burned the information into their minds.

"Come back any time you want," Sentius said, leading them to the exit of the room.

"*Multas gratias,*" Layla said. "We will hope to return soon."

****

Will and Layla walked swiftly down the broad street leading away from the Forum. They arrived at the inn after just five minutes.

Carmen saw their approach from the window. "It's them!" she shouted.

They charged up the stairs. Jonathan opened the door.

"Come on in," he said. "Have you saved the world?"

Will hugged his friend. "We didn't," he said. "But a lonely librarian forty years ago did."

They told the others the account of how they had to prove their knowledge of the field and all about the almost undiscovered book.

"We have a debt to that single scholar," Will said in conclusion. "He compiled information thought worthless at the time. But these records will help people two thousand years later to save the world from destruction."

"The name Sentius Augurinus deserves to be spoken in the same breath with Archimedes and Aristotle," Layla stated. "And he thinks his book was a waste of time because no one ever read it."

"Instead, this will all stay Ultra Secret even if we get back home safely," Carmen added.

Will nodded. "And so that's now our only mission. We have two orders of business. We leave tomorrow morning. We have a thousand miles to cover in twelve days. On our way, we bury this information at the drop point. Let's not let our guard down."

The group relaxed with a nice dinner at a nearby *taberna*. No one slept well that night, in the excitement that the next day would begin the journey home.

Chapter Thirteen

The group woke early the next morning and received horses at a *mansio* by the western gate of the city. Several miles outside Rome, they arrived at the ruins selected for their attempted burial.

Looking in every direction, they saw rocky ground and scattered brush.

"It looks the same right now as it will in two thousand years," Jonathan said.

"Start digging," Will ordered.

They took turns scooping dirt away at the previously determined spots. Will and Layla worked on a hole five meters north from the scattered columns. Carmen and Jonathan dug a second hole five meters beyond that. When each hole reached a meter in depth, they stood up and prepared the jars. Layla and Will looked over the papyrus notes they had written the previous night and confirmed the accuracy of the information. They put them in the jars, the insides of which they had already coated with wax. Jonathan lit an oil lamp and the team took turns holding pieces of wax over the flame, dripping it around the lid and sides, completely sealing the jars. When they were satisfied with the job, they carefully laid a jar in each of the holes and refilled them with soil. They went around, kicking stones and tufts of weeds onto the spots.

"Even if someone sees this later today, they won't know anything was buried here," Will said.

"And that means it's possible we've saved the world even now," Carmen declared.

The group looked at each other in a moment of proud silence.

"You're right," Jonathan said. "In fact, there's an excellent chance that one or both of these jars will be preserved until the year 2013."

"It would be sad, I mean for us, if we don't make it back to the extraction point. We'd never know for sure if we saved the world or not," Layla said.

"We saved the world," Carmen said. "Dr. Valquist said the CIA had already gone to see if anything was there. I'm betting they found both jars perfectly intact. The only thing left for us is the thing even they don't know."

"Whether we make it back," Jonathan said.

"Let's get home so they know everything that happened here," Will said.

****

As the sun was setting on the first day of their journey back, the students spotted the familiar yellow glow of the windows from a *mansio* beside the road.

"This is as far as we dare travel today," Will said.

"Good," Carmen said. "This horse has been limping a bit for several miles. She needs to stop."

They rode to the stables they knew would be on each side of the road toward the main building. Getting off their horses, they handed the reins to slaves waiting to receive them.

"Can this horse be set aside for a few days before being assigned?" Carmen asked. "She needs a break."

"That should be fine," the man said.

"We'll need four fresh animals to leave first thing in the morning," Will said, unfolding and displaying the diploma to the main attendant.

The man examined the document according to custom and nodded. "I'll set them aside and have them ready at sun up, sir."

They entered the main room and were greeted by an old man.

"How many rooms, sir?" he asked Will, apparently sensing his leadership role.

"Three," he replied, looking around the largely empty space. "When does dinner begin?"

"In an hour. We're a bit behind schedule today because we know that a group of officials are coming a little later. We hadn't expected your arrival at all."

"That's fine," Jonathan said. "Can I just get a little bread?"

He clapped his hands. "*Panis*!" he screamed.

A door flung open and a young boy scrambled out, carrying a bowl with several loafs.

"Here you are," the boy said.

Jonathan nodded and took a loaf. He broke off pieces from the side and stuffed them in his mouth. "This will get me to dinner."

"Let's get cleaned up, people," Will said.

They retired to the upstairs, where they found wash basins and even had an hour to rest in their beds before they heard the commotion of dinner and several more arriving guests.

"Will, Layla, I'm heading down," Jonathan said, rapping at their door.

Layla emerged instantly. "I'm starved," she said.

"I'll be down soon," Will called from inside their room.

Layla knocked on Carmen's door. "Hungry?"

"I'll be right there," she answered.

Jonathan and Layla descended the stairs and stood before the newly set up tables. Three of them were already surrounded by the groups of guests who had just arrived.

Layla reclined on a couch next to the only open table.

Jonathan reclined on a different couch. "Your hubby should be next to you," he said.

"Is this all weird for you and Carmen?"

"Not really," Jonathan replied. "We knew you two were in love for years. Now, it's funny but you really do come off as a comfortably old married couple."

She grinned. "That's how it feels. It makes me think that people in our time are making a mistake to postpone marriage into full adulthood. I mean, traditional societies must have known what they were doing to marry people off sooner rather than later."

A slave quickly dropped several platters of various foods on the table. Another set glasses and a pitcher of wine before them. Jonathan helped himself to both.

He drained his entire glass and refilled it. "You know, Layla, I know my limits and don't ever feel like I need to overdo it like Carmen was doing. But I admit I've become pretty accustomed to having a few glasses of wine with my dinner."

Layla laughed. "I know what you mean. Say, let's add 'Change the drinking age to eighteen in the entire United States' to our list of demands."

Jonathan nodded. "I suspect even the President can't really make that happen just by executive order."

As they ate, they began to overhear a conversation at a table next to theirs.

"I can't believe how angry Cornelius was when we saw him last week," a man said.

"He's a monster," another added. "Even so, I sure wouldn't want to be those four when he finds them."

"How does he know that their diploma is a fake?"

"You didn't hear? He went to Britannia and asked every official he could find what they knew about this group. I mean he doesn't actually know it's a fake, but he believes it is, which for him, as you know, is the same thing."

Jonathan and Layla locked eyes in the mutual recognition that they themselves were the topic of conversation.

"What's this group look like?" a guest at a different table called out.

"Young, but normal, except for one of them, a strange little white-haired girl with bright blue eyes."

"He swore an oath by Jupiter that if he ever saw them again he would kill them on the spot."

Just then, Jonathan and Layla saw Will's feet coming down the stairs to the main hall. They could hear that he was talking to Carmen, descending directly behind him.

Jonathan bounded from his couch and headed up the stairs. He wrapped his arms around Will and started walking him backwards.

"What are you doing?" Will asked, annoyed.

"Code Red," Jonathan whispered.

Will turned around. "Okay. Carmen, we're going back up."

Jonathan continued up until all three stood in the hall just away from view of the dining area. "Get in your room, Carmen," he whispered. "Quickly."

Will looked at her and nodded. They followed her in.

"Do you want to tell me what's going on?" she asked.

Jonathan took a couple of deep breaths. "People downstairs are talking about us."

"What?!" Will said loudly.

"Shhh," Jonathan said. "Listen. They're talking about how a man named Cornelius is angry at four young people."

"How do you know that has to be us?" she asked.

"One of them was described as a 'strange white-haired girl with bright blue eyes'."

Carmen nodded. "Probably too much to be a coincidence. What are we going to do?"

Will sighed. "For starters, you stay in your room tonight. We'll bring some food up for you."

"I understand."

"When we leave tomorrow, we'll try to cover your head somehow."

"We'll be fine in the morning," Jonathan said. "We'll get on the road before other people even wake up."

"Agreed," he said. "Hold tight here, Carm. We'll be back up in a few minutes."

After they quickly ate, Jonathan and Will went back upstairs with some food for Carmen. Layla was assigned to position herself at a couch, hoping to learn more about the situation. She listened in on the various conversations while she ate.

"So what's his plan?" a man said.

"He assumes, since they had come from Britannia, that they'll be coming back on the Via Aurelia. And so he checks every *mutatio* and *mansio* all along the route."

Layla's heart raced. With the exception of going the route of the Alps for just a portion of the return trip, there was no other way back to the extraction point than to be on the Via Aurelia. The team was officially in crisis.

"Think," she whispered to herself. "Will needs to bring them all home."

****

The following morning, Jonathon rapped gently on the team's doors. He heard them stirring and soon they began to emerge.

Carmen came out first, a veil drawn completely over her head as they had agreed.

"*Bona dies*," she whispered.

The other two were soon standing in the hall and ready to move. Will gave the nod. The group came down the stairs in silence. They found the dining hall empty.

"Would you like some breakfast?" a slave asked, seeing them walking across the space.

"Just bring us several loaves of bread," Will said. "We have to get going."

The young slave quickly entered the kitchen and emerged with a loaf for each of the travelers.

They nodded and each took their food, immediately tearing into it.

Will led them out of the *mansio*. As they approached the stables, they saw an attendant grooming four horses.

"These are ours?" Will asked, rubbing the neck of one of the animals.

"*Sic, Domine*," he said. "These are some of the best horses we've seen in some time here. They were left by a general and his entourage a few days ago. If you're heading north on horseback, you'll probably catch up to them."

Will smiled. "Perhaps. We'll be going now."

The four climbed atop their horses and kicked them into motion. When they were a distance down the road, Will slowed so all four riders were riding abreast and able to talk.

"Obviously we have a security crisis here," he said.

Carmen laughed. "That's an understatement. What are our options?"

"We can go through the Alps, right?" Jonathan asked.

Will shook his head. "This is all a gamble. We are behind schedule, so we need to make excellent time all the way home to have a chance at returning. The Alps were supposed to be used on our way to Rome and reassessed if they were too hilly for fast travel homeward."

"But it could be a spot where we sidetrack seeing Cornelius," Layla noted.

"It's probably a little more than a fifth of the whole journey back," Carmen elaborated. "It slows us down, but it's worth it to possibly miss him."

"We do still have to have a strategy for avoiding detection," Will said. "It is true that a man who can recognize us at sight intends us harm. We have to try and minimize the possibility of that happening. How do we do that?"

Jonathan groaned. "Much as I hate to say it, for starters that will mean that we can't stay at *mutationes* and *mansiones*. That's the most likely place where we'll run into him."

"Or at least someone who recognizes me as the 'strange white-haired girl'," Carmen said.

"You're never going to live that down, you know," Layla said, smiling.

"I hope we joke about it at our ten year high school reunion," Carmen returned. "Because that will mean we somehow got out of this mess."

"Alright," Will started. "It's agreed that we can't stay in the facilities anymore. We're going to be camping somewhere off the road every night for the next two weeks."

"What about the possibility of just running into him on the road?" Jonathan asked. "If he's coming south while we're coming north on the Via Aurelia, he's going to see us. That's guaranteed."

"If we were to get off the road a distance every time we saw an oncoming traveler, we are never going to get back in time," Carmen said.

"You're right," Will said. "Hiding from every oncoming traveler for the next thousand miles would add a full week to this trip that we just don't have."

"We're not going to surrender to him if we see him," Carmen said. "Every time we pass someone, we will have to be ready in the blink of an eye to defend ourselves, if necessary."

"Another way we could reduce the risk of seeing him would be to do more traveling at night," Jonathan said.

"That just trades one danger for another," Layla noted. "We can hope we won't run into Cornelius, but we will face bandits when we travel that way."

"And someday we could get unlucky and lose badly," Carmen said. "Even so, Jonathan, you have a good idea. We can at least reduce the amount of sleep we get and ride a little into the night and get up at dawn. Cornelius will probably be getting drunk at a *mansio* by late afternoon and then sleeping it off till midday."

"That's a good plan on paper," Layla said. "But I don't know how many days in a row we can really do that."

"Don't forget that we will still have to go to *mansiones* to trade in our horses," Jonathan said. "And that needs to be during business hours."

Will nodded. "Now, if any of us actually *sees* Cornelius as we travel, we need a signal for everyone to move to full speed."

"Right hand in a fist, held high," Carmen said. "And right hand held high and open will signal that we are coming under attack."

"Good," Will said. "We've put together a decent *modus operandi* for the trip home. There's no way to make this entirely safe anymore. So everyone be on guard."

They spread out and formed a line again as they continued their travel. After a few minutes, they spotted a cluster of wagons and horses in the distance coming toward them.

"This will be a test of our vigilance," Will said. "Be nonchalant as we pass, visualize pulling your swords in response to the sudden realization that we are face to face with Cornelius."

"Gotcha," Carmen said.

They continued and soon they were moving toward the right-hand side of the road to pass by the other travelers. They all felt their hearts racing with fear and stress as they looked at every face on the wagons and horses. When they had passed the procession, they breathed a sigh of relief.

"I don't think I can survive two weeks of thinking we're about to be attacked twenty times a day!" Layla said.

"Unfortunately," Will said, "we're likely to get a bit more lax about all this every time we pass a group that doesn't include Cornelius. And we can't afford to. So I am going to call us all to task and remind us of the dangers regularly."

"Again, understood," Jonathan said.

They rode the entire day. At a few spots, they stopped outside a *mansio* for just a moment so one of the team members not easily identifiable as a 'strange white-haired girl' could run in to fetch some food and drink skins. They quickly made horse exchanges at a time when they assumed guests would already be at dinner. About two hours after sunset, they were moving through a forested area.

"It's time for us to camp," Will said. "Follow me."

He led his horse off the road into total darkness. After they had gone far enough that they could no longer see the road through the thickness of the trees, they came to a stop at a clearing.

"It's no fun to find firewood in the dark," Jonathan said. "In retrospect, we should have gathered our kindling in the light and brought it with us."

"We live and learn," Will said, getting off his horse. "Alright, people. Scavenge for wood."

A half an hour later, the four sat around a small fire. They were wrapped up in the few blankets they had. Their stomachs were in knots from eating mostly bread that day. The hard ground under them already spread pain through their joints and limbs.

"I don't think there's really any reason for us to do the guard duty thing anymore," Will said. "The horses will make some noise if anyone approaches. And we need as much sleep as we can get."

"Is this really safe?" Carmen asked.

"I think it's a necessary concession to our critical situation," he said.

"Alright."

They stared at the glowing embers in silence for the next hour and then huddled together for warmth and slept through a fitful night.

Chapter Fourteen

The following morning, the students quickly broke camp and resumed their travel north. The experience of bracing for combat every time another traveler appeared in the horizon went from an initial terror to a general sense of vigilance. They all found that not having a guard duty stint somewhere in their night gave them a feeling of deeper restfulness, even though they were getting up earlier and traveling much deeper into the night. By the time they reached the Italian Alps, they had already reduced the number of days they were behind schedule. As they arrived in Genua, they set out on a northern road into the Alps which would bring them back to the Via Aurelia just south of Lugdunum.

With mountains soaring on each side of them, the students saw white-capped peaks in the more distant horizon.

"This is the most beautiful place we've been," Carmen said, twisting around and taking in the scene.

"And the air!" Jonathan added. "Compared to Rome's stench this is so welcome."

Will nodded as they continued to trot forward. "Notice that the roads wind around a lot more than our map would have suggested. I'm still worried that this little alpine vacation will take more time than we really have."

"Maybe we'll have to ride through the night a few times," Layla said. The moment the words left her mouth she regretted them. The last time they did that was an occasion of Carmen needing to take a life. Even though Carmen had again killed a bandit during their escort of Irenaeus, a night trip meant the possibility of facing that action again.

Carmen seemed to sense her friend's turmoil. "If we have to we have to," she said. "And I'll do what the situation requires. Don't feel bad."

"*Gratias.*"

It was just past noon when they spotted a *mutatio* with an adjoining stable ahead on the road.

"We might as well trade horses and load up on some food while we have the chance," Will said. "Veil up, Carmen."

She sighed and dug out a band of blue cloth from her bag. She draped it over her head and pulled the ends into a knot below her chin. "If only they had some good hair dyes in this time. We wouldn't have to go through all this."

"What color would you choose?" Layla asked.

"Well, my prom date seems to have a thing for red heads."

"Oh good Lord!" Jonathan exclaimed. "I'm never going to live that down, am I?"

They stopped their horses in front of the stable and dismounted.

"I'll check them in and choose new animals," Carmen said.

"Alright," Will replied. "We'll go in and get some supplies."

A slave came from within the stable and approached Carmen as she stroked the neck of one of the horses.

"Greetings, my lady," the slave said. "How can I be of assistance?"

In that instant, the constant fear of attack, the beauty of the earth around, and the burden of her conscience, Carmen decided she could no longer treat a slave so distantly.

"*Salve*," she said. "*Quid agis hodie*?"

The slave looked at her curiously. "*Sum bene*. Why do you ask? Do I look sick?"

"*Non*," Carmen said. "It's just that where I come from people ask one another such things."

"Even of slaves?"

Carmen smiled. "Where I come from there aren't any slaves. So I can't treat one as anything less than a free person."

"You need horses?"

She nodded. "We'll trade in these four and we need four nice replacements. Could I please see your stock?"

"Why do you say 'Please'? It's my *job* to show you the horses."

"I'm just being courteous."

The slave laughed. "I'd risk death to run away to where you come from! Follow me, we have four that have had three days off. They're nice and strong and they'll take you two days through the Alps if you need."

He led her to a section of the stables where the animals were standing separate in a chamber eating hay.

"They'll do nicely, *gratias*."

"*Gratias*? What's the name of this country you come from?"

"It's called the United States of America."

"Never heard of it."

"It's very far away." She pushed up a lock of hair that had fallen from beneath her scarf.

"Four of you, huh?"

"That's right."

The slave nodded and closed his eyes.

"What's wrong?" she asked.

"What would you give for your freedom?"

She puzzled over his question. "I'm not a slave."

"And if you were? Is there anything you wouldn't do to become free?"

Carmen thought of an appropriate response. "I would fight for my freedom. But there are things that I wouldn't do."

"Would you take a life?"

Carmen saw the faces of the men she had killed flash before her eyes. "I wouldn't take an innocent life. But I have taken life before."

The slave swallowed hard. "You're in serious danger. Don't go into the *mutatio*. They know about you in there."

"What do you mean?"

"That loud-mouthed man, I think his name was…"

"Cornelius."

"That's right. He was here just a week ago. He tells everyone who works along the *Cursus Publicus* to be on the lookout for a group of four that has with them a…"

"Strange white-haired girl."

The slave smiled. "Right again. And he's offered a very large reward for anyone who captures you."

Carmen nodded in understanding. "A large enough reward for you to buy your freedom. So why did you warn me?"

"Because for the first time in my life, someone treated me like a human being. And I can't live with helping him catch you."

"So what's the danger?"

"There's a group of men waiting about four miles up the road to ambush you. I overheard their plans. They learned about the reward and they've been camped out there waiting for a group of four people fitting the description."

"How did they find out we were coming this way?" Carmen asked desperately.

"They don't really know you're here. But the reward is big enough that they said it was worth waiting and watching."

"And they didn't wait here at the *mansio* because…"

"Because they assumed you'd be smart enough not to send the whole team in together."

Carmen looked into the sky, her eyes suddenly flooded with tears. "How many?"

"I don't know. About seven."

She looked at the slave. "I have no way to repay my debt to you for this."

"You don't have to," he said. "Now, you lead two horses and I'll take the others. We'll go down the road a bit. I'll tell your friends the horses are ready."

She leaned over and kissed him on the cheek. "I will never forget you for as long as I live."

"May that be many years and so may the memory of me be eternal."

She smiled and nodded. "Let's go."

****

The other three walked out of the *mutatio* with several bags of supplies and started down the road toward where the slave said Carmen was stationed with the horses.

She waited until they were close enough to hear her in a normal voice. "Mount your horses quickly," she said. "We have an issue."

"Do as she says," Will said, climbing his steed.

They began down the road, Carmen leading them at a slower than normal pace. When they had ridden a half mile, she stopped the group and explained everything she had learned.

"So we're about four miles away from an ambush," Layla said. "Can't we just travel off the road far enough to escape detection?"

The group looked around them at the towering mountains through which this Roman road had carved a way.

"Not really, sweetie," Carmen said.

"We have to go through this," Jonathan declared.

"What's the plan?" Layla asked.

Will rubbed his forehead, straining in anguished thought. "There's no point in offering the duel with Carmen. They're waiting to kill us."

"You're right," she said. "But thanks to that slave, they no longer have the element of surprise."

"If anything, we have it," Layla noted.

"Exactly," Will said, starting to grin. "Let's go with that. We know that a group of about seven men are out there. And when we're approaching them, they're going to be pretending that everything's normal."

"And we know it's not," Carmen said.

"And so our strategy?" Layla asked.

Will took a deep breath and held it. He slowly released the air as his face turned to a deep sadness. "We approach them as if we suspect nothing. And when I give the word, we attack with intent to kill each one of them."

Carmen nodded slowly. "Before they even realize the battle is on, we could even the odds."

"There's no other way?" Layla asked.

Jonathan put his hand on her shoulder. "You can do this, Layla."

Will snapped the reins of his horse and continued forward. The others followed.

"The word is '*charge*', in English," he said. "When I say that, you draw swords and attack your closest target with intent to kill quickly and move on to another."

The horses trotted upon the cobblestone road, their hooves echoing back from the tall mountains all around. A few miles more and the group saw men on horses keeping station on each side of the road.

"How many are they?" Layla asked.

All peered forward and tried to assess the count.

"I think it's only six," Jonathan said.

"It is," Carmen stated.

"And we can really be sure that's the group?" Layla asked.

"No," Will said quickly. "But I don't know what else those men are doing out here, if they aren't the ones set on killing us."

"If we don't keep the plan, we lose the element of surprise," Carmen said. "Stay strong, Layla."

"No one acts until I give the command," Will reminded them.

The group continued forward, Will and Carmen moving up to take the lead, with Jonathan and Layla right behind.

"Can Layla kill?" Carmen asked Will softly.

"I don't want her to," he whispered back. "I've done it. I wish I could spare her the burden."

"Set me loose, Will."

"What do you mean?"

"You know exactly what I mean."

He looked at her seriously. "We're safer as a group."

"I don't care about my own safety anymore," she said. "I want to save Layla from the pain we carry."

"What's your plan?"

"I charge and attack and I kill as many as I can. They'll be more surprised by my single assault than by any attack from our whole group. When you arrive, you will only need to help mop up."

They were close enough to their enemy that they could hear the other horses neighing.

"You can really do this?"

"Will, I'm sober and my mind has never been clearer. I can take this whole group. They'll never see this coming."

"Do it," he whispered.

Carmen charged forward. The horsemen watched her approach with mere curiosity.

"What's going on?" Jonathan asked.

"You'll see."

Carmen rose to her knees on the back of her horse. She raced directly into a group of four men clustered on the right-hand side of the road. Just as her horse reached ten feet from them, she turned the reins and jumped into the air, pulling her sword out of its sheath. She landed on one of the men, her sword driving through his chest.

All the horsemen drew swords now and turned toward their comrade. Carmen left her sword buried in the man and pulled her dagger from beside her boot. She shot toward a horseman just a few feet away.

"Charge!" Will shouted.

The students drew swords and raced toward the action.

Carmen knocked the man off his horse. As he stood, he pulled his sword back. She kicked forward and struck him in the face. The man crumbled and Carmen thrust her dagger into his chest. Another horseman had jumped off his beast and thrust his sword toward her.

She stepped out of the way and shot her arm forward. Her dagger cleanly entered the man's neck. Yet another opponent was upon the scene and swung his weapon toward her. Carmen dropped to the ground just in time to escape the enemy's blow, picking up the sword dropped by the man she had just killed. She kicked the man between his legs and then thrust the blade into his chest. Her enemy dropped to his knees, as Carmen pulled her sword from his body.

The last two men had jumped from their mounts and were charging at Carmen. Jonathan arrived first and leapt from his horse, tackling one of them. The enemy punched Jonathan hard in the stomach. He lay stunned upon the ground, struggling for a breath. The man raised his sword. Jonathan quickly pressed his hand against his ribs and drew in a deep breath, recovering his strength. Just as the enemy began to bring his weapon down, Jonathan reached for his dagger and thrust it into the man's stomach. The opponent fell to the ground.

Will stayed on his horse. He was about to drag his weapon down upon the last opponent, when Carmen threw her sword, spinning end over end, to bury itself in the man's chest.

A moment of confusion turned to a silent recognition of an ended battle.

Layla brought her horse toward Carmen. "Why did you do that?" she whispered.

"To save you," Carmen replied. "In every way."

Layla closed her eyes and silently grieved.

"It's okay, sweetie," she said, smiling sadly. "Now I just have to save eight hundred and ninety-nine lives."

"Assemble," Will shouted.

The group gathered, surrounded by horses wandering about and bodies strewn upon the ground.

"We're going to search these people for money and supplies in a minute. We are no longer safe to enter the *mansiones* or *mutationes*. We will still need to swap animals on the *Cursus*, but luckily we have the two hundred *denarii* from the General. We'll need them to buy food at *tabernae*. Every time we can, only two of us will trade in for fresh horses. Carmen and someone else will continue down the road as if they weren't part of the group and wait for us. The next time, we trade in the other two."

"The distance we're traveling is hard enough on these horses," Carmen said. "We're going to be hurting them."

"We have no choice," Jonathan said.

"Operation 'Sneak Through Gaul' has a new set of rules," Will declared.

****

The nights in the Alps were cold. Even with a fully stoked fire, the students shivered until dawn to begin anew the stressful circuit of their travel. They found the Via Aurelia after two more days and started north. Their animals did suffer from the new plan. Between Lugdunum and Augustodunum, one of them took a severe limp. Carmen wept openly as she forced the animal several miles to the next stop. Needing to still make up one more day, they rode through the night between Augustodunum and Durocortorum. As if showered by an unexpected grace, they encountered not a single soul on the road during that night. They were getting back on schedule and on the road toward the shore of Gaul.

Chapter Fifteen

As the students came closer and closer to the coast, the air itself was alive with a hint of brine. They had managed to get themselves one day's travel from the extraction point with just one day left of their trip.

With the sun ready to set, Will pulled the reins of his horse to bring her to a stop. "We went without sleep the last two nights. We can't do this again. We need to sleep just a few hours. We've got just about five more miles to Gesoriacum. I say we get off the road and camp here for the night."

They climbed a slight hill to a ridge off the western side of the road. Just over the crest of the hill, thick trees met them. They continued a few hundred more yards and found a natural clearing.

"This will give plenty of cover," Jonathan noted. "No bandits will be able to see us from the road."

Jonathan and Carmen foraged for materials to build a fire while Layla and Will dug a fire pit.

"I'm so tired," she said. "To think that we could actually be home tomorrow."

"Well, according to the chronometer, we will either be home tomorrow or welcome to your new home here."

"Where would we go in the event that something goes wrong and we don't make it out?"

"What do you mean?" Will asked.

"I mean, let's imagine that something happened, and we get stranded here forever. What's next?"

"I'd say we should go back to Rome and take Sentius up on his job offer."

She smiled. "As good a plan as any."

"Here's the stuff," Jonathan said, carrying an assortment of different sized sticks and logs.

Carmen followed him, carrying even more.

They set the materials down and Will began striking the flint against his dagger. Soon flames were licking their way across the wood.

The four sat and passed around various dried foods they had. Will sent the wine skin around as well. Jonathan passed it hesitantly to Carmen, who immediately passed it to Layla.

"Still holding off?" Will asked.

"I'm not saying I'll never drink again," Carmen replied. "But tonight is officially sixteen days with no alcohol. I didn't think I could do that. So for now, I'm content to stay away from it."

"I'm so proud of you, Carm," Layla said.

"Thanks," she said, looking into Jonathan's eyes.

He smiled at her and nodded without a word.

"Alright," Carmen said. "I'm off to bed, people."

"Me too," Jonathan stated. "But I doubt I'll sleep much with the excitement of going home tomorrow."

****

In the middle of the night, Will sat down on a log beside Layla. He blew into his hands and rubbed them vigorously together. "You can't sleep either?"

"Not a wink," Layla said. "Are you cold?"

"I'm alright."

A silence hung between them. The closer they came to returning home, the more they knew this life they had forged would require some explanation back in their own time.

"My parents are going to be so pissed," she said, sensing his thoughts. "I'm almost worried about going home."

"I expected as much."

"They're going to say it's not real. That it never happened."

"It's a valid marriage," Will said seriously.

"I adore you, Will," she said. "But what's our plan when we get back?"

He looked at her seriously. "If you wonder what I think about us, I am currently looking at the woman I have loved for years and now am blessed to call my wife."

"Are we really married back there?"

"I honestly don't know if it has any civil force back home. People from other countries are considered validly married in America as long as their marriage had civil validity in the country they came from. Ours is both valid civilly here and, more important to me, it's sacramentally valid. But if we have to, please marry me all over again when we get home."

"I will," she said. Layla laced her fingers through his. "You need to get us home, Will."

"I'm trying."

"There's now another reason, my dear. We got married right about the middle of my cycle. My periods are like clockwork. I'm some days late right now. I've never been late before. And I feel very weird inside."

"You're serious?" he asked.

"I'm pregnant, Will. I'm positive. And I think Irenaeus predicted this to me."

He took a deep breath. "You're expecting our first child?"

"First?"

He laughed out loud. "Are you happy?"

"I am," she said, smiling. "So get our family home, Will."

He kissed her tenderly. "*Te amo, mi* Layla. *In saecula saeculorum.*"

****

Will awoke and was surprised at how bright it was already. Looking beside him, he saw Layla still asleep. He gently stroked her cheek and then carefully and quietly got out from beneath the bedroll.

As he stood, he saw Jonathan and Carmen already up and sitting some yards away on the other side of the smoking embers of the previous night's fire.

"Good morning," he whispered, approaching them.

He took the chronometer out of his pocket and leaned toward the screen. "Fourteen hours and some minutes. We should actually get there with some hours to spare."

Carmen laughed. "We were days behind schedule at one point. Thank God."

Layla sat up. "Will," she said softly. "I want our friends to know."

"But do you really know for sure yourself?"

"I do, with all my heart. Guys, I'm pregnant."

"Oh my goodness," Carmen gasped.

Jonathan laughed. "Are you guys happy about this?"

"I am," she said.

"We are," Will said.

"Then this is simply awesome," Jonathan replied. He walked to Layla and wrapped her in a hug.

After a moment, Carmen peeled Layla away from Jonathan and pressed her forehead against that of her friend's. "This trip has been nothing but pain and death. You're turned it back into life."

"People," Will said loudly. "We need to be back on the move."

"If that Briton's not there waiting for us, what then?" Jonathan asked.

"We've got so much money left over that we'll find someone else to take us across the channel."

After quickly packing their belongings, the group set out from the woods. Their horses moved slowly as they descended the rocky terrain toward the road. Once on the paved surface, they brought their animals up to the accustomed trot.

The group continued in silence as the sun rose in the sky. The still air warmed steadily. They saw a marker that indicated they were just five miles from Gesoriacum.

After clearing a gentle hill, the city became visible in the distance. A row of mule drawn carriages was heading toward them away from the city. Will, in the lead, guided his horse to the right-hand side of the road, to give the oncoming traffic room. The team followed him single file as they saw carriage after carriage loaded with what seemed to be wares from Britannia. When Will reached the last carriage, he saw several horses. His breath stopped when he recognized the face of one of the riders. It was the man who had beaten Carmen. It was Cornelius.

The Roman locked eyes with him just momentarily before Will rode past. Will kicked his horse's sides and raised his right fist into the air, the pre-arranged emergency signal for a full sprint.

"What's this?" Layla asked herself, next in line. She recognized the signal and complied, raising her own fist above her head.

Jonathan also broke into a full gallop.

Carmen brought up the rear, already beginning to race as she cleared the carriages. She saw the rider and immediately knew why Will was racing.

"*Tu!*" Cornelius screamed. "You're not getting away from me!"

Carmen felt her heart exploding from her chest as she pressed her horse into its highest speed. She shot her head back and saw the man turning away from his team of carriages and beginning to pursue.

"He's following!" she shouted forward to the rest. "What's our plan?"

Will's mind raced faster than his galloping horse. "How many are there?" he shouted back.

Carmen quickly turned and saw several men on horses in pursuit.

"Too many to fight!"

"Then we try to outrun them!" Will shouted.

The four continued at their highest possible speed, knowing the animals could not maintain it forever. Eventually, and a bit before they reached the city, they would have to drop their speed. This was going to be a match of the animals.

As they pressed forward, Will was seeing the signs that his horse was straining under the pressure of the run. Carmen kicked her horse to come up beside him.

"They can get us to the city at this speed," he shouted, the rush of air on her ears almost deafening the words.

"Not without killing them!" Carmen shouted.

He looked at her and saw her face convulse in grief.

"There's no other way," he said.

They continued racing toward Gesoriacum. As they looked back, they saw Cornelius' group continuing in pursuit, but not gaining on them.

"My animal's about to die underneath me, Will," Jonathan shouted. "What are we gonna do?"

"Just a bit more…" Will blurted through gritted teeth.

They reached the city gate. Since it was peace time, the massive wooden doors were wide open. The presence of pedestrians mulling around the area, however, brought their speed to a standstill.

"Dismount!" Will shouted.

He jumped off his horse and began to run down the main avenue into the city center.

"This is good," Carmen shouted behind him. "We can outrun them on foot and they can't ride their horses fast through a busy city."

The four ran down the main road and turned onto a side street, before again heading left and north toward the harbor itself.

"I think we've lost them," Layla managed through staggered breaths.

They brought their speed down to a jog and saw ahead the glistening water of the channel.

"So here's the thing," Jonathan said. "We won't have time to bargain with someone for passage across the channel. Our lives now depend on that swarthy Briton being there ready to take us back."

"That would be awfully nice," Carmen said.

They poured out into the open space leading to the rows of military and commercial ships moored in the sprawling complex of docks.

"Find him, people!" Will shouted.

They stopped and scanned the scene. For what seemed an eternity as they knew their enemy was advancing on them, each one examined seemingly identical boats.

"I see him!" Carmen finally shouted, breaking into a sprint.

The others followed after her quickly.

They ran down a crude wooden pier and all soon recognized the boat that had brought them to Gaul.

Will jumped across three feet of water to land beside the napping captain.

"We have to move!" he shouted. "Right now!"

The Briton shook his head, trying to push away sleep. "Now? I waited ten days for you here. I decided to wait one more because that you gave me the money anyways. And now we are needs to leave now?"

"Now!" Will shouted in his face.

Jonathan jumped across and immediately began pulling down the ropes and preparing the ship to sail.

Carmen and Layla boarded and started to help.

"We've picked up some enemies on our trip," Will said. "And they're right behind us."

"Why you not to say so?" The Briton drew a knife from his cloak and sliced through the rope anchoring the ship to the pier. "We go now."

A gentle breeze was soon filling the sails and pulling the ship steadily away from the continent. After several minutes of adjusting the ropes to maximize their speed, the group finally stood on the deck and relaxed. After another half an hour, they had begun to dare to calm their spirits.

Will breathed in deeply and released a sigh. "We escaped."

Layla hugged him from behind and kissed him on the neck.

He put his hands on hers. "We're almost there."

Carmen stepped to the back of the ship and peered into the distance. "We might not be out of the woods just yet."

"What do you mean?" Will asked.

"What's that?"

Jonathan squinted and saw two black sails on the horizon. "That would be a double sail coaster."

"What is it, exactly?" Will asked, stepping toward them.

"It's a type of boat. It's faster than what we're in. It might overtake us sometime before we reach Britannia."

"Is that..."

"The guy who kicked my face," Carmen said bitterly. "I think that's a safe assumption."

"And he probably has a dozen soldiers with him in that ship," Jonathan said. "We are officially in trouble."

"Damn it," Will whispered.

"Do what?" the Briton asked. "What do you want me to do?"

Jonathan shook his head. "Stay the course. We can hope for the best. They're a ways back. We might beat them to the shore. We can hope we're that lucky."

The ships continued the twenty miles across the channel. The black-sailed ship steadily gained on them, but soon they saw the shore of Britannia in the distance.

Will stood silently on the bow of the ship, looking back and forth between the British shore and their pursuers. Jonathan approached him and leaned his back against the bow.

"Are we going to make it to shore before they take us?" Will asked.

"No."

Will closed his eyes. "You have an idea, I know. And I don't like it."

Jonathan sighed. "There's a way out of this mess. I can handle this ship. And I can handle it alone. You're close enough to swim to shore and..."

"You're talking about turning around and ramming them?"

"It'll save the mission. You'll make it to shore and that ship full of soldiers won't. But this needs to happen sooner rather than later for it to work."

"But you won't either. I made a promise to myself when this mission began that I would bring every one of you home."

"It's not your fault that it's a promise you couldn't keep."

Will turned to his friend, his eyes full of tears. "I'll try to do it then."

"You don't know how," Jonathan said smiling, his own eyes now flowing forth. "And you have a pregnant wife, Will. Plain and simple. You go home. I don't."

Will looked down and shook his head. "There has to be another way. We can stand up to them and fight."

"That isn't going to work and you know it."

Will nodded slowly.

"Don't tell the girls about this, Will. You give the order to abandon ship and swim for shore. They can be on their way before they realize I'm not with you."

"Agreed." Will pulled Jonathan tightly into a hug. "Make me a promise."

"Yeah?"

"Promise me that the second you know you have impact on them, that you will try to get out of there and meet us at the extraction point."

"I'm not on a suicide mission," Jonathan said. "Of course I'll try to make it. But it's not likely that..."

"I know," Will said.

"Now you promise me something," Jonathan said, holding his friend at the shoulders.

Will looked at him seriously.

"When you get home…" Jonathan choked up and took a deep breath before continuing. "When you get home, I need you to tell my uncle something for me. Tell him that I loved him. And that I know he loved me. And that I'm grateful he became my second father."

Jonathan buried his face in Will's shoulder and sobbed.

Carmen looked across the boat at the two young men. "Oh God," she whispered. "I know their plan."

"What's going on?" Layla asked.

Will stepped back. "If I don't do this right now, I will change my mind."

"Go," Jonathan said softly.

"Abandon ship!" Will shouted, running the length of the boat and diving off the bow.

Carmen turned Layla in that direction. "Follow Will!" she shouted.

Layla ran and dove after Will into the water.

"What is it happening?" the Briton asked. "Why you to do this?"

"He's turning the ship back," Carmen said. "Do you want to go along?"

"Do I still get paid?"

"We'll pay you for the boat."

The Briton dove into the water without a word.

Carmen stepped toward him. "Jonathan…"

"Get off this ship, Carmen," Jonathan said, pulling a rope to swing the sail around.

They locked tearful eyes. Each knew that there was too much unsaid to say in that moment.

Carmen turned around and dove off the ship.

"*Te amo*," she whispered through the waves.

Jonathan pressed his weight against the rudder and turned the ship sharply. He looked forward and focused his boat on the black sailed vessel. Jonathon saw the oncoming ship begin to steer a bit northward. He compensated. They switched direction again. He matched their course and soon he could hear the water churning from the bow of the other ship. They made one last attempt to avoid collision. Jonathan delicately guided the rudder to close the gap.

Just when he knew that nothing could prevent the collision, he ran the length of the ship and dove through the air.

On the other vessel, Cornelius had seen the plan, jumped off his boat, and began swimming toward the shore.

As the two ships crashed together, the back of the smaller vessel lifted up, catching Jonathan's feet as he sailed through the air. He lost his momentum and tumbled into the water. As he started to swim, he saw that Cornelius was already far ahead of him, moving swiftly toward the shore.

****

Layla arrived at the beach first, followed closely by Will. She turned around and looked into the distance. There on the horizon she saw the two motionless ships, listing in the waves, each one smashed open in its bow.

"What happened?" she screamed. Looking around, she saw Will stepping out of the waves and Carmen swimming right behind him. "Where's Jonathan?"

"Get moving!" Will shouted. "We have to get to the extraction point."

"What and where you go now?" the Briton shouted, pulling himself onto the shore. "You ruin my boat!"

Will tossed a bag to the man. "Here's enough money to buy two more. Have a good life."

The Briton felt the weight of the bag and nodded, a huge smile forming on his lips. "*Valete, mi amici.*" He started running eastward along the shore, toward his village.

Carmen stood and pulled her legs through the water the final feet toward shore. Once on land, she peered into the distance. "Damn!" she said. "That's Cornelius way out there!"

"Follow me," Will shouted, running up the grassy sand dune toward the road.

Layla mourned as she figured out the events that had taken place. Carmen put her arm around her friend's shoulder and helped her along as they both broke down in tears.

Just up the slope, they found the road which would lead them westward to the crag and the extraction point. They ran in silence. As they continued, they passed the spot where Carmen had killed the bandit thirty days earlier. She shook her head, her mind pulling back all the memories of the ordeals they had faced.

After jogging for another hour, they reached the rocky incline and followed the path back to the top of the crag. The wind howled as they stepped onto the flat granite slab.

Will looked at the chronometer. "Still a few hours left," he said softly. "Come on, Jonathan."

They stood gazing into the distance, hoping to see their friend appear.

The time and their hope rapidly diminished. With just mere minutes before the extraction time, they saw a figure in the distance.

"It's Cornelius," Carmen said. "And he'll see us up here. What's the plan?"

Will looked down. "We can fight him, but we can't risk being off this spot when the extraction time comes."

"No. I'll stop him," she said.

"What about last time?" Layla asked.

"I'm not talking about beating him," she countered. "I'm talking about delaying him long enough so you two get out of here safely."

"No!" Layla protested.

Will nodded. "Go. I know it's the only way."

Carmen stepped forward and turned around. "I'll try to beat him and get back. But if I don't, you two have a wonderful life."

Will buried his face in his hands. "I didn't bring them home. My heart is broken."

Layla wrapped her arms around him. "Pray, my dear. It's all that's left."

Carmen ran down the slope and came to a stop on the road below. Will and Layla could see her stretching her arms upward as the figure approached.

"I'm so happy it came down to the two of us," Cornelius said, interlacing his fingers and cracking them forward. "You're the only one that fought like you had a single prayer of even facing me."

"I'm sober now," Carmen said, sinking into a defensive pose. "You'll find that's a bit of a difference."

"For what it's worth, I'm sober at the moment too," he said.

She looked up at Will and Layla still assembled on the extraction point. "Stay put, Will," she shouted. "No matter what happens, you two get out of here."

"I do need to throw this timepiece away before that happens," he shouted back. "I'll send it the other direction, but I don't know exactly how big it will blow."

As Carmen turned to Cornelius, she saw a figure past him in the distance. "Oh my God," she gasped. "It's Jonathan!"

Cornelius turned around quickly and then looked back at her. "Let's make this a fair fight. I let the little man join your group but you stay here to fight me."

She nodded.

Jonathan slowed before his approach. "Give me my orders, Will!"

"Assist Carmen!" he shouted.

"No!" she returned. "I've promised Cornelius a fair fight. Join them, Jonathan," she said calmly.

Jonathan walked slowly past Cornelius and climbed the hill to join Layla and Will.

"Thank God, you made it," Will said, embracing Jonathan.

"What about her?"

"Pray. Hard."

"Let's do this thing," Carmen whispered.

Will looked down at the time piece. "Two minutes, Carm!" he shouted.

"I'll let you throw the first blow," Cornelius said.

"That didn't work so well for me last time," Carmen replied. "You go."

He immediately twirled and sent a foot flying toward her face. She ducked out of the way and shot out her left foot, striking him in the ankle.

As Cornelius fell toward the ground, he reached out and seized her hair. He pulled her toward him and put his hands around her neck.

Carmen pulled her two arms back violently and drove her elbows sharply into his stomach.

Cornelius gasped as she spun away from his grip.

She stood a distance away and sunk again into her stance. "Come," she whispered.

"The gods damn you to Tartarus!" he screamed and charged.

Carmen dropped to the ground on her back. As Cornelius leapt toward her, she shot both feet up, crashing into his ribs and propelling him over her to tumble into a nearby thorn bush.

Carmen rose quickly and scrambled up the hill. She ran into the center of the group.

A beep sounded.

"Give me the watch, Will," Carmen said calmly.

He set it in her hand.

"Present for you, Cornelius," she shouted, tossing it down the hill toward him.

The Roman struggled forward, still stuck in the brush, and caught the object.

"*Quid est?*"

A flash of light filled his vision. The people up on the hill had somehow vanished.

"Where did you go?!" he bellowed.

He held the object and watched as it flashed and beeped ever quicker and ever louder. He did not understand the symbols changing on the shining screen.

The blast was heard as far away as the coast of Gaul.

Chapter Sixteen

They felt a sensation of falling, then suddenly the students were gripped by a paralysis, as if all the cells of their bodies were frozen. Spots covering their vision slowly subsided and they knew they stood once again in the darkness of the time travel chamber. The portal opened.

As they stepped out, the students saw that the men were in the exact stance in which they had observed them last.

"Welcome home," Dr. Valquist whispered.

They shook off the slight sickness that the time travel left. The four students turned to one another and were unable to speak.

Will finally took a deep breath. "Can...we...be alone for a moment," he managed through a weak voice.

"Certainly," the President said. He opened the door toward the hall and stepped outside, followed by the others.

The door closed behind them, leaving a perfect silence in the space.

They turned toward each other and began just shaking their heads, unable to accept that it was over. Smiles came quickly, followed even more quickly by chuckles. This, though, gave way to tears. The four fell into an embrace and held each other as they shook in sobs simultaneously of elation and grief.

When they finally left the room to join the others, they found a note in Dr. Valquist's handwriting taped to the outside door.

"When you're ready, a car will bring you back to the house. We'll all be waiting for you there. And take your time," they read.

Stepping into the bright day outside the building, they paused and gazed down upon the plain.

"Look," Carmen whispered, pointing into the distance. "You can still see the outline of where the road was."

"And there's where Cornelius was when we disappeared," Jonathan said, indicating the spot.

"Was that wrong, what I did?" Carmen asked, forming a smile. "Because I kind of needed to kill just one more person where I could really feel good about it."

"You did well," Will said. "You made the second century A.D. a better place for everyone. And I don't think you have to make up for that one at all."

The four faced each other.

"What can I possibly say right now?" Will whispered. "Every one of you saved this mission somehow."

"None more than you," Carmen said. "History will never know what we did. But it doesn't matter. That only means that the four of us are the most privileged people that have ever lived. Because we know everything that happened back there."

"Is anyone else hungry?" Jonathan asked.

"I am," Layla said, laughing. "But, Carmen, Jonathan, if you'll pardon me for a moment."

She stepped toward Will, put her arms around him, and pulled her husband into a deep kiss.

Carmen and Jonathan stood looking at them and then turned to each other. She leaned forward and kissed him on the forehead. "You saved my life, do you know that?"

"You saved mine too," he whispered. "More than once."

Carmen suddenly kissed him on the lips and stood back.

He looked at her curiously. "I half expected that to feel weird. But it didn't." He leaned in and pressed his lips to hers for a lingering moment.

"Hmm. Not weird at all," she said. "Where have you been all my life, Nennius?"

****

When they arrived at the house, they found attendants standing in the foyer with trays of appetizers and assorted drinks.

"Have a snack if you desire," one man said. "Then get cleaned up and meet the others in the main dining hall when you're ready."

They proceeded to rooms they had not seen for a month, still reminding themselves that the people here had seen them just hours earlier. After taking their first real showers in a month, they put on the formal clothes that had been laid out and came downstairs.

The President, Prime Minister, Dr. Silver, and the faculty stood from their seats as they saw the students enter the room.

The Prime Minister stepped forward. "I am speaking on behalf of a planet that will not know your sacrifice. The world thanks you and is in your debt."

They exchanged handshakes and hugs, laughter and more tears.

Seated at the table, the President smiled. "I know that starting tomorrow you'll be undergoing extensive debriefings. But for tonight, we relax and celebrate your accomplishment."

"You can tell us now," Jonathan said. "You already got the information we buried outside Rome?"

"Yes, we did," Dr. Silver replied. "In fact, we got it last week and we've already deflected the trajectory of Planet X. You've saved our world. But until you reappeared in that chamber, no one knew if you would make it home."

Will caught the gaze of the other students, who all nodded for him to speak for the group.

"Listen," he started. "We've got some demands."

The President and Prime Minister looked at each and laughed.

"We figured you would come back with some ideas of how we should repay you for all you did," the Prime

Minister said. "And that's fair. It's the least we could do."

"What do you have in mind?" the President asked.

"For starters, we want the school year to finish so that the other students get credit toward another high school."

The President smiled. "We were not expecting that. You all have bank accounts set up with 10 million dollars in them a piece. That was what *we* considered the least we could do."

"Are you serious?" Carmen asked.

"They are," Dr. Valquist said.

"We're not saying that we're buying your secrecy over all that happened here," Dr. Silver said. "But from a security standpoint, we can't allow any one of you to be in financial straits at any point in your lives."

"We also want a prom," Carmen said.

"A prom?" Miss Maple repeated.

"That's right," Jonathan said. "I think I'm dating Carmen now, by the way. Based on two kisses we just shared."

"Let's see how prom goes first," Carmen said, grinning.

"Are we still allowed to go to college if we want?" Layla asked.

"Of course," Dr. Valquist replied.

"Then I want to go to Oxford, Mr. Prime Minister."

"That's within my power," he said.

"But why Oxford?" Dr. Valquist asked.

"Because Will and I got married."

Dr. Valquist laughed. "I didn't see that coming."

Dr. Silver cleared his throat. "Um, Layla, do you...?"

"I know, yes."

"Know what?" the President asked.

"She's pregnant," he said. "I took a quick scan of the control panel. It monitors the DNA signature of everything that goes and comes back. I mean, we'd need to know if one of these kids returned with Bubonic plague."

"Why did that tell you she's pregnant?" the Prime Minister asked.

"Four distinct human DNA signatures went back. Five returned. Would you two like to know the gender?"

"No, thank you," Layla replied. "Let it be a surprise."

"Anything else you want?" the President asked.

"We want a graduation ceremony," Will stated. "We would like you world leaders to attend, but we want Dr. Valquist to give us our diplomas."

Their teacher's eyes filled with tears. "Done."

"That's all we planned on asking for," Jonathan said. "But thanks for the ten million as well."

"You're welcome," the Prime Minister said with a smile.

"Can we eat now?" Jonathan asked.

"Yes," the President said. "And afterwards, you can all call your parents."

"And I'm calling my uncle," Jonathan said. "That's not negotiable. And I insist you clear him for Top Secret so he can know something of what happened here."

The President nodded. "Done."

****

Dr. Valquist stood on the stage, flanked by Miss Maple, Mr. Cole, and the other teachers from the academy, all dressed in academic regalia. On the other side of the stage stood the President, the Prime Minister, each one accompanied by his wife.

Pomp and Circumstance blared through the auditorium, played by the United States Navy Band.

The small audience made up of the students from the lower grades and their families were whispering wild speculations about why the world's leaders were present for this event. The strange report had also surged through the lower grades that somehow Will and Layla were now a married couple.

The four seniors walked into the auditorium in a procession. They came up the center aisle, past a set of chairs where their families stood, and took their own places in the front row before the stage.

Dr. Valquist conducted the required ceremonies toward calling forward the Valedictorian and Class President, Will.

He stepped up onto the stage and went to the podium.

"Four years ago," he began, "we four students started our studies here at the Fairfax Classical Academy. It would be an understatement to say that our time here was not everything we expected."

Everyone in the room with at least a Top Secret clearance laughed knowingly. This included Jonathan's uncle, who had been briefed along with the rest of the parents.

"I'm sure these speeches which are taking place all across the country this time of year talk about how we need to go into the future with energy and optimism. Well, this place was all about the need to go back into the past. That's why we studied Latin and the other ancient disciplines. And we found, as time went on, but mostly this year, that in the past, we would find the answers that the future desperately needs. But we also found something deeper. We found that as a team, we had a strength which could take us into the deepest and darkest places. But we struggled through them together.

"We thank the faculty of the academy for their instruction and companionship on this journey.

"And to my fellow seniors. It's a curious thing to have done the most important thing you'll ever accomplish before you even graduate high school. But that's who we are. I found a quote on the internet by a writer who lived in the city of Lugdunum in Gaul back in the second century A.D. This man, St. Irenaeus, was a priest and then a bishop who became famous for his scholarship. His words for us resonate almost like those of a friend. Here's what he wrote. 'The glory of God is to be found in any human who is fully alive'. We are fully alive, my friends. And there were times when we wondered if we would even survive. So let us now live and let us love. My fellow students, we know we are the most privileged people to have ever lived. No words can further describe what we did here."

He stepped off the stage to an applause that was hesitant on the part of those who did not know the story.

Dr. Valquist stepped to the podium.

"Thank you, Will," he said. "Before I confer the diplomas on these worthy students, it has come to my attention that a strange rumor has circulated among the student body, to the effect that the Fairfax Classical Academy would be closing after this year."

A murmur rose from the crowd of younger students and their families.

Dr. Valquist looked at his four students. "This rumor is untrue. It has been the greatest honor of my life to have had any part in training the four young people who graduate tonight. And I can think of no better work than to continue training young women and men in their footsteps."

After the students received their diplomas, they stood in a row on the stage.

"I hereby declare," Dr. Valquist said, "that these students have completed all the requirements for graduation from the Fairfax Classical Academy. Congratulations, class of 2013."

They took off their caps, threw them into the air, and fell into an embrace.

.